The Century's Scribe

Brendan Walsh

Black Rose Writing | Texas

ISBN: 978-1-68433-542-8 (Paperback); 978-1-944715-88-5 (Hardcover)
PUBLISHED BY BLACK ROSE WRITING
www.blackrosewriting.com

Printed in the United States of America
Suggested Retail Price (SRP) $18.95 (Paperback); $23.95 (Hardcover)

The Century's Scribe is printed in Garamond

*As a planet-friendly publisher, Black Rose Writing does its best to eliminate unnecessary waste to reduce paper usage and energy costs, while never compromising the reading experience. As a result, the final word count vs. page count may not meet common expectations.

ACKNOWLEDGEMENTS

This is the fourth time I've done one of these, and I fear they're getting repetitive. Nevertheless, there are very important people I need to thank for helping this novel come to be, and I've been through a lot since I finished The Serpent League.

First off, I want to thank my wonderful brother Robert. Without your constant reading of my work along with your tolerance of my creative anxieties, I would never have finished my first novel back in 2015. Even though you were away for most of the time I was writing this, your support made you feel like you were only a couple rooms away. My dear friend Scott Wagner, though I did not have the pleasure of seeing you in person in 2019, it still surprises me how you were so supportive of me back when I was working on The Raven Gang, even though we were not yet close friends. You are kind, brilliant, and I feel lucky to still have you in my life.

When The Century's Scribe was only a few chapters old, I had the privilege of joining my good friend Jose to see an early screening of the film Rocketman back in March of 2019, two-and-a-half months before its release. I adored it. Not only was it my favorite movie of the year, but it had an indelible influence on my creative ambitions. This novel was not originally going to be so personal, but the movie encouraged me to believe I had something intimate that was worth telling. Dreden is more myself than any other character I've written, and some scenes were difficult to write, because of how true-to-life they felt, but I don't regret them. They're my favorite scenes. So, Elton John, Dexter Fletcher, Taron Egerton, and everyone else involved in the birth of the outstanding film, thank you.

I'm also extremely thankful to Black Rose Writing for taking an interest in this novel. I don't love the querying process. It's long and full of rejection, but getting a yes can be one of the best feelings ever. I have enjoyed our relationship so far and am eagerly looking forward to more in the future, as well as getting to know more great authors on our Facebook group.

I originally wrote The Century's Scribe and its sequel as just one novel, meaning that I'm going to be writing another one of these again. Don't worry, I never get tired of thanking you all.

The Century's Scribe

PROLOGUE

Minkompa sometimes imagined he could be anything he wanted. That was the power of books. Books could transport him into a whole other world, to a world of fantasy and magic, where the narrator could be a creature that didn't look anything like him. Considering Minkompa's species, that was something he definitely had to get used to.

If you happened to be the kind of creature that used a cave as a library and a permanent residence, like Minkompa, the art of bookkeeping might get frustrating at times, since the kind of creatures that had a reputation of doing so were typically very large. Even though he was a chronic bibliophile and had the kind of reading addiction that would earn glances from the most knowing of modern physicians, he was not immune to chucking a book across the cave or incinerating one on the spot out of rage.

His massive legs were extended with his clawed toes splayed at his latest find. Going up from his bulky frame, up to his forelegs, he held a giant book in his scaly paws. Sadly, it wasn't a *giant* book, as in its physical dimensions, but it was long, as it was the most up-to-date almanac he could get. Minkompa never left the underground, but the massive cavern system below the city of Brunswald served nicely for exploring and even the occasional adventure. Because of that, nearly all his knowledge of modern culture came from reading, and when he wanted brand new information, he had to crawl along the caverns and try to use his good reptilian ears to hear what the people above were saying.

From horn to toe, Minkompa was ruby red, with a significant area from his neck down between his legs being black. The complimentary nature between both colors of his hide gave him almost the look of a burned raspberry tart, which was a type of sweet dessert, as his books informed him. He had a fat tail which he would chomp at in fury whenever it acted out of his accord. It was long and lined with large, defensive scales that decorated his spine, making it irksome when he wanted to sit down and lean against his cave walls, since they would cut into his back. If that happened, he'd crane his neck around and snip at the annoying bits with his fangs, which he made a habit of polishing and cleaning with pointy jewelry. Above those, his ears almost looked like tiny wings just below the top of his head where his goat-like horns were ever-pointing to the cavern's roof.

His eyes were wet with a soul, and, while his eyesight was keen, he often had to rest a book on the top of his snout, but the words in his almanac were big enough for the book to only be just above his reptilian lips.

Minkompa was a dragon.

Leafing through the pages, careful not to make a slice with a claw, the dragon found the spot where he left off last time. He was reading about a juicy story involving an affair between troubled former aristocratic families. The almanac told the story matter-of-factly, so Minkompa had to apply the scandalous excitement in his mind.

"A former Gween noblewoman found her husband under the sheets with a Hawkler?" as he scoffed, a small puff of smoke escaped his throat. "That mole-faced fribble is too dumb to start another fight over. No one likes those ever-shrill Hawklers, and the fact that it was in the back of one of their own private carriages makes it all the worse."

Minkompa had always wanted to see a carriage. The idea that humans could domesticate a big animal like a horse and make it carry a large wheeled structure was amazing to him. "But it's only the best they can do, since they can't fly like dragons." is what he always said.

Talking to himself, while it made him happy, was something he tried to stop himself from doing for most of his life. He knew that if he had more people to talk to, it wouldn't have developed into a chronic quirk.

His only guests were tiny cave-dwellers like bats, rats, insects and the occasional frog. He thought they weren't very talkative, and they often left their droppings on his stuff.

Turning the page, he continued aloud. When he got into an excited reading stride, he never noticed that he was speaking to himself. "Ah, rightfully so! A divorce is the best choice. Cut this atrocity at its source, and if they're lucky, the Hawklers won't sever their ties to the family's steel factories. They're going to need all the business they can get, since the Edland family is now owning just about everything."

Excited, he clutched the book against his snout, devouring the words with his tail flapping like a puppy's. With the kind of thrill such stories gave him, he didn't notice when an hour had flown by. It was already midnight. That was typically when Minkompa liked to lay his head down for the night. He never went to sleep without a small snack first.

The dragon felt around the ground near his rear. His claw caught a small sliver of metal that made up his bed. It was a round, solid gold coin. The mere size of the beauty would have been enough for two kingdoms to go to war in the old days. Scores of soldiers, knights on horseback, and cannons going off, cutting off entire bloodlines that would have lasted for centuries, all of that just for a piece of metal shiny enough for Minkompa to see his own reflection through. Even now, in the grip of an industrial age, a large gold coin like that, in as great condition as it was, would have been worth several paychecks.

He spun the coin through his claws. There was an engraving of an ancient bearded man, someone who was probably a king. Minkompa didn't know who it was. All old hairy men seemed to look the same when they got to a high enough rank.

There were still places in the world where people would have sold their livers for the coin. The entire city of Yanberra, a former political power in the old days, now fallen on hard times, would have been affluent enough to give all its residents food for a day.

His ears perked up. He twiddled the coin some more between the claws on his foreleg. The *cling-cling* of metal against his leathery skin along with the scratch of a nail against the coin always reminded him of what he was. Depending on his mood, that either pleased him or depressed the fire out of him.

The invaluable coin settled on his thumb claw. Carelessly, he flicked it into the air above his head and watched it spin and spin, seeing if he could get a last glance at the old hairy king before he opened his jaws-

-and it fell into a slimy abyss. Minkompa raised his head and felt the weight of the metal ease its way down his esophagus. Every time he swallowed a coin of that weight, he always heard it settle in his stomach. Now and then it would hurt, feeling like it got lodged somewhere unhealthy, though that was nothing a quick shaking of his massive belly couldn't fix. To his knowledge, dragons weren't as numerous anymore, so he had to rely on orally passed down wisdom of reptiles before him.

Minkompa dragged his tongue across his lips, washing the taste of the gold away. It was written in one of his books on legends that gold was said to be good for a dragon's immune system. There was no way of knowing for sure if that was true, but gold had never given him problems before.

Satisfied with the snack, the dragon lumbered on all fours to the bulk of his stash. Gold, Silver, Platinum, rubies, emeralds, basically every kind of material mankind could have an excuse to covet were sloppily clumped about the far side of his cave. Altogether, the mound of jewels formed to make a loose image of a bed, or at least what would have been comfortable for a beast that stood fifteen feet high, even when standing on all fours.

Not being picky with where his jaw rested or where his toes dug into rare coins like sand, Minkompa closed his eyes and hugged a pile of diamonds and swords like a child's doll, and went to sleep, excited to read more about modern men when he next woke.

"I'm not the man they think I am at home."
-Elton John and Bernie Taupin

CHAPTER 1

The cobblestones under Dreden's boots had not been recently polished. It was the middle of the week, and the time the university maintenance crew did most of their work. Even though it was still early in the day, and there had yet to be a stampede of scholars down the cleaned-up road, the walkway didn't look as good as it used to on maintenance day. Certain people probably had to take another pay cut, but that wasn't something anyone was going to talk about.

Although, sometimes *not* talking about things, as obvious as they were, like a roach in milk, gave one intel that would otherwise not have been granted. He tried to ignore it. Most of his classmates were able to, but they didn't have as personal of a connection to Faeriebridge University as he did.

He felt a wave of warm air upon opening the classroom door. It pleased him. Since it was early winter, he typically had to go about his morning in a coat with fur sleeves, holding a metal teacup. Luckily, the administration had allowed for fireplaces to be built in classrooms during the past semester. Closing the door behind him, the crackling of flames licking against scraps of parchment and wood was sweeter than a tuned lyre.

The weight of eyes from turning heads came on him. He felt too guilty to make eye contact with anyone. Especially with the professor.

"Mister Sharpstand," the professor greeted him, emphasizing his last name.

"Professor," Dreden found a seat in the back row of desks. "Sorry, just returning from breakfast."

His teacher raised an eye. "Tardiness appears to be a common trope with you, not unlike some of the more frustrating characters of today's study."

Bouts of chuckles swept the class. Dreden smiled. Even when he was the focus of the joke, which was common, his professor's sense of humor was never aggressive to him.

Desks around him were capped with *The Mage Unlimited*, a small yet dense piece of culture from half a millennium or so ago. It wasn't a long read, but its staunch lack of dialogue or plot made it a chore on par with reading a dictionary.

"Alright, can one of you remind me where we left off last session?" asked the professor.

A young woman with plum-colored bangs raised her hand. "We were on page sixty-six. The poor lunatic was going off again."

More laughter sounded, amplified by the thick stone walls of the classroom. The professor smiled, turning his glasses down and flipping to the page. "Right right. I'm going to assume that none of you did the reading for this morning, taking advantage of our failure to finish the discussion last week, so we'll just be behind a bit. No worry."

He raised his eyes from the text, surveying the students. "Would anyone like to read the next two paragraphs?"

A silence came over the class as the professor waited.

He was a middle-aged man whose clean, rugged face always looked like it had the ghost of a beard. He had long and thin black hair that hovered above his collar like cobwebs when he walked. Like many of the people in Kroonsaed, the color of his skin was closer to the brown of mud than to the white of snow. With the exception of a couple months in the summer, Kroonsaed was never sunny, but long ago, its bright economic prospects attracted humans and avehos from all over the world.

A hand finally came up. It belonged to the girl with the fruit hair.

The professor smiled again. "Ah, Miss Merris, do start. From the top."

Naphel Merris began, "Yes professor, '*The answer of the friends comes deep from the outside. Your end is too old to be wise, so one needs to have a fresher look to wash one's spirit from decades or centuries of awareness from the deep abysses of the soul. Being an elder isn't a crime so don't call me foolish or try to attack me standing here while I assure that I don't attack your experience but do not forget that death is simply another gateway not unlike a spell to wipe a mem-*'"

The professor noticed that nearly everyone's head was away from the text, so he raised a hand and Naphel paused.

"Is there something about this specific passage that you all find even more unpleasant than usual?"

Several students looked at him, trying to hide their lack of attention. One near the front, a chubby nineteen-year-old, sighed as he completed his fourth yawn of the day.

"Mister Maglant, would you care to speak for the class about this?"

He did a double take, making sure he was the one who had been called during his daydreaming. "Um, I wasn't paying attention,"

The professor nodded to himself. "In other news, grass is green, and this university still hasn't won the Pellermack Literary Grant since I was born."

Maglant fingered his hair. "Exactly. Anyway, to continue, I think I speak for at least some of us here when I say that... well... this book doesn't seem important."

The professor started walking along the aisles of desks. Some students who didn't already have their texts out rushed to grab them and turn to the right page, hoping to avoid bad marks in participation.

Dreden wasn't looking at the professor. He didn't want to seem like the rest of them, as good meaning as their humor was. He knew things about the school that they didn't. It was much more than any of the students assumed because of his relationship with this literature professor.

"Sharpstand," the professor said, stopping above his desk. Some of the students farthest away smiled, and a couple released accidental snorts of laughter.

"Seriously? Must this always be the case?" He spun around with his arms raised to the class. His teaching robes rose and fell with quickened breath. "Just because my son is by far the best student in the class doesn't mean that he gets any special treatment. In fact, you all can learn a thing or two from him. This is a university. Not primary school."

Dreden showed his teeth for the first time in the class and raised an inked quill. "Actually, Professor Sharpstand, I find that in this case I'm going to agree with Maglant."

His father's jaw hung open for a moment as the entire classroom went quiet. As Dreden's smile grew and it became obvious that there was no serious tension between the father and son, several students broke the silence by sitting up straight and putting quills to parchment.

"My! My own damn son has a problem with my assigned reading." The professor's palm fell over his heart and his fingers swished his hair back, feigning distress. "Oh, I think the pain will prove too great for me. Go on, Dreden, tell me what your issue with the text is. It will mean more from you because I *know* you've read it."

His son flipped through the earlier pages of *The Mage Unlimited* as he eyed his notes with highlights and underlined words. He wanted to make sure he had the right spots and notes of textual abnormalities.

Dreden paused on one of the pages of the latest assigned section of reading. "Ah, here! To start, based on the small section that Naphel read, it is easy to tell that this text is pretty dense, and it splits into different concepts and philosophies very regularly, as if the book is a brain and we the readers are trying to soothe its maladies."

Professor Sharpstand raised a brow. He walked back to his desk, surfing through his own copy. "Yes, good observation, Dreden, but you're pointing out the obvious here. It is dense because it is written in what, in literature, we call *the soul's flow.* Can anyone tell me what that means?"

A few hands darted up. Sharpstand ended up pointing to the one belonging to a woman with sunken enough eyes to rival a sloth.

"It's the style in which the writer attempts to translate wondering, unconscious thoughts an individual has onto paper." answered Dalil, the woman chosen by the professor.

"Very good. This style is known for causing professors to rub their heads against blackboards for days."

Dalil continued, "Maybe, professor, students of literature such as us aren't suited for analyzing this test. Perhaps the students interning at the nearest sanitorium will be more successful."

For what was already the fifth time that day, the class collectively burst into laughter.

"If I'm allowed to redirect the conversation," Sharpstand resumed with a smirk. "I think my son wasn't done with his attempt at it."

Dreden blinked. He had almost forgotten that he was the reason for the latest lecture tangent. His hand leafed through several more pages, back and forth. He made a mental note to improve his note-taking system. It was nearly as hard to decipher as *The Mage Unlimited.*

"As I was saying," continued the professor's son. "this text, even just the chunk from this page, goes from topic to topic with little logic, and we're not left with any resolution from any of them. I think this was because the author couldn't keep track of everything they were saying. If my intuition doesn't deceive me, I believe that by the end of the text we will start seeing rapid answers the author is coming up with for his own problems," He took a second to observe everyone watching him. They were flicking pencils and quills against their chins, giving their attention to him. "because they knew they were nearing the end of the work, and it was easier to reread recent entries than to go back over the entire thing. Maybe, this could deceive the reader into thinking there is more resolution to the work than there actually is, since the reader will lose track of the early topics and questions as they inevitably would find their minds wondering due to the so 'hard-to-follow-ness' of the majority of the work."

His father shot him a resigned smile. "On that account, I think the semester will be ending a little early this year." A few rogue claps surrounded him. "I know, I know, you'll have much more free time now that Dreden Sharpstand is your professor, but while I'm still in charge, there will be reading to do, regardless of how hard it is to follow or if there's a satisfactory resolution or not."

The rest of the lecture went smoothly. Dreden's argument was the last time he spoke that period. He left the rest of the discussion to his father and the other bright pupils such as Mister Maglant, who was now more attentive with his five brain cells than the whole previous semester, and Naphel. It was Dreden's only class of the day, so he was happy to get some drinks for himself after class and hang out with his two best friends.

"Remember, young ones," professor Sharpstand warned after a college employee came around ringing the recess bell. "The rest of *The Mage Unlimited* will not be impossible. If you made note of the specific sections we've talked about since the start, you will be fine for an exam. Promise. Have a good day!"

His classmates shuffled out of the room, snickering at some gossip. Dreden stayed put at his desk, watching his father flick back his thin, webby hair as he organized the books on his desk. When everyone was gone, he sighed and turned to his son, who was silently watching him, waiting for his father to say the first word.

"You did very good today." his father said. "I get more impressed every week with the kind of arguments you pull out of your rear and thump everyone with."

Dreden chuckled, rising from his seat. "Come on, father, you know I made a good point. I know it's one of your favorite texts, but you must see without accusing me of not having enough data that what I say has weight. Besides, the book is about a wizard. As university students, I'm sure you can imagine that texts with magic and other make-believe stuff are not things everyone is going to enjoy as much as you do."

"Of course I do, Dreden. Let me tell you, if I had the kind of book-smarts that you do right now at your age, I wouldn't be teaching right now. Heck, that's probably a good thing. One fewer alleged intellectual to wreak havoc on the masses."

His son rested an arm against the classroom brick wall. He frowned. When his father started talking like that, something was always wrong. The elder Sharpstand was an expert in the art of evading uncomfortable conversation topics, but like all social skills, if one observed him for enough time one would recognize when the skill was being implemented.

"Is something the matter?" Dreden asked.

The professor continued to shuffle a few more papers on his workspace before meeting his son in the eye. "Help me with the wall a moment. Even though we are by ourselves here, I don't think this is a topic for the classroom."

His son nodded. He grabbed the other side of the wall and began to shove it towards the professor. His father pulled from the other side to make the job easier. As the pair moved the wall, allowing it to rest against the classroom bookshelf by his father's desk, the secret part of the building was revealed.

There was everything that a small family needed to be content. Two beds rested on opposite sides of the room, acting as a sort of room-divider between the bedroom/lounge and the kitchen and dining room. A row of cabinets lined the far wall, above where the oven and the fireplace were.

The elder Sharpstand closed the wall behind them as the two of them stepped inside. To Dreden, it seemed like their home got smaller and smaller every day.

"I take it there's crappy news?" Dreden asked. "We always come in here for that. Not that there is ever any good news."

His father took a seat on his bed and took off his professor robe. "I won't argue about that. My application for tenure was denied. It looks like we're going to be stuck here for another while."

"How is that possible?" Dreden exclaimed. "I can't point out a single classmate that doesn't like you. This is nonsense! The university board must be insane!"

"Try to think of it from their perspective." he urged. "Every year the university gets less and less money. If they want to continue keeping up the appearance of a prestigious institution, they're going to have to reward their employees less and less."

His son paused, thinking to himself as he took out some of his class supplies and put them in the drawer by his bed. He knew what the reason for the school's budget deficit was. Hell, everyone knew. It was an unspoken truth, like knowing your wife was cheating on you but not saying anything in order to keep up a happy illusion. Nobody ever mentioned it, but it would be hard to find someone who didn't know, considering it impacted the lives of everyone in Kroonsaed, and not just the university. The enigmatic Sunitian Sea.

"I know." Dreden said, drooping his head as he sat on his bed. "I know. It's just… we deserve better than to be living in one of your classrooms. *You* deserve better than this."

Approaching his son on the bed, the professor had a gentle smile. "Well, it makes me happy to hear that." he exhaled. "I'd like to think that my colleagues are just as worthy of better accommodations, even though most of them are better off. It's not a competition, at least it shouldn't be. That's what some people don't understand. It's what most people don't understand."

"Have you ever wondered what you would do if you weren't a professor?" his son asked.

"Is a shark a shark if it doesn't eat fish?" asked the professor. "I think that even if I didn't get paid for it, it's who I am at heart."

Dreden stood up from his bed. His father watched him as he put on wool pants and a different, warmer jacket.

"Going out tonight with the usual crowd?" his father asked.

"Yeah. Gerrika and Chanin told me this morning that they would meet me at the tavern after my class with you."

"Have you told them yet about how you're turning my class against me?"

"No." Dreden laughed. "Chanin is always studying, so she's probably not much different from me."

"But not Gerrika." his father shook his head. "I assume that that's not a problem the aveho has ever had?"

"Totally. The bird's hollow bones would crumble upon even the slightest notion!"

"I have a lunch meeting with some of the other department professors. I likely won't be too long, but if you're going to be out late, just leave a note under the door to let me know."

"Will do." His son gave him a thumbs-up as he opened the wall again and saw himself out.

"And remember to finish the next chapter of *The Mage Unlimited*" the professor shouted before his son was gone.

In Another World...

"This is how I like it." Cipre said.

"Fine, I won't push anymore." Her colleague, Matry, said. "I guess I'm just awfully quirky that way."

"You're telling *me*?"

Matry turned from her and filled up his mug with water from their floor's drink bowl. He took a slow sip, testing it. Satisfied, he socially stood against a vacant desk right across the aisle from Cipre.

He took another sip and licked the water off his lips. "I just want you to be the best manuscript reader you can. From my experience, it's hard to do that when your desk is so cluttered."

"I told you," She shot him another smile. "I'm aware that it's a mess, but at least I know where everything is. Besides, it would mean more coming from someone who didn't lose things all the fucking time."

He playfully scoffed. "Excuse me?"

"Don't pretend that you don't know what I'm talking about. I hear you asking some of the other readers for pens all the time."

"That's true." Matry confessed. "I guess I just think that if I can keep my work completely organized, soon my entire life will follow suit."

"I hope it works out for you. You're a good reader, Matry. I hope you get a manuscript that becomes a great book." She eyed the clutter of pages on her desk. "I hope *any* of us do."

"You say that as if you're not the one in charge of *A Mad Past*."

"I have...reservations about that book."

"Don't let me bother you anymore. I need to get back to my desk and... ask Callen if I can borrow a pen with red ink."

She put her face in her palm, chuckling as she watched Matry leave her office and go out of sight. Adjusting herself, she fixed around some of the loose pages from the clutter, put them back to their proper place, and continued reading some of the latest submissions the printing company received.

Cipre didn't dislike her job. She enjoyed it. She *wanted* to love it. Their printing company, Mirthinout Printing, was the best in the city, and one of the best in all Skaltbard. At least that was how their reputation had presented them. Nowadays, she wasn't so sure.

Most of the fiction manuscripts she'd read in the last two years had painfully lacked originality. She couldn't remember the last submission she read that wasn't about a wealthy family dealing with the problems of being wealthy.

She read so many pieces over the past couple years that it almost seemed as if every original observation about the condition of society and life had already been made. Every new story was simply a shallow and pale version of a philosophy that an earlier author had beaten them to. It never helped that the only people who could come to the variety of observations and epiphanies were always the same types of people, and Cipre knew that all those tropes were now everywhere. Life imitating art, indeed.

A man in a well-kept suit and cravat approached her at her desk. He had a giant file under one of his arms, and a smile that was about as warm as the cup of fresh tea in his other hand.

"Radoff, I see you're getting to work earlier than usual." Cipre said to him.

"Oh, yes, I ended up going to sleep sooner than expected last night." the man replied. "I had an event with the wife and kids in the early evening yesterday. It had me beat."

"Tough being so obligated to such things, I imagine." Cipre smirked.

"How envious I am of you, woman." he replied. "Not a care in the world, when you leave this place and go home, except to continue your slavish devotion to fine literature here at the company."

"Don't let me keep you from your work. Most people will be startled to see the boss here so early in the day. I can already smell the sweat of the slackers dripping."

Radoff Dell laughed, giving her desk a hearty tap of approval. The boss took a big sip of his tea and started off to his office at the end of the room. Before he turned for the hallway, Cipre leaned back in her chair and called for him.

"Radoff!"

Her boss's head came back around. When she didn't start talking right away, he knew she wanted to have a more serious discussion. Radoff put his files down against the wall by Cipre's desk and took a seat opposite her.

"Is this about wanting to pick up extra hours again?"

"No…no." she said. "It's more complicated than that."

"That's for me to decide." he grinned.

His employee smiled in reply, seemingly to delay the uncomfortable nature of what she wished to talk about. "I love my job, you of all people know that. But still, I'm finding it hard to keep up the pleasure of being a professional manuscript reader and editor."

Radoff nodded. When he didn't reply, Cipre took that as a sign to say more.

"Not that I think I'm too good for a job like this. No way. Most people would kill to be in a position like mine," she cupped her hands together, pensively. "but… it almost appears, from my desk here, that the cultural advancements of our nation have ceased."

"Interesting observation." He crossed his legs. "Do go on. You have my curiosity."

"I'm a hard worker. I read many submissions every week. In my early days here, every story I read had something original and unique, and the characters felt so real. So many of them, the ones that took place in Brunswald, made me fall deeper in love with this city of ours." She paused to take a view out of the window. Through the corner of her vision, she saw her boss do the same. Of all the cities in the countries in all the world, Brunswald's skyline was a thing of envy. The balance between its culture and industry made it inimitable in the unsteady modern world.

"If I'm getting you correctly, and I think that I am," Radoff interjected. "You're saying that you don't believe people these days have any interesting ideas anymore."

She nodded with a mix of shame and confidence.

"Honestly, I don't know if I would agree with you, but if you're right, you're not the first reader in my business to come up with that hypothesis."

"I mean, not that they're not *some* good stories coming in, because most of them definitely are, but they're all about the same types of people. It's been too long since I've seen a story of a character who was… new. A character destined for a new kind of adventure."

Cipre could hear his boss gulp. "You're saying for certain that you don't think Morell Edland's *A Mad Past* is going to do it?"

"I'm not sure. I haven't finished it yet, but I suspect that I won't feel any differently about it compared to all the other submissions."

"I mean…" her boss continued, hesitant. "I'm not going to try to influence the way you feel about his work, but I also don't want to lie to you. Whether or not you're right about the lack of recent original ideas in our submissions, the public, aware of it or not, might share your feelings."

She didn't need Radoff to say anything else. As world-famous and successful as they were, Mirthinout had been steadily losing money over the last few years. With the steady decline that they had been monitoring month after month, they needed a big winner on their hands.

And if Morell Edland wasn't going to be their new literary star, then no one was going to be.

"Don't worry," Cipre told him. "you don't need to worry about influencing how I feel. I can almost hear the jingling of change in the Edlands' pockets with every word of his novel that I read."

"I guess that can't be avoided." Her boss said, shaking his head in defeat. "The Edlands might be the richest family in the country, but that certainly doesn't mean that their son has talent. Tell you what, send his manuscript my way once you're done with it. This opportunity to get in that family's pockets is too sweet for us to risk."

"Will do, Radoff." she said. "I'll finish it up today and be ready for the young man himself when he comes in for his meeting."

Taking his cup of tea, which had stopped steaming during their conversation, her boss set her free to work.

She reached into the bottom drawer of her desk and took out the young Edland's novel. Not wanting to let her boss down, or herself, she read his words, looking for a new adventure.

CHAPTER 2

Dreden could always tell from the sounds of the crowd if his friends had beaten him to their usual hangout spot. The tavern they frequented didn't have the best business as of late, and Chanin and Gerrika had easily decipherable voices. Gerrika was the easier one, because of the fact that there weren't as many avehos around, and his species typically spoke in a higher pitch, yet sounded like their voices could have been made by a ringing cello.

Chanin Adderfoth was a different story. She was a human like most of the people in the area, but some of her features were not what one would have assumed a young woman would have. Her eyes were more sunken in, making her brow arch notably over them, like an ancient biological cousin of humans. She had brown hair, cut short, making herself different from every other girl at Faeriebridge. Her eyes had a tendency to grow twice in size whenever she was studying history or when either he or Gerrika were telling a fun or personal story. Gerrika and Chanin were both odd and they knew it. He was often a lone aveho in a university of humans. She was a human who didn't play by convention. They clung together.

The pub crowd wasn't booming. It gave Dreden some solace. For all the struggling his hometown was going through, at least he didn't feel like he was the only one going through the hard times.

Gerrika and Chanin were sitting in their favorite spot. It was a table in the far corner from the entrance near where the servers poured their ale out of the barrels.

"Hello, Dreden!" Gerrika cheered upon seeing him. "You're just in time for the second round of drinks."

Dreden greeted the black-feathered humanoid bird with a wave. Chanin turned to him as well and gave him a smile which he returned.

"Second round?" he asked, taking a seat at their table. "Guys, I'm even a few minutes early. What could have possessed you to start drinking without me, and to drink so quickly?"

Chanin bumped arms with Gerrika. "Don't blame me. It was his idea. I don't think he did too well on his philosophy exam."

Gerrika crossed his arms and huffed. "I didn't. Forgive me if there are a few subjects I'm not the top student in."

The crow-looking aveho was wearing a rugged unbuttoned brown jacket with a pair of black pants that he needed to get a special size for, since he was thin even for his own species. Below those, he sported his usual large black rain boots, which he wore regardless of the weather. Avehos had large feet for the bodies, compared to humans, with three toes on each foot, even though their hand-talons had a full five fingers. One wouldn't have expected it from a civilized creature, but aveho talons tended to rival an eagle's in their sharpness.

Taking a few sips of her dark ale, Chanin had spilled some tiny specs onto her red cotton long-sleeved shirt. Her legs were crossed under the table, and they were covered in brown leather pants. She wore boots as well, but only today because of how cloudy it looked when she woke up. She typically preferred to wear open-toed shoes.

"Besides, who wants to study philosophy these days anyway?" Gerrika asked.

"Maybe if you used that topic for your term paper, your professor would give you a perfect score." Dreden said.

The aveho turned to him, frowning. Even though his friend had a beak, an aveho's face could be just as expressive as a human's, even if it was covered in dark feathers.

"Sadly, not all of us have our parents as professors." his friend replied, lightening up.

"You've got the wrong idea." Chanin said. "I think Dreden's dad goes harder on him than he does anyone else in his classes. You should have heard him last time I visited their place: '*Do the reading. Son, do the reading. Remember The Mage Unlimited!*'."

Dreden shrugged with a smirk. He called the bartender over and asked for his usual fruity wheat beer.

"You two," he started. "he's a passionate man. What can I tell you? He's someone who has his own ideas and philosophy figured out, and I think he wants me to sort of share his obsessions."

The bartender, a pale shaggy man named Irin, came over and delivered Dreden his beer. He thanked him.

"Besides," resumed Dreden. "it's not like it bothers me. It would bother me if I weren't a good student. If I weren't, I would think that he was just constantly pestering me about my grades, but because I'm one of his best students, I just take it as him always being a father."

Gerrika tapped his boots against the wooden floor. "If that's what being a good father is all about, then my father is severely lacking in his practice."

"I would disagree. We all know you turned out excellent." Chanin smiled.

"The credit is mostly my father's, despite all the crap I get from him, but thank you very much. You're wise for a mammal."

Dreden took a healthy gulp of his beer and wiped some foam off his lips.

"You've hardly touched your second beer, pal." Dreden said. "Something on your mind?"

"No." replied the avian. He cupped the corner of his yellow beak in his hand. "I've just had enough already."

Chanin picked up Gerrika's beer glass and held it close to the tip of his beak. "Come on. How else are you going to be as puffy chested as the rest of your species?"

"Yeah." Gerrika snorted. "I don't mind being scrawny, even for an aveho. Heck, all that strength and speed our biology gifted us with, and we hardly do anything with it. I'd like to think I'm ahead in the race."

It might have been what his pal had just said about not drinking anymore, but Dreden was starting to feel exhausted. His after-class meetings with his two best friends always stimulated him and got rid of any boredom still lingering in his mind from school. Sometimes it wasn't enough. It looked like it was going to be another one of those days.

"You two got any plans for the rest of the day?" Chanin asked.

The pair shook their heads.

"Not much. If I don't find something to do, I'll probably just sit at home with tea and a book." Dreden took another big sip of his beer. He knew it was already his final sip of the day.

"We could go see a play." Chanin looked at her two friends with a twinkle in her eyes.

"The last one was a dud." Gerrika tapped his glass pensively with his feathered fingers. "It didn't do much that was productive. Just some cheap laughs."

Chanin grabbed the aveho by the shoulder. "Come on, please! If I don't do anything else, my mom is going to set me up on another blind date."

"Oof." Dreden grimaced. "She's still on about that?"

"Yeah, and it's bugging the shit out of me. I mean, hasn't she ever seen me? Who would want to date someone who looks more like a boy than a girl?"

"I think you're pretty." The bird said under his beak.

"Thanks, sweetie." she smiled. "But it would mean more if that came from a member of my own species. You know, someone who I could physiologically make a child with."

"I think you're pretty." Dreden echoed.

The woman lowered her head, trying to hide her smile. "You're both very nice, but the fact that I'm twenty and not in a relationship is a burden to my family. They probably think I'll only get uglier and more ape-looking with age."

"Don't worry about it, Chanin. I know what could help. Gerrika, come on, let's see a play tonight."

The aveho paused, crossing his arms over his chest. "Ugh, alright. But nothing so uptight like the last one. I swear, even for a town like ours, they seem to forget that avehos have written plays too. Everything is always by a human."

None of them took another gulp of beer, but the trio did end up getting a round of water before heading out to get tickets to the play. As much as Dreden cared for his two friends, he felt that their hangouts were starting to get repetitive. As if they always ended up on the same topics of conversation. That was life when money was hard to come by. That was life when much of the land was infertile from all the colorful gas looming over former farming areas.

The gas was called the Sunitian Sea, and it was as mysterious as it was breathtaking. It typically glowed a bright green with intermittent flashes of red and violet as if it were a thick rainbow that no one asked for. The people of Kroonsaed would have loved to learn more about it, but it had a tendency to suck the oxygen out of one's lungs if they got too close.

And that was a problem, since the Sunitian Sea had expanded more inland over the last few years. Thankfully, according to university studies, it currently was at a standstill.

15

Shaking his thoughts away, Dreden and his friends went down the street. They didn't know what play the local theater was putting on, but they didn't really care. None of them were bothered at the idea of staying out late so they could avoid feeling so stranded in their own homes.

Her latest literary catch was sitting right in front of her. Cipre's eyes were diverted as she skimmed the final pages of the young man's manuscript. She was conducting her usual last-minute hunt for grammatical errors to mark for her future polishing of the story. She had finished on time, as she promised Radoff.

Morell Edland arrived right on the dot for their meeting.

"Everything looks good, Mister Edland."

The writer brushed his hand through the air. "Are you always so formal with your clients?"

"Yes." she said. "I always like to think of these meetings as if they were the start of a vital business."

"Well said." Morell's youthful yet chiseled jaw formed a smile of a proud man. "I think civilization can never have enough stories. It might not rank among some commodities such as food, shelter, and water, but stories are commodities for the soul. Anyway, Mister Edland is what my father and my grandfather are called. I'm just Morell."

Cipre smiled at him. "That's a very nice name."

"It's been in my family a long time. Even before the time of the last monarchs. It was a name they gave to the sons my family believed were destined to be great warriors. I'd like to think I'd suffice, even if I'm simply a warrior of the pen."

Morell gave a light chuckle. Cipre didn't want to insult the printing company's newest gem, so she laughed along with him.

"Of that I've no doubt." she replied. "This is such a great accomplishment for someone as young as yourself. I assume your parents are thrilled by the talent of their twenty-three-year-old?"

"Very content. Though when I first brought up my creative ambitions my poor mother nearly lost her marbles. Though what did she know? She didn't become a cultured reader until she saw through me what storytelling could do. How it could mold the minds and morals of an entire people, one day winding up treasured mythology… but enough of that. I apologize, I think I interrupted you a while ago."

"No no, it's fine. This is all important information." Cipre gave the large pile of parchment a couple taps. "Now, the story. I wanted to just ask you a couple questions about it."

Morell leaned back in his chair and lowered his eyes at her. "Anything."

"Your protagonist, Lady Hanning, she overcomes her poverty…" she flipped through the last half of the novel, swiftly reading through the tabs she marked for herself. "Yes. Yes. She falls from her high status when it's revealed the marriage between her and Lord Hanning is a farce, and she is outcast…"

Cipre didn't say anything for a few moments. The only sound was the creaking of Morell's chair as he shifted around in it. Another few seconds passed before the young writer said: "Yes?"

"Basically," she continued. "One of my main questions focused on the dichotomy between herself and society's more vulnerable populations. And… it didn't end up going at all where I thought it was going to go. That subversive nature is one of the best things *A Mad Past* has going for it."

Morell nodded, his arms still crossed, looking like a cat proud of fishing a minnow out of a wine glass.

"If I've read this correctly, I think that this story is almost revolutionary both because of how self-aware it is and how knowing it is of its setting, of its morals and where they came from."

"They told me you were one of the best readers here, and now I see that I wasn't deceived." Morell said, nodding amicably.

"Very kind of you to say." Cipre showed her teeth. "This journey Lady Hanning takes, from her wealthy education and upbringing, to the disgrace of her aristocratic parents, to the disease-ridden roads of outer Cilsa, only to discover that she was a princess, the true heir to the throne in the end, it was a feel-good story, and means more than it seems, because damn, this is…"

"Rediscovery?" Morell said.

"Yes, that's the word I was looking for." Cipre replied. "The way culture follows your characters. Relics from centuries ago are used as these totems of time, and it works because I believe you've put into words, albeit *many* words, something that we've all been thinking about in this city but haven't known yet how to say it."

"And not just Brunswald… I think the whole country of Skaltbard suffers from this cultural and emotional impotence."

Cipre tapped her pen on her desk in accord. "Evident by Lady Hanning's journey across coast to coast of the old country. Now, if there was one concern I had about this story's impact, it would be about what certain parts-"

The whole five-story building of Mirthinout Printing shook like a bowl of gelatin in a carriage. The clicking of desks against the wooden floor and the jingling of metal mugs and glasses in the hallway cabinets sounded like a dam about to burst. Mirthinout's workers began to huddle out of their rooms and offices in a worried mash.

"What the hell is happening?" Morell cried out as he gripped the edges of his seat for balance.

"It must be an earthquake!" Cipre shouted.

Her chair didn't have the steady arms that her client's chair did, so the best she could do was to hold on to the heavy drawers filled with files and novels and other important things for her job. It didn't do much, but it kept her rear secure in her seat.

In the chaos, with the loud murmuring of her colleagues and the shuffle of objects around, she didn't need perfect hearing to solve the earthquake mystery. Sunlight was drained from her window. It was being shadowed by an immense dark form. The form was moving too fast for Cipre to see more than a misshapen blur, but the first thing she could see was a massive tail. She didn't know if her eyes were being deceived by how fast the thing was moving, but the tail looked dark, long, and thin. Farther up along the blur were five shapes that protruded from the base. Whatever this being was, it had legs, arms, and a head.

With how fast it was moving, the sun should not have been blocked out for more than a portion of a second. But the creature changed course when it had reached the roof of Mirthinout. It was now flying *towards* the sun, keeping the window in shade for an extra few seconds. When the creature got far enough, the sun returned, as did the structural integrity of everything in the building.

"Well, if that wasn't a sign from fate, then I don't know what it was." Morell said.

"How do you mean?" Cipre said. She struggled to organize things back to normal, though she was still shaken up.

"Perhaps the Creator Himself is giving me one last chance to back out of a deal with you." he laughed.

She returned a laugh to him, awkwardly. From the sound of it, they were the first ones to return to business after the quake. Many people in the offices behind her had fallen on the floor or had objects from shelves tumble onto them. Regardless, there was a lot of groaning coming from the floor, and the cleaning crew was being summoned from the basement.

"I should probably be assisting my coworkers with the aftermath of... the earthquake."

Her client nodded. "Good on you. I think we had a great meeting, and it seemed like it was about to end anyway."

Cipre smiled and shook his hand. "I'll have a letter in the mail for you regarding another meeting, but I can nearly assure you for certain that your story will be our biggest priority this year."

"That news will make my folks happier than a basket of bunnies." he replied, flashing her more of his perfect white teeth. "Thank you once more for having me today. I only hope that next time there's no earthquake. I'd hate to think that supernatural forces are against me."

With a last wave, Morell Edland was heading downstairs, back to his carriage.

There was a parade of thoughts going through Cipre's head. With everyone else being so busy during the quake, it seemed like her view out the window had made her unique. *Could I be the only one who saw the creature?* she thought. *Morell Edland was sitting right next to me, and he didn't bother to correct me when I referred to the incident as an 'earthquake'. Whatever it was, it moved almost too quickly to be seen.* She knew he was also not as taken aback as she was by the incident. Then again, by the sounds of it, there might have been some injuries.

She didn't have much more to do at work. The addition of the quake caused by the mysterious behemoth's flying probably meant that she would mostly be doing cleaning the rest of the day. Cipre resolved to keep her secret to herself. Surely *someone* else on the city streets or in the other buildings saw the creature too. Perhaps she would ask Matry about it, but that could wait.

Time for office hours, thought professor Renny Sharpstand as he left his bedroom. *I wonder if anyone will show up tonight.*

While he did hope that at least one person would come, it didn't bother him much when he was alone the entire time. They were good kids. They all were. They scored high on tests, were respectful of him and all the other professors, and, hell, they even sometimes laughed at his jokes. With each semester, he never knew what he was going to get, or even what the curriculum would be in some of his classes, but with all that going for him, along with the presence of his son, this semester was one of the happiest ones he had in a long while. He couldn't recall many happy times since the death of his wife back when Dreden was still too young for school.

He sat down at his desk and brushed his black cobwebby hair out of his nose. He had meant to cut it a while back but part of him worried that if he cut his hair, it wouldn't grow back. Made sense. That was simply aging. Of course, that wasn't something to be ashamed of. Many people in Kroonsaed didn't grow up to be old.

He flipped open his copy of *The Mage Unlimited*. If he was going to have another empty night, he figured he would put it to good use. His next lesson on the text wouldn't be for a couple days, as most classes only met every other day with a short break every so often.

As his fingers leafed through the pages and he perused his notes, he thought about his son. Dreden was one of his best students, if not his best. That made him happy, though he knew that that happiness was a drying creek. In just few months, he would not know what his son would be doing, or what any of his friends were doing.

Chanin perhaps had it best, if one took a grim look at it. She was a woman. While not conventionally pretty, she had the capacity to marry into stability. That was a possibility neither his son nor Gerrika had. He certainly wasn't rich, so no major marriage prospects were going to come from his son. Because of the ratio between avehos and humans in Kroonsaed, Gerrika may as well be rotten meat. Sure, there were a lot of avehos in Kroonsaed, and a handful of them attended Faeriebridge, but Gerrika never flocked with his own kind. His father was a hunter, probably the best in the country, but that wasn't enough to give them the money to move somewhere where there were more avehos.

That was what Honja, Gerrika's father, wanted.

The professor dwelled on the subjects for about an hour when he heard his door creep open and the sound of heavy boots follow. He didn't bother to look up, as he was nose deep in his notes. By the sound and rhythm of the footfalls he knew it wasn't a student. He knew who it was.

"Professor Sharpstand," a man's voice greeted.

He looked up to see his visitor. The man was neatly dressed in a white shirt and brown vest. He had a pair of black cotton pants, and his jaw was just as defined as the wrinkles on the arms of his shirt.

"Garad, very nice of you to come in during my free time, as opposed to during class time."

Garad let out a gentle snort. It was his version of a grin. "Yes. At the suggestion of the university council, my etiquette has improved."

"Well done." replied Sharpstand. "That makes me smile, but something tells me that you didn't come here to give me a simple life update."

Garad nodded. "Professor, how long would you say we've known each other?"

"Upwards of ten years. Ever since I started teaching here."

"Or 'professing' as you call it. Yes. Ten years sounds about right. I've been the Lord of this institution since before your time here. It was a less trying time back then, but there were still troubles."

Sharpstand had a feeling he knew where Garad was going with his speech. He didn't want Garad to get to the point. "Yes, and your chest is just as visible through your shirt, and your chin can still be mistaken for a blunt object."

The other man showed no sign of amusement. He approached Sharpstand even more and put a hand on his shoulder.

"I've always appreciated your presence here." Renny Sharpstand's face fell at those words. The school's Lord noticed, and his brow furrowed. "Lately, it's been *too* hard. It's the kind of thing we tell ourselves that we won't have to worry about, because it'll be the problem of the grandkids of our grandkids. Well, my friend, *we* are the grandkids now."

"You're going to fire me. Isn't that right?"

"That will be a subject of my next meeting with the university council, but it isn't looking good. Sharpstand, you know if I weren't pushed into this position that this is something I would never do."

The professor sighed, folding his arms. "I suppose that warms me up an itty bit."

"Times being what they are, it's going to get a lot worse before it gets better, *if* it gets better."

"Same old stuff I assume?" asked the professor. "Adults in Kroonsaed aren't having enough kids, and our economy is becoming more unstable and resources are dwindling. That kind of stuff?"

"That's not all. We had some people in the natural philosophy department do some research, and the Sunitian Sea isn't retreating like we hoped. Last time turned out to be a major miscalculation." He lowered his voice, as if worried the gases themselves would hear him. "That sea is getting closer. It's already taken so much from us and it's decided it hasn't taken enough."

Sharpstand didn't know what else to do but nod silently. What else could he do? It was news to him, but it wasn't surprising. *How long have the natural philosophers been at it?* the professor wondered. *Isn't this knowledge that is supposed to be given to the public as well?*

"How many people know about this?" he asked.

"Not many. The results were given to me earlier today. Unless there's some other covert team out there conducting the same research, the only people that know are in the natural philosophy department, and yourself."

"What do you plan on doing with it?" asked the professor.

"I assume the best thing going forward would be to haul ass and divert more funding to research."

"No, I meant regarding informing the public about the Sunitian Sea."

Garad paused. Sharpstand could see in his boss's face that it wasn't something he had yet thought about. "I don't think it's smart to rush things. That's all I can tell you right now."

"If I may speak," said the professor. "hopefully as someone that is still employed by this university, I think it is something that should be published. The people of Kroonsaed have had it hard enough as of late. In case things take a turn for the darkest, I think people should have time to do the best with whatever they have."

"I'm glad you have a positive attitude about this, my friend." Garad said. "This... won't be easy for a while. Our diverting of funds to the natural philosophy department is no luxury for anyone."

Now, with his back fully turned, he stepped one foot out the door. "You probably have another couple weeks of lecturing before any decision we make is finalized. If I were you, I'd start planning your final lesson and advice to your students. I'm afraid that's by far the most likely outcome."

"That's plenty of time." Sharpstand replied, with a forlorn smile. He brushed his hair out of his eyes. Suddenly it seemed even lighter. "Good luck to the rest of you. I'm almost glad I'm not one of you."

CHAPTER 3

The Prime Minister of Skaltbard couldn't put his novel down. The story was incredibly engaging and thrilling, but a meeting was about to start, and everyone would have appreciated it if he were paying attention.

"Right. Right." Prime Minister Charles Dowlepot shoved his book under his desk, dog-earing the page on the chapter he'd just finished. "Thank you all for coming."

The secretary of war nodded his head obediently. Dowlepot caught it. It made him wonder how much people actually cared to critique his writings and speeches.

"Aren't you forgetting something?" asked one of his aides, Mister Skitt. He was a mousy man with a thinning hairline.

"Whatever are you-?" Skitt poked him on the shoulder and pointed to the Prime Minister's wife, who was chatting up with the assistant to one of the ambassadors. "Oh. Hon, we're about to start here..."

Venka Dowlepot was an unusually tall woman. She was several inches taller than her husband, and the fact that she always wore heels didn't help. Despite the fact that she had been bred and raised in Brunswald, there was almost something foreign about her. From her speech pattern to the way her hair brushed against the sides of her smooth face, she had the look of someone who didn't want the political life, but became a part of it like a caterpillar to a butterfly.

So it was no surprise that ambassadors and diplomats in the room couldn't get enough of her.

"Excuse me, Venka." Charles turned over his shoulder.

Her eyes caught his, in the middle of one of her laughs. She managed to keep it, despite knowing very well what he was going to tell her. "Yes, Charles?"

The Prime Minister coughed sheepishly. "The meeting is about to start, so...do you mind getting refreshments in the common room? We hopefully won't be too long."

"No problem. No problem."

The meeting was scheduled to begin at noon. It was two minutes after. Venka knew it, but she took her time with the diplomats on the way out. She put her hands on their shoulders, bending over slightly to be eye-level with them, and allowed them to kiss her hand before finally showing herself to the door.

Now they could start.

"Alright. I appreciate you all being able to meet today." Charles's shoulders felt heavy from all the eyes on him. "I hope you're not too bothered by the delay. Like I said, I think this isn't going to take long anyway."

He saw a hand fly out from all the way across the table. There were two representatives blocking his view, but he could tell from the wrinkled, pasty palm that it belonged to Ogdell Bloom of Borgetta, the man who was clearly the oldest among them.

"Ambassador Bloom," greeted Charles. "do you have a question already?"

"In fact, I do." The Prime Minister relaxed at seeing everyone's heads turn to the old man.

"Please, do deliberate."

"How much of this meeting will deal with your conflicts with Andayt?" asked Ogdell.

"Most of it." he replied. "If not, the papers are going to have my ass again."

A soft grumble swept the room.

"Okay, we're already talking about it." Charles exhaled. "What angle of my foreign policy does your question deal with?"

"The one about how Borgetta is contractually obligated to sell you weapons despite our peace with Andayt."

The Prime Minister adjusted his collar. The room was already getting hot. "I thought I had my envoy clear that up with you last week?"

The old man prepared to stand up. "Fat job he did! I told that kid I wasn't signing anything without speaking to the Andaytian representative himself!"

"Mister Bloom," interjected a middle-aged man named Thatch, another one of Dowlepot's aides. "We've made it clear to you in the past that that is extremely difficult to arrange. All talks with them went out the window when they closed their borders to us."

"But they never did such a thing to *my* nation!" Ogdell shook his arms about, looking like an albino monkey. He turned to Charles once more. "Prime Minister, surely you can sympathize with us. Borgetta has no qualms with Andayt. Sure, they might fit your definition of a 'rogue' nation, but that's none of our concerns. We have to take care of our own people, and with the economy we have right now, it's getting difficult."

A few heads turned to the far corner. The Skaltbard corner. It was obvious that several other representatives were ready to swoop like hawks to discuss the grievances of the escalating conflict.

A new voice rose above the murmurs. "If I can just say one thing..."

The voice belonged to the ambassador from Gontland. Gontland, along with Andayt, was one of the few major nations that was still a kingdom, and the ambassador was a strange presence in the room, considering his youth. Charles would have expected someone Ogdell Bloom's age from a comparatively 'backwards' nation.

"Mister Pulk, you have the floor." said the Prime Minister.

The young man named Pulk rose from his seat. *Excellent*, thought Charles, *we're not even in the room for five minutes and we already have someone standing.*

"Ambassador Bloom," he began. "Gontland has been a neighbor of Borgetta's since pretty much the dawn of written history. Would you say that we've largely been a good neighbor to you?"

Ogdell adjusted himself in his seat. "Yes, but in this instance, that is neither here nor-"

"And in that time," he didn't skip a beat. "our two nations have had similar economic troubles. Our shores are restless, and storms thrash our major ports many times a year. We've been able to make it work by being such cooperative allies for thousands of years."

The Prime Minister knocked on his desk twice, getting the young man's attention. "Mister Pulk, I trust that this romantic rambling is going to lead to an argument."

"It is, Minister. As I was saying, ambassador, the legislative changes of *your* Prime Minister back in Borgetta seem to suggest that your leadership isn't familiar with history. For the first time in nobody here knows how long, your leadership is ignoring the cries of the Gontish people, in favor of nourishing the pettiest of your needs. Your congress awarding themselves another raise? Making sure the big dogs in your government all have enough money to maintain their personal yachts at the expense of the needs of the working class? What do you say to that?"

"I say," the old man rose. Charles was worried that the poor brute was going to have a stroke. "That times change, and sometimes one person or maybe an entire state needs to change with them. The Borgettan government isn't about to mindlessly adhere to a tradition, no matter how great, for the sake of funds received from a future war that could end up killing Andaytians, a people Borgetta has no anger towards. *That*, is what I say, you pestilent fool!"

Charles couldn't think of a single thing he could do to take back the meeting. It was like a flaming chariot tumbling down a mountain with each horse charging in a different direction. Former quiet ambassadors and representatives lit up along with the outraged young and old men, demanding that the Skaltbard leader give them time to the floor as well, and when someone kept talking over another, they accused Charles of not taking their issues seriously.

He was wrong. The meeting ended up taking the entire afternoon. Venka was probably going to be fresh with him afterwards. Hopefully she would understand that the elected leader of Skaltbard, the most powerful nation on the planet, was under great stress.

When all the men finally shuffled out of the room, the sun was setting. Charles felt ten years older as he lowered his head to the desk and put his hands on the back of his neck. *This thing*, he thought, groaning. *This thing could end up becoming a world war. The* first *world war. How did this happen?*

The weather's not that bad, Dreden thought. *If only it was this nice last night when we went to that play.*

Of course, he didn't make that observation out loud, as he and his two friends had already exhausted all conversations about the weather for the night, as they rested their behinds sitting in the Town Square. Sometimes it seemed like none of them had any idea of what they wanted to do, only that they were content with each other's company.

"Why is that?" asked Gerrika.

Dreden blinked. "Why is what?"

The aveho smirked with his eagle-like beak. "Did you get lost in the clouds again?"

"I guess I did." he forced a laugh. "Can you remind me what happened?"

"You made a comment about how it so often seems that none of us has any idea how to spend our time. I agreed, and we all went silent for a while as we pondered our answers."

"I think I know." Chanin said.

"What's your theory?" Dreden asked.

"It's simply that we spend too much time together."

The response earned laughs from Dreden and Gerrika.

"You might be right about that." Dreden said. "My father does tell me I should branch out and make more friends."

"That wouldn't sit well with *my* father." the aveho replied. "He'd rather I not have friends at all. He detests humans."

The humans nodded to themselves. Even though it was a joke, there was truth to it.

Gerrika's eyes darted the other way, looking like he regretted saying so much. "Well, not enough to stop me from hanging out with you guys. But he'd rather I stick with my own species. Hard, since I've never had an aveho friend."

The aveho seemed antsy to change the subject. Dreden didn't want to put any more pressure on his friend than necessary. Despite all their times hanging out together, Gerrika never told Dreden and Chanin much about his home life.

"I mean," Chanin started. "while we're on the subject of 'things we do all the time' we may as well head over to our spot right outside Heathback Caverns."

The other human shrugged. "I'm down for that. I could go for a nice breeze right about now."

"Solid with me." his friend replied. "I think the people living around here would want us to go about now anyway. No use in Dreden's father getting any more complaints about our loitering."

The sun finished setting while they were on their way to the cave. It was about a three-mile walk, but they never minded. The trio knew how to get home, despite the supreme lack of lighting along the way as well as the bumpy dirt mounds they needed to traverse.

Heathback Caverns was the largest cavern system in Kroonsaed. It was once speculated that there was a fortune to be found deep inside, but adventurers and daredevils only ever found pieces of old bones once belonging to extinct beasts, as well as a cold water stream that let out into a river a couple blocks away from the edge of town.

After a while the Magistrate, Kroonsaed's governor, had to deem the entire cavern system off limits due to the ecological disruption explorers were causing to the indigenous fauna, as well as the inevitable natural destruction caused by scores of inconsiderate groups. Because of the law, the three friends couldn't actually go in the caves, but they could hang out inside an altar-shaped slice on the rear side of the rock formations facing the forest.

Dreden, Chanin, and Gerrika got to the cavern slice in just under two hours. It was always strangely cool there, as if the stream ran right through their little hovel. And when it was hot, they took off their boots and planted their soles on the cold rocks.

"Finally," Chanin said as she stepped into the alcove.

The two males let out breaths of relief. Even though they were used to walking the distance, sometimes it still made them long for their beds.

"And we'll have to make the trip back too." Dreden smiled. "That's going to be wonderful."

Gerrika took a seat on one of the larger rocks and crossed his legs, kicking off his boots as he rested his bare avian feet on the cavern floor.

"Ahhh," sighed the aveho. "I know that it's plenty cold right now, but the additional chill on my feet is giving me energy."

The trio was sitting on the most chair-like rocks available. They passed the time by talking some more and kicking pebbles back and forth to each other. After only a few minutes, they landed on the topic of food.

"You guys aren't hungry?" Dreden asked.

Chanin brushed her hair back, leaning forward with her broad shoulders. "I could eat something, but that would mean walking all the way back to town."

"Fine by me." Gerrika said, fixing his feathery tail under him. "The alternative is catching something around here, and I'm not in the mood for something uncooked."

Dreden looked defeated. "Really? We just came all this way, and now we're going to go back?" He shook his head. "Come on. Let's at least watch the bugs along the walls. That's always fun."

"I can't quite think of something I want to do less than that." Chanin replied.

"Maybe we should, Chanin," Gerrika said. "If not, Dreden is probably going to go on another one of his 'meaning of life' talks and drag us down with him."

He shook off his friend's comment with a smile. Gerrika wasn't wrong. Whenever they started to struggle for things to talk about, Dreden typically pushed the two of them into a philosophical dialogue. Chanin and Gerrika usually humored him, but sometimes they weren't in the mood.

Philosophy wasn't their thing, and he knew it. A part of him sometimes longed for other company. He knew that spending time with people who were as well-read in philosophy as he and his father were would make him happier, but Dreden was never good at meeting new people. Besides, Gerrika and Chanin were great.

"Are the bugs edible at least?" Gerrika asked. "Like, they're not going to burn my stomach?"

"What is it with you and food tonight?" Dreden laughed.

"I'm hungry, okay! I should have eaten something before we left town."

"Doesn't your father ever cook for you?" Chanin asked.

"He offers plenty, but I don't like what he hunts. I prefer traditional human food."

Wow, Dreden thought. *Gerrika told us two details about his personal life tonight. That's definitely a record.*

The trio went quiet, like they were contemplating deeply what Gerrika had said.

He wasn't sure what Chanin was thinking, but Dreden couldn't help but look down at the cavern floor. Usually taking the whole walk all the way to the caverns made them all awake enough to have personal discussions to last until many hours after the sun went down. He figured it was something in Gerrika's mood. He was usually the one in the best spirits. He supposed that the fact that something seemed to be bothering the aveho was keeping them all down, like he was their emotional lifeboat.

A splatting sound of boots on mud came from outside the cavern. The three of them perked up.

It was rare for anyone to come near their hideout.

"Think it's a group of nomads?" Dreden asked.

Chanin paused, making out the rhythm of the footsteps. "Probably not. It doesn't sound like they're high in numbers. Also seems like they're traveling light."

The trio backed against the wall, instinctively. To the humans' side, Gerrika motioned to put his boots back on. As he was picking up his footwear, a thundering blow caused him to drop them back on the ground.

The aveho yelped, leaping back to his friends. "What was that!"

Dreden felt Chanin grab his arm. He reached for Gerrika's, but he was already up against him.

The footsteps on mud and grass were in sync, and they were getting closer. A long metal stick was the first thing they saw of the coming intruders, and they were grasped tightly by thick pale hands. Human hands.

There were three of them. Dreden didn't think he had ever seen a group of plainer looking people in his life. Their skin didn't have wrinkles, and there was a lifelessness to their gaze like a taxidermied animal. From head to toe they wore the same clothes. They had sharp, blood-red pants and full-sleeved coats. Their boots were darker than the mud they troughed through to get there.

They were all about the same height. Two of them held long metal sticks against their chests.

The leader held his stick against the ground like a walking cane. He walked with a limp and had the teeth and narrow hungry eyes of a wolf.

"Hello there," the first one said, getting the attention of the other two. In the moonlight, Dreden could tell he had the palest skin of the three.

"Hi…" the human replied.

The three strangers paused, surveying the inside of the cave. Gerrika was the last thing their eyes caught, and, at the sight of him, their eyes showed the first spark of life.

"Oh…" the second, tallest stranger muttered. His mouth drew into a smile. "A strange creature here? I'm sorry, but we cannot allow this."

"Allow what?" Chanin moved forward. "The three of us have been hanging out here for a long time. Why is this suddenly a problem?"

"A confession?" The darkest one laughed. "Wasn't expecting our jobs to be that easy. Did you think it would be this easy?"

He nudged the third stranger with his elbow, and the silent one still made no noise. He only smiled, the corners of his mouth nearly touching the back of his head, showing even his molars.

"And since when do chickens wear clothes?" asked the tall one.

The aveho's eyes widened. Even the blue feathers on his chest stood up. "Umm… I'm not a chicken, you stiff creeps. I'm an aveho."

The dark one laughed again. "A what? That's one of the dumbest fucking words I've ever heard!"

"Yeah," agreed his tall friend. "We're not going to remember that, so we're just going to call you a chicken. Fine with that? Good."

The three strange men stepped into the cavern entrance, causing Dreden and his pals to retreat farther inside.

The third one kept his smile. His teeth were as white as his lifeless eyes.

The one with the limp looked around at the cave's roof. "How deep does this thing go?"

"It's just this room." Dreden kept his friends at his side, as they reached the deepest wall of the cavern "The main cavern system is mostly underground. If you want an entrance, you have to go west about another mile."

"Just as I suspected. This place is way too dangerous. Yep, you, the girl, and the chicken all need to leave right now. I'm afraid we cannot let you come around these parts anymore."

"Why the hell not?" Chanin asked. "We've been coming here a long time. We've never harmed anything and bothered any wildlife. All we do is come here, talk, and enjoy the scene. And who are you to tell us that we can't come here? Who do you work for anyway?"

"Who do we work for?" echoed the leader one.

"Who do we work for!" the darker one cheered.

"Who does anyone work for? We work for the Prime Minister."

"Prime Minister?" asked Dreden.

"Those words don't mean mouse shit to us." Gerrika took a seat on a rock, putting his boots back on. "I don't know who the 'Prime Minister' is, but only the City Guard can tell us what to do. We won't play your made-up games." The aveho grabbed the arms of his two human friends. "Come on, guys, let's get out of here."

A second bang stopped them dead. Dreden could feel his heart jump as Gerrika's grip on his arm tightened, and his talons pricked his skin.

Chunks of cave wall splattered right by their heads. The trio ducked down as pieces fell and knocked them on the backs of their heads.

The bang sounded like a firework exploding right by their ears out of nothing but silence. Dreden looked to the metal stick in the grasp of the smiling, silent man. Smoke filtered out of the mouth of the object like water through a pipe.

"What did you do?" Chanin shouted at the quiet man once she had regained her wits.

The leader pointed his weapon back at them, putting his weight on his good leg. "No respect. These animals never give us any respect."

"The Prime Minister likes a well-cooked bird." The dark one pulled back a small lever on his metal device, making a click, then leveled it at Gerrika. "We'll just shoot us the chicken and we'll be on our way."

A rock sailed above Dreden's head, catching the darker man on the side of the head. The stone landed on the cavern floor, breaking in half, as a thick line of blood dripped from the man's head. He tumbled over, his finger catching the trigger of his small machine. Dreden heard the sound first, instinctively diving out of the way, bringing Chanin and Gerrika down with him. From behind, the splatter of rock and wall caught their ears again.

It came from those long metal devices, thought Dreden as he hit the floor. *It shot something faster than my eyes could perceive. How?*

The next thing he knew, Chanin was on her feet and lunging behind them. He turned to see her pick up another large chunk of the wall that had settled on the floor. He didn't know if there was going to be another bang from any of the men's tools, but there was no time to wait.

He grabbed the only chunk within arm's reach. As quickly as his body would allow, he was on his feet, and Chanin was at his side with her best weapon, ready to strike again.

Two of the mysterious men grabbed Gerrika by the arms. The aveho's eyes were wide. He opened his beak to protest, but Dreden saw the quiet man and the dark man jab their loud shooting sticks into his sides, and he was silent.

"Put those rocks down, kids!" said the tall one. The faces of the three men grew hostile for the first time. Even the quiet man no longer showed any teeth. "Put them down or the bird gets it."

To his left, the darker skinned one jabbed the tip of his weapon harder into Gerrika's side. His friend let out a cry, closing his eyes tight.

"Fine, fine!" Dreden lowered his arm. Chanin followed. Neither of them wanted to see their friend in terror for another second.

Indecisiveness gleamed in the eyes of the armed trio. After several seconds of tense silence, Gerrika's captors threw him forward, and he stumbled onto the cave floor. He didn't try to get up. His talons gripped any loose stone he could find, and his eyes remained shut.

The three of them smirked, turning their exploding metal sticks away from them. "Just remember, kids," the tall one smiled. "we could have killed you, but we chose not to. There was a clear cause for self-defense."

"*We* were defending *our*selves!" Chanin roared at them, wrapping her arms around Gerrika's trembling neck. "You had just fired at us with those metal sticks!"

"We've killed for less. Now, the three of you better get on out of here and never show your faces around here ever again." He narrowed his eyes, focusing on Gerrika. "Especially *you*, chicken."

The three men turned around and exited the cave, walking side by side in uniform. When the sound of their boots against the ground could no longer be heard, Gerrika and Chanin no longer hid their voices.

"Who did they think they were?" Gerrika covered his eyes with his talons, hiding his tears. "What the fuck did we do to deserve that?"

"Nothing. We did nothing." Chanin sniffed, holding the aveho tight against her chest. "They're gone now. They're gone."

Dreden closed his fists as he watched his two friends. He felt his lip start to bleed from his own biting.

The human picked up his stone and rushed out of the cave.

"Dreden!" Chanin screamed.

But he didn't go back for her. What he had just seen, besides the near loss of his and his friends' lives, was something he never wanted to see again. Chanin and Gerrika didn't deserve to weep and be bullied.

We're not done, bastards, he told himself, as he rushed through the field after the three men, *your weapons have made their last booms.*

Their tracks were easy enough to follow. Thankfully the recent rainfall had gifted their path with cake after cake of mud.

He rounded the final bend of the cavern system. He knew they were right around the corner. The sounds of their boots were back. He had them.

Rock tight in hand, he dashed around the massive wall of rock.

And he almost choked on his own throat.

Dreden had never seen it up close before. Only from a long distance. Only from the height of the city or from the mountains.

A light green sea of gas raged like a hurricane in front of him.

The Sunitian Sea.

The enigmatic sea of gas was a menace to all inhabitants of Kroonsaed, as well as anyone else who had needed to evacuate because of its advances. The gas was so thick, so dense, that anyone who got too close had a risk of their lungs breaking.

Dreden covered his mouth and nose.

He was too close.

Backing up, he saw the three men continue to walk in sync, as if they had become mindless. They approached the sea with unfeeling purpose. They were getting too close.

They're killing themselves!

Dreden found himself wanting to shout for them to run away and hold their breath. By the trick of the light, or some illusion from the gas, the three men started to dematerialize. They began to fade, as if they were going through foggy water. Their skin, their clothes, weapons, all began to lose color as they approached the border of the sea.

And like the jaws of an angry whale, the sea raised itself, almost forming a head, and clamped down on the men, who had just finished fading into nonexistence.

The Sunitian Sea instantly retreated. It went from being only a few hundred feet away from him to almost a mile in a single second. A second later he couldn't even see it anymore, and the entire area in which the sea had just encapsulated returned to its normal self, as if it had never been there.

Just like the three men.

CHAPTER 4

They kept what had happened to themselves.

At least that's what Chanin and Gerrika decided.

Neither of them had great relationships with their parents. Gerrika's father was cold, tough, and didn't care about Dreden or Chanin. Chanin's mother and father weren't so uncaring, but any bad news about their daughter having a near-death experience would make them pull her out of her relationship with the two of them.

The trio had made the walk back in silence, hardly giving each other even a tap on the arm in goodbyes. There would be no classes the next day, as it was the end of the week. Their Saturday tradition involved meeting at the campus alehouse for a late breakfast and either catching a play or going on a hike near the caverns. Though based on their latest experience, they weren't going to be going anywhere near the caves.

Dreden wasn't sure if either of them was going to show up for a meal. He was the first one there, arriving just after ten in the morning.

He ordered a few eggs and two slices of bread. The young man behind the bar came over and gave him a beer on the house because, according to him, Dreden 'looked like he needed it'.

He was halfway through his eggs when Gerrika showed up. His friend still had a haunted look in his eyes. He ruffled his talons through his head as he entered, looking more like an extinct reptile than a bird.

The two of them didn't make eye contact until the aveho was seated opposite him.

"Hey," Gerrika sighed.

"Hey,"

The same man came around the bar again once Gerrika was seated.

"Anything I can get for you, sir?"

"Uhh…" the aveho swiped the menu away, towards the server. "Ham with a lot of gravy, please, and all the coffee you've got."

"I'll get you a beer instead, man." The young man winked. "You two have a good night last night?"

Dreden and Gerrika exchanged sour glances at each other.

"No," replied the former. "it was surely not."

The server nodded, taking the menu away from the table. "It'll be right out, boys."

The pair watched as the young worker walked back behind the bar and gave the chef Gerrika's order. They wanted to make sure he was out of earshot before they began.

"You feel any better than you look?" asked the human.

"Maybe. I didn't look at myself in the mirror this morning."

"Sleep?"

"Yeah. A few hours. You?"

"Same." Dreden took a sip of his free beer.

"Do you know if Chanin is coming?"

"No. Probably not. I don't think she's ever arrived at a place after me, so it'll be a first if she comes."

Gerrika sighed again, running his talons over his sunken eyes and beak, which appeared more pale than its usual yellow. "Man, Dreden, I just can't get over any of what happened. What were those metal death sticks that popped and broke the cave walls?"

"I have no theories myself." He flipped pieces of his eggs over idly with his fork. "Or about anything else they said. What the hell is a Prime Minister?"

"Maybe something like a governor? Maybe some kind of religious leader?" the aveho shook his head. "Maybe they were fanatics of some kind."

Their server rounded the corner with Gerrika's food. The smell of the steaming ham and gravy made the aveho perk up. Dreden could see at least a little spark in his friend's eyes from the appetizing scent.

"Thank you," Gerrika nodded to the young man, as he also plopped the wheat ale alongside the plate of meat.

Not wanting to dwell on the subject any longer, Dreden and Gerrika ate in silence. Dreden was the first to finish, since he had gotten a head start. Gerrika was guzzling down chunks of ham as if he hadn't had a nibble in weeks. Dabs of gravy spilled on his black wool shirt with each stuff of his mouth.

Dreden was wiping his mouth when Chanin came through the door. He saw her before Gerrika, since his back was facing the entrance. She looked to be the most put-together of the bunch. There was no sign of insomnia in her eyes, and there was even a hint of a smile as she returned a wave from Dreden.

"You boys feeling okay today?"

Gerrika nodded, using his whole body. "Food is such a wonderful invention."

"This guy seems to be on the uphill since walking in here," Dreden gestured to the aveho. "I'm fine. Didn't get much sleep, considering…"

Chanin wiped her hair away from her forehead and raised a finger to get the server's attention. "You tell your father about what happened, Dreden?"

"No. He was asleep by the time I got home, and he was gone when I woke up. I think there was another professors' meeting today."

"And you?" She eyed the bird.

Gerrika lowered his head, rolling his eyes to her, as if saying '*Did you seriously ask me that?*'.

"Fair point."

The young server returned once more. "And for you, miss?"

"Just tea for me. I'm not hungry yet."

Dreden was relieved when the alehouse employee didn't protest her order and say he was going to bring her a beer like he had done to him and Gerrika. He wasn't in the mood to feel tempted to say something rude to the guy.

"Since the three of us are here now," Gerrika started. "I figure we need to talk more about what happened." He put his fork down on the table and sucked the gravy off his avian fingers. "Dreden, have any more thoughts on our attackers' disappearing act?"

Dreden had told the two of them what he had seen when he dashed off to pursue the men while they were on their way back to town from the cave. Initially it hadn't sat well with either of them, and they told him that it was just his fear and adrenaline playing tricks on him. But he kept to his story, insisting that he knew what he was talking about.

"There could have been a number of reasons why it got hard to breathe." Chanin said, remembering what Dreden told them about his proximity to the

Sunitian Sea. "You could have just been out of breath. You're not exactly an athlete, friend."

"I know what happened." Dreden said. "Even if that's true, how can I imagine the colors and sounds of the Sunitian Sea? I know what it looks like. I've seen it before, like everyone in Kroonsaed has. This time it was up close, and loud, and the three men were swallowed by it."

"So they fucking killed themselves?" asked Gerrika.

"I'm not sure about that. Before the sea claimed them, they started to vanish. It was like I was looking *through* them during the last couple seconds. It didn't look much like a death to me. More like a transport of some kind."

"I guess wherever they went, they went with the sea." Chanin replied. "Even if what you're saying is true, what happened to make the sea come this far inland, and what caused it to retreat back in the blink of an eye?"

Dreden shrugged. The trio grew quiet again as the server returned with Chanin's tea. She gave him a 'thank you' nod, and he went back to his post.

As the three of them finished their food and drinks, a thought gnawed on Dreden's mind. He hadn't remembered it at first, but having his two friends together with him again brought it back clearly.

"Why did they pick on you?" he asked the aveho.

Chanin and Gerrika perked up. "What do you mean?" asked the former.

"Remember when the three men first entered the cave?" Dreden started. "I was the first one they saw, then you were the last. Their tone changed after they saw you and called you a chicken." He paused for a second, surveying their faces. "And at the end, after their devices popped a couple holes in the walls, the tall one looked at you as if you'd been in a blood feud for centuries. He said: 'especially *you*'. Why were you so offensive to him?"

"Beats me." Gerrika scratched the last scraps of ham off his plate with his fork. "Besides threatening to feed me to whatever a Prime Minister is, I don't know what else they could hate me for."

Chanin wrapped her arm over the aveho's neck and rubbed his shoulder with a consoling hand. "We won't see them again. If we do, they're going to have a lot more to hate us for. I'm not going anywhere without a dagger from now on."

Gerrika gave his first smile of the day. "And I should stop wearing boots and trimming my claws. My talons can do some serious damage when I know how to use them. That being said, I'm about as useless with them as fur on a fish."

Dreden thought about ordering another beer, or anything to stay a bit longer with his friends, but he hadn't seen his father since yesterday afternoon.

He didn't like keeping his father out of the loop. If there was anyone else who had a right to know about what had happened the previous night, it was Professor Sharpstand.

And last time they talked he got the feeling that there was something his father wanted to tell him.

The lights in the classroom were off. As expected. There were no lectures on Saturdays, but the classroom was the only way to get to his home, as were the current states of things for the elder and son Sharpstand.

Dreden slid the bookcase along the side, giving way to the two-room home where he and his father made their living.

Over on the far-right side of the room with the kitchen was the desk that functioned as his father's study. And there sat his father, reviewing his literature and making notes for his classes the following Monday.

"Good morning, Dreden." His father said to him as Dreden shut the bookcase-door behind him. "You get breakfast at the alehouse?"

"Yeah, we did. The usual thing."

The professor shut his book. "Damn, I should have asked you to get me some bread and jam. Oh well, I'll probably find my way to the winery later anyway."

Dreden paused, rubbing his fingers along the side of his pants like a nervous child. His father took a sip of his morning coffee and turned his chair around to face his son, putting his long, graying hair behind his ears.

"Is something the matter, Dreden?"

"A little bit…"

He inched his way over to his bedside. The two rooms of their home were only divided by half a wall about five feet high. From his corner, the professor could still clearly see his son, even as he took a seat on his mattress.

His father got up and rounded the wall into his son's room. "Can I get you anything? I still have some coffee in the pot. Or maybe a beer?"

"No no, I've already had enough this morning. Dad, you know how Chanin, Gerrika and I like to go hang out at Heathback Friday nights?"

"By the caverns?" His son nodded. "Despite my ideas about you finding something in town like the other kids?"

"We were there again last night," he continued, ignoring his father's jest. "but something was different...we were ambushed."

"Ambushed?" His father's body went stiff. "Were you robbed? Are the others okay?"

"We're fine. No, they didn't take anything from us. They just taunted us, and they might have tried to kill us at one point. It was terribly unclear."

In the next second his father was rushing to the door. "Attempted murder? On *my* son? I think the City Guard would like to know about-"

"Wait!" Dreden darted off his bed. "They'll never find them. Please sit down. The rest of the story gets even more strange."

His father reluctantly obeyed, taking a seat on the floor as he listened to the rest of his son's account. It took Dreden longer than he would have liked to finish telling his father the story, but the professor kept insisting that they alert the authorities. After the description of the assailants' metal sticks that popped small objects at supreme speed and about how they simply vanished into the Sunitian Sea, the professor was convinced that his son was right.

"Nobody comes out of the sea." said his father. "They're gone."

Dreden put his arms on his knees to calm himself down. "It was the most frightening thing that's ever happened to us. Gerrika's taking it the hardest. One of those bastards shoved the nose of one of the popping tubes into his ribs."

"You *sure* you're fine?" insisted the professor once more.

"Yes. I'm...I'm not sure how I'm supposed to be after something like this happens. We all don't. What do we do?"

"You're certainly not hanging around Heathback again."

Dreden smiled nervously. "Right about that."

The professor got back on his feet, and his eyes turned to his desk. "Prime Minister?" he asked to himself, remembering the title his son said the men claimed to serve.

"Sound familiar?" asked Dreden.

"Maybe. When I'm stumped like this, you know what I do?" The professor extended his arm, gesturing around his side of the room. "I take to my study."

Dreden followed his father to the corner of the room, by the ceiling-tall bookshelf where all the professor's histories and literature were saved. It was an incomplete collection. He had to sell a lot of his volumes to make ends for his family, but everything he deemed important and relevant to his profession as a lecturer was always kept.

Bending down to the lowest level of the shelf, his father dusted the outside of the pages and the face of a heavy leather-bound volume. He picked it up, wiping the back of it clean as well before letting it fall onto his desk.

"A dictionary?" Dreden asked.

"I figure it'll make my job easier." The professor licked the tip of his finger, sliding through the later entries. "I doubt there is a word in any of my collections that doesn't appear in the Faeriebridge Dictionary. Now, let's see…" He paused, as the entries now started with the letters 'pr'. "Primateship…primeval, primarily, prime, primer," he flicked his fingers back, retracing his eyes. "Primage, primal…primed…primas…No, I don't see any definition here for a Prime Minister. I mean, it doesn't make sense that it wouldn't be here…"

"Do you have something that would have the definitions of religious words?" asked his son. "Gerrika wondered if maybe a Prime Minister is a religious figurehead."

"Possibly. Even then, all the terms for those types of titles should all be in here too."

Dreden turned away, looking down at his feet. His neck began to feel wet. He wanted to get to the bottom of his attack as much as his friends, but he didn't want to see his father taking the hits the hardest. Everyone knew he had enough on his plate as it was.

"I think we can work on this later, dad," Dreden said, defeated. "I think getting too preoccupied won't do either of us any good."

His father looked at him for a few seconds, silently. Exhaling, he flipped the thick dictionary closed and shoved it back into its proper place on the shelf.

"Okay," he sighed. "but remember what I said. Please *please* do not go near Heathback anymore. Any other *slight* sign of those strange men around here and I will rush out naked as an animal to the City Guards if I have to."

Dreden smiled. "I don't think it'll come to that. Besides, I think Chanin's parents would beat you to it in that situation. Or even Gerrika."

"But not his father." the professor said, not as a question.

"You ever meet him? Gerrika's dad?"

His father's eyes froze. "Yes. Once, and that is all I ever need."

"Yikes…"

A pain of sympathy hit his chest. He knew that Gerrika didn't have a good relationship with his father, but not much else, since Gerrika didn't like to talk about him. Whenever it came up, he could see the pain in his friend's avian eyes. Especially when the topic of his mother came up too.

"Yes. Honja is as frightening a civilized creature as I've ever met. I wouldn't put savagery past him. He probably enjoys jam made from human livers."

As Dreden laughed again, the professor threw his hand in the air, as if what he said were an annoying insect.

"I'm sorry, son. That was a rather nasty joke."

"I didn't think so." Dreden replied. "Why do you say that?"

His father blinked. "Consider the not-to-distant history between our species. Avehos hunted humans all the time." As his son's face lost its joy, it was his father's turn to smile. "Do you seriously not know about it?"

"No…" He scratched his head.

The professor turned around and walked across the room, back to his bed. He picked up one of his record books. "I'm sorry about that. It's true. In fact, according to my records, the last chronicled incident of an aveho killing a human for food was twenty-two years ago."

"Only *that* long?" Dreden couldn't believe it. That was almost in his lifetime.

"If we are going to question the records that are cited in history classrooms and that are preserved for the general knowledge of society, then Faeriebridge University as an institution ceases all credibility." He said, fixing his thin hair again. "I suppose I can't be too surprised. Since the majority of avehos are part of society, it would be a sore subject to bring up in primary school, and even secondary school."

His son grunted, already deep in thought.

"Dreden," the professor laughed. "If you're starting to think that your friend fights a primal desire to eat your flesh every time you hang out, then you're madder than a bat in a hat."

"That's not it." Dreden's tone grew awkward. "It's just…I'm realizing that there is so much I don't know. About everything…" Now Gerrika's line about hating aveho food stuck out in lights in his mind.

"I know the feeling." His father relaxed his palms on his mattress. "How do you think I feel? I'm a *professor*. Even in my own department I sometimes feel like an invalid."

Crossing his arms, Dreden allowed himself a genuine smile. "You're great, dad. Everyone in the class knows it."

Giving a thankful nod, the professor walked back to his desk. He grabbed a couple books along with his lecture notes under his arm as he made it to the sliding shelf-door. "Look at the time. I have a meeting with a student in fifteen minutes. I shouldn't be long, Dreden. Maybe we can get dinner if you have no other plans."

"Good idea." Dreden replied, watching his father exit through the classroom and out the door.

He didn't have any plans. Chanin and Gerrika had left him without any.

He couldn't help but worry.

CHAPTER 5

I really don't think I have the brain for this.

Cipre flipped through another page of Morell Edland's story. She had been at it for hours, with only enough work to show for about twenty minutes.

She had grown up with two kind, nurturing parents along with two lovable yet mischievous brothers. Her family, the Lanes, may as well have been the very image of Brunswald's middle class.

Could that be why I'm having a hard time properly understanding this manuscript?

Morell Edland was wealthy. His family owned the most successful steel company in all Skaltbard, and over the past decades they had succeeded in slipping their fingers through the cracks in almost every new development in science and technology. Before that, the Edlands were constantly fighting the government for more control over their workers and factories. Cipre assumed their struggles even dated back before the modern government, in the days of monarchs and feudal lords.

Now there was seemingly no limit to the profits his family was taking in. And, even though she hated to admit it, his story, *A Mad Past*, reeked of prestige.

Cipre knew it was something special. Something different that Mirthinout never had the pleasure of printing before, but she couldn't kick the feeling that the average book-buyer wouldn't cling to it. She hadn't lied to Morell during their meeting, but she wasn't entirely forthright either. She was still struggling with the text.

She sighed. *I can't bring myself to believe Lady Hanning's transformation. She travels all across the country, seeing the richest of the rich and the poorest of the poor. But, in the end, as she attains her birthright and becomes a princess, there's no more signs of empathy or revolution in her. I mean...she has a beautiful final monologue about all the wonderful places and people, castle-cozy and street-sleeping alike, but we don't see any further resolve from her.*

Could this story be regressive?

A moment from her last conversation with the author came to her. It wasn't supposed to be literally about a revolution. It was a *rediscovery*. Just like Lady Hanning rediscovered her roots. It was a *moral* rediscovery.

That was it. She tapped her pen against her desk in triumph. *Now* it was something that she could get behind. But how long would that satisfy her?

With resolve, Cipre put her pen down on the paper and began once again marking the manuscript.

Her pen slipped out of her grip. A line of ink washed against the corner of the page.

Something was happening again.

This time was different. Her eyes turned out the window. There was no mysterious flying behemoth outside. Last time, before seeing whatever it was, she thought it was an earthquake.

The bases of the buildings next door crumbled like a pie crust.

"Emergency!" One of the other editors came shouting out of his office. "Everyone get under their desks! This is not a drill!"

Cipre didn't listen, and everyone else was too preoccupied with their own survival to notice that she was still standing, half her body out the window, taking the destruction as it happened. The people caught on the street wobbled like pins as they tried to keep their balance, not wanting to risk injury by running as the ground itself bellowed.

Carts, carriages, and stations of street food toppled over onto the people hoping to use them for cover. Like dominoes, the buildings crumbled one after the other. When it was the Mirthinout building's turn, she had to fight to keep her hands on the ledge. Her desk screeched as its legs dragged across the floor. Cipre had to leap out of the way to avoid having it clobber her in the back.

The screams made the sound of the quake and crumbling less deafening. In a world that was falling apart, she was the only silent creature within a mile.

But if the building began to go down, she knew she would no longer be quiet. With Mirthinout being the tallest building on the block and her desk facing the window, she was going to have the best seat for her floor's collision with the street.

Her grip tightened against the window's edge. Her desk hit the far corner of the office.

Cipre closed her eyes.

And nothing happened.

Mirthinout no longer felt as if it were a raft in the middle of a sea storm. She didn't want to look out the window anymore to survey the damage, out of fear of a sudden aftershock ending with her being splattered on the pavement. Based on the sudden silence following the disaster, it was at least over for now.

She allowed herself to breathe. Turning around, Cipre saw her desk in shambles, and Morell Edland's manuscript was littered across the floor. She didn't care. She just hoped everyone was okay.

The people around her slowly got back on their feet. It seemed no one wanted to speak until they had taken in all that had become of their workplace. A handful of people had their shelters slide out from over them. Several desks were slopped together against the entrance from the main staircase, and rows of bookshelves from the far corner had taken tumbles, looking like the wreckage of a tornado.

Cipre approached the center of the room for a better view. Three of her coworkers were lying on the floor, unmoving under the fallen bookshelves and a couple shattered desks.

A long, thick streak of blood dressed one of their arms.

"He's hurt!" Cipre shouted.

"Who's hurt?" Came a question from one of the younger editors. When she saw the body, she gave out a scream which the prior silence only amplified. "Callen! Help! Someone telegram the hospital! Callen isn't moving!"

The manic parade that followed made her feel dizzy. She had to sit down. Not having the strength to put her desk back in the right place, she just sat down in her chair with a hand on her forehead, not making a sound in the panicked sea. Every few minutes someone would notice the way she looked and ask her if she was okay. She replied by telling them all the same thing: "I just need to sit for a while."

After ten minutes, her friend Matry, done helping the fallen, came to check up on her.

"You were going to die!" he whispered, fighting hysterics. "I didn't see any of it, but everyone said they saw what you were doing."

"Oh?" She brushed her eyes.

His jaw was as widely open as his eyes. "Lara said your corner of the building was teetering like a see-saw, and that you were *right* on the window. You could have easily fallen out! Why the hell didn't you move?"

"I guess the same reason why I was the only one who wasn't screaming." Cipre paused, taking in the progress of the floor's panic. Several men in white hospital garments were helping the bookcases off the injured people. Once the shelves were off, the bodies were no longer still. Everyone was alive. "I couldn't believe what I was seeing. I couldn't believe my body, and the way I was being tossed around. I…think I might just need to get out of here."

"Okay. Okay. I don't think that'll be an issue." Matry patted her on the shoulder, smiling. "With the street as broken as it is, this building isn't going to be safe for a while."

She nodded, feeling as if the earth were once again moving under her. Her heart felt like it was in her throat.

She hadn't noticed before, but she was trembling.

"Come with me," Matry grabbed her gently by the elbow. "Let's go get you a hot drink. The stairs might not be a safe bet anymore, so we'll have to take the emergency pole down to the first floor. Can you do it?"

She nodded in reply, crossing her arms over her lap. Now she was cold.

"It looks like everyone is going to be fine. In a minute or two they're going to start guiding everyone away as it is, so the least we can do is make their job easier for them."

Following her friend's hand, she rose from her seat, keeping behind Matry.

As they negotiated the debris and the emergency workers helping the injured editors and publicists, Cipre's mind was somewhere else. Her arms and legs instinctually moved with the rhythm of Matry's lead. When they got to the room with the pole, she waited for him, but he didn't want her to go second, out of fear of having her stay up on the third floor in her current condition.

And then she remembered what had truly caused her silence amidst the terrified cries.

When she was gazing out the window, she saw the street split open like a piece of bread. Tall buildings and one-story homes alike crumbled at the source as if they were nothing more than sugar, and that wasn't even what stuck with her the most.

Underneath the cracking brick streets, her eyes caught the proof that this wasn't just any natural disaster. Philosophers and religious men alike could talk about God's will, or the will of the many gods, but there was a will involved here that her eyes knew made this a clear physical, *terrestrial* will.

Because between the cracks of the leveled streets, Cipre's eyes caught the sight of the immense spine of a subterranean creature. That behemoth had left a trail of destruction all across her quarter of central Brunswald.

Meaning it could be caught. The story wasn't over.

It was the worst national disaster to hit the nation's capital in more than a hundred years.

The last fifteen Prime Ministers didn't have to give the kind of speech he was about to give. It certainly was no luxury. *Of course, it has to be me,* thought Charles Dowlepot.

Giving a speech honoring the victims of the Brunswald earthquake was going to be a nightmare. He didn't even have access to past speeches leaders gave when addressing deaths of a natural disaster, since the hall of records was one of the hardest-hit buildings from the quake. It was going to be much different than consoling families of fallen soldiers during wartime. At least those people *knew* what they were going into. The average civilian doesn't worry about becoming a casualty while walking into their office or getting a loaf of bread from the bakery across the street.

Damnit, I'm a wreck.

He cursed his own disappointment. He felt guilty that he was taking the speech as a chore, rather than a duty. But what could he do? Skaltbard was getting closer to war with Andayt, and tensions were rising with the neighboring nations of Borgetta and Gontland. It seemed that he now had to watch every arm of a clock tick, every flicker of his own eyes if he wanted to avoid future deaths.

A knock came from his office door, and Skitt, his aide, entered before Dowlepot could even tell him 'Come in'.

"Is speech-writing any easier than speech-giving, sir?" he asked.

The Prime Minister slapped his pen down on his mahogany desk, sighing as it clattered. "Isn't there someone I pay to do this for me? What's the point? No one would know if I was the one who wrote it or not."

The mousy man nodded, closing the door behind him. A flicker of irritation flushed through the Prime Minister. He hated when people assumed he had time for them.

"Sir, forgive me, but your speech to the victims and the families of those killed is going to need to be put off."

"Postponed!" Dowlepot cried. "Skitt, do you realize what you're asking of me?"

Skitt raised a trembling hand. "I...I realize...but."

"What's the estimated death count now?"

"Forty-six."

Dowlepot could almost hear his hair grow gray. He slapped his hand on his desk, cursing. "Forty-six? Forty-six Skaltbardians are dead and you want me to delay the speech?"

"I assure you, sir," Skitt adjusted his glasses. "that there is a very good reason for it. There are people here to see you, and they aren't the types to dilly-dally with their own time."

"There is no one who is more important than what I have to be doing now. Now shoo, Skitt."

Before his aide could reply, the door to his office opened again, this time without a preliminary knock. The Prime Minister looked up, already holding an irritated face to grace whoever thought they were good enough to simply walk into his office during a crisis.

When he recognized the pair, his face fell.

"It is good to see you again, Prime Minister Dowlepot," a woman of about fifty-five greeted him.

Dowlepot sprang from his seat, rounding his desk to greet the husband and wife. "Janely and Keeting Edland. Please, accept my apologies. I couldn't have had less of an idea that you two would be paying me a visit at this time."

"Understandable, Prime Minister," Keeting Edland replied, taking off his black bowler hat.

The Edlands could best be described as looking like they had never been in the same room as a speck of dirt. Clean cut down to a hair, both of them, they were two of the most enviable people in Skaltbard, and the world. Their family had been in the business of big capital for almost a century. Going from one market to the next, their family had settled on their steel manufacturing, and, considering the increasing industrialization of the economy, they were making millions.

The Edlands were the first immensely wealthy family to have no aristocratic blood. They didn't play by the rules, and many in the government considered them dangerous.

And here, with Keeting in his red suit and yellow slacks, and Janely in her comfortable, loose-fitting orange sundress, they only emphasized their hobby of subversion. Fashion be damned, they did what they wanted, even in the presence of power.

Janely extended a warm, pale hand to Dowlepot. He shook it with both of his hands, then repeated it with Keeting.

"First off," started the former. "I can't imagine the kind of pressure you must be under right now."

"Nah," sighed the Prime Minister. "it just goes with the job. It's a privilege, really, to be the one that gets to do this for the people."

"We're happy to hear that," Janely, who was a couple heads shorter than her husband, looked up at him, urging her husband forward.

Keeting cleared his throat. "Sir, this is a sensitive time for Skaltbard. For everyone in the nation, and not just the people who lost family and friends today."

Dowlepot raised a brow. "How so?"

"The economy is growing at a rate not seen in a long time." Keeting adjusted his collar. "Part of that, both happily and tragically, is because of increasing automation. People have been evicted from their homes and had their property seized to make room for factories with more help in the form of grinding gears than human flesh and blood."

Dowlepot fought back a laugh. *And who do you think is responsible for people being evicted? Money-hungry businessmen like you, sir.*

"Sure, it's one thing when your home or business becomes history to make room for something new," continued Keeting. "but when a terrible natural disaster takes it out?" He shook his head. "That's a factor economists and political theorists can't predict. Where will these people live? Where will they work? Do they have the right skills in various trades to be able to adapt if necessary?"

"If I may, sir," the Prime Minister frowned. "the people are expecting my condolences, and it doesn't seem like that's what you're here to discuss. You can always approach the papers yourself for any concerns for your capital, but that's not what's going to be the focus here."

"You misunderstand us, Charles," Janely said, stepping forward. Dowlepot privately scowled. He was hardly ever called by his first name, with the exception of his wife. "We came here to tell you that we think you should *adapt* your speech to the new information we give you."

Dowlepot blinked. "That being...?"

"Despite some efforts, earthquakes are unpredictable." Keeting crossed his arms, looking more like a university lecturer. "The best thing we can possibly do is have our scientists find new ways of testing the rock beneath the planet's crust. Now, the center of Brunswald has historically been a common place for quakes, and as we saw today, it looks like they're only getting stronger. How do we expect our nation's capital, and our people, to have a consistent living if their homes and businesses are at risk by what could best be described as simply an act of God or even magic?"

The Prime Minster tried not to smile, but he guessed he failed, considering Keeting's next words.

"I know it's silly, sir, magic does not exist, and any loving God would never forsake the poor as such, but the fact remains, there is a part of town by the peninsula where there has never been a natural disaster in all of recorded history."

"And where would that be?" Dowlepot asked.

"The corner of the Andenberg District, where the main Edland Steel Plant happens to be."

Keeting flinched out of the way as the Prime Minister threw up his arms in disbelief. He turned his back on the Edlands for a few seconds as he regained his composure.

He faced them again, putting his hands together as if in prayer, and pointed them at Keeting. "Mister Edland, I must have misunderstood you, because what I just heard was that you wanted me to tell the friends and family members of the recently deceased that what they could do to best ensure their future safety is to go work for you."

"Now now, it's much milder than that when you hear *our* reasoning." Keeting replied.

Janely took her husband's hand and held it in her own as she spoke. "Some people have nothing anymore, sir. They have no jobs. Shit, some people live in the same places that they work. No home and no source of income? That's terrible! We're not going to sugarcoat it for the sake of our pride, Prime Minister. Business has been *very* good for us. With our new factories opening up across the district, we need more laborers, and considering how new some of our buildings are, there is still time to make homes for the less fortunate. It will be temporary, of course, until Brunswald is in better shape, or they're relocated to a better place, but until then, *something* needs to be done about this."

Begrudgingly, Dowlepot felt that there was truth to what the Edlands were saying. What he hated most was their pride. The *audacity* of two of the richest people on the planet to swoop in and be Brunswald's saviors, all-the-while serving their wallets.

Regardless of the ulterior motives of the Edlands, he couldn't deny the fact that they made a good point. A *great* point. He had a job to do...

And a speech to deliver to grieving friends and families.

"Very well." Dowlepot met Keeting Edland's eyes. "I guess, if anything, this meeting has finally given me more to go on, so my speech-writing is no longer so stunted." He allowed himself to smile. "For the future, would you two mind scheduling an appointment ahead of time with my secretary? I pay her for a reason."

Keeting returned a friendly grin, pleased with Dowlepot's shift in tone. "We must let you know, Charles," *Again* with the first name. "we can't promise that. It wouldn't make sense to set up a meeting with you *before* the earthquake. We have no idea when they'll come. To us, disrupting the schedule of a public servant like yourself is just our civic duty. If we can better the lives of our citizens by discomforting you, then we'll do it every time."

Keeting put his hand on the middle of his wife's back, ushering her out of the Prime Minister's office. With a smile and a wave, they exited, leaving Dowlepot alone with his unfinished speech.

His foot struck the corner of his desk. The mahogany creaked as the pressure from his kick rippled through the wood. It was too heavy a desk for a kick from the Prime Minister to have moved it, but he felt the pain in his toes.

He cursed himself. How dare the entitled millionaires talk like everyone is simply a pawn to their whims.

Maybe the newly homeless and grieving widows and friends belong to you, he thought to himself. *But not me. NOT me.*

CHAPTER 6

Dreden tried not to think about what was troubling him anymore.

But it was so hard when there were so many things troubling him at once.

Hanging out with his friends usually did the trick. After what they went through with the three strange men at Heathback, they didn't want to leave town. So the trio decided on a play. It was Gerrika's idea. He was the one that was the fondest of plays, despite his earlier complaints about the domination of human works. Dreden found it fairly amusing, since the aveho was never seen reading books or making stories of his own, but the theater had a way of entrancing him.

None of them spoke during the performance, lest they get angry looks from the surrounding spectators. That was part of why Dreden was struggling to have a good time. Just sitting there, not talking, having nothing but the play to distract him from his own grim thoughts. And he wasn't finding the show that interesting, so it was a losing battle.

When the crowd stood and applauded, Dreden was already out of his seat. Taking note of their friend's exit, Chanin and Gerrika followed.

"Up for a drink, gang?" Chanin asked.

"Sure," Dreden said. "The Faeriebridge Pub?"

"At this time? We're going to have to wait an hour for a goddamn seat!"

Gerrika sped up, catching up to the two humans. "At least it's always a good time. Besides, they like us there. We'll have special treatment I'll bet."

The crowd was letting out into the street, splitting across the road like a river. Considerate carriages were paused, and their horses still. Several hands from the corner of the wave of playgoers flew up to give thanks to the paused driver and he returned the gesture.

"You didn't seem like you were having much fun." Gerrika said, turning to Dreden.

"No. Sorry, I guess I was just stuck in my head the entire time."

"Something the matter?" he asked the human. "I mean, anything *new* the matter?"

Dreden shrugged. When they had finished crossing the street they paused, planting their feet outside of a candle shop and an apothecary. "More of the same. You know, just dwelling on everything."

"No hard feelings from me if you guys want to clock out early tonight." Chanin said. "I'm with you there, Dreden. I wouldn't mind another twelve hours in bed. Besides, that play wasn't especially good."

"No, you're kidding! Really?" the aveho beamed.

Dreden smiled. "*You* really?"

"Did you actually like that play?" Chanin asked, mimicking Dreden's amusement.

"Yes." Gerrika shyly tucked his talon-hands into his coat. "The acting was good, and the comedic timing was all on cue."

"I suppose…" mused Chanin. "but it was still a bit immature. It was one of the more unsophisticated plays this theater has put on in a while."

"You guys can never just have *fun*, can you?" Gerrika sighed. "Of course, it isn't something that Dreden's father would ever do a lecture on, but that doesn't make it bad, or it doesn't mean it isn't culture."

"Okay." Dreden threw up his palms, and the trio came to a halt. "Help us help *you*. What was it about it that you liked?"

"It was funny."

"Not very clever, though." Chanin commented.

They moved out of the way, clearing their side of the shop walkway. There were still a bunch of people exiting the theater, and they didn't want to impede the pedestrian flow with their grilling of Gerrika.

"Did it need to be?" asked Gerrika. "Sometimes you humans are all the same. Oh, everything must be intelligent, *oh*, everything must be utilitarian, *OH* I must not enjoy this lest I bring shame to my species."

During his rant the aveho had been using his eyes to move the rest of his face, imitating human facial expressions and waving his hands to show off his slightly less opposable 'thumb' talons. It looked so ridiculous to the two humans that they couldn't fight off their laughter.

"See?" Gerrika begged. "What I just did was really stupid, and you thought it was funny!"

"Maybe it's because we know you." Dreden said. "That could be the difference."

"What about the story?" Chanin asked. "Anything about the story you liked?"

Gerrika nodded. "I thought the talking pig was a good plot device. I think you guys are dismissing the play too easily. The two leads, the man and the woman, want to get their sister a dog for her birthday, but the brother accidentally buys a pig, and it can talk! But despite its ability to be a human through its verbalizations and the fact that it could bark better than a terrier, it is *still* a pig, by biology. Yet the sister was aware and was fine with it. I think there's something smart there."

"So," Dreden smiled. "do you think that the play excels as a commentary on the politics of human/non-human relations by taking a stance on the inevitability of our inability to reconcile the intrinsic biological differences between rational animals because of an innate desire for primate hegemony on the part of the human man?"

"What is wrong with you?" Gerrika covered his amusement with a hand on his beak. He could almost feel his friend flushed under his black feathers.

"I think I got most of that." Chanin gave Dreden a light kick in the shin. "We get it, Dreden, you're your father's son. We're all *so* impressed."

Having finished their conversation, the trio reentered the flow of traffic along the walkway. The center of campus was only three blocks straight ahead, and that was where they usually said their goodbyes for the night, since it was practically at a focal point between Chanin and Gerrika's homes.

On the corner of the final street just in front of the university, a man was sitting with an almost empty newsstand. Since it was night, he didn't have much left to sell, and wouldn't be getting new materials until the following morning. His bottom shelf was full of small leather-bound books.

"Hang on a sec," Chanin tapped her friends' shoulders. "there's something new at that stand. Come on, I want to see what it is."

They approached the stand, which may as well have been invisible since no one passing by even gave the shelf a look. It wasn't often that a stand still had so much material so late in the day.

The man sitting behind the shelves had his hooked nose in some thick book. Chanin had to knock to get his attention, because he didn't realize that she was speaking to him.

"Yes, sorry, what is it?" he asked.

The moonlight showed the age of the man's face, or based on his teeth, it was probably more the tobacco.

"Would you mind telling me what you still have so much of down there?" Chanin pointed to the section at the man's foot.

"Those?" he grunted. "Oh, that's just nothing. They're just a bunch of plays by some nobody."

Gerrika came forward. "Plays?"

"Yeah. Since the theater across the way hasn't been doing too hot, they thought having the plays printed for advertising purposes would be a good idea."

"Do you have the one that just played?" Gerrika asked.

"I think so," the man adjusted his foggy glasses. "what was it called?"

"*Pigamist.*"

The man leaned over on his stool, leafing through the thin little books of plays until he found what Gerrika asked for.

"I keep forgetting that they're in alphabetical order." he laughed. "Here you go."

The aveho took the play from him. In his talon hands, it looked almost no larger than the booklets given out to the playgoers with the actors' bios in them. "Do you have any others by the same writer?"

"Yes. Plays by Winds Wilk are all I have right now."

"Winds Wilk…" Gerrika said, as if the very name of the author had cast a spell on him.

Chanin tapped him on the shoulder. "Sorry, G, but I'm tired enough to pass out on the street right now."

"Sorry. Sorry." Dreden could sense Gerrika blushing again. "Umm, I'll take three others by Mister Wilk as well."

The man bent over, groaning along with his wooden seat as he bent down again. "Which ones?"

"Any of them. I don't know the names of any of his others, so just surprise me."

The salesman just took the first three that were in alphabetical order. It seemed random enough. The quality of a play was most likely not determined by the first letter of its title.

"Okay, so four plays for the young aveho." He finally smiled, probably happy that he was getting four sales from one customer at night. "That'll be forty tints."

"Wait," Gerrika dug into his breast pocket and took out a small metal plate. "I'm a Faeriebridge student. Is there a discount for us?"

He nodded. "Very well. Thirty-two tints."

Gerrika paid the man, giving him a quick handshake in goodbye. Once they were free from the crowd and on the university side of the block, he turned back to his human friends, proudly displaying his new buys as if he'd grown rainbow colors on his tail.

"And you guys were just talking about how I don't read." he smiled.

"Didn't you say you were tired of plays written by humans?" Chanin asked.

"If all this human's plays are as good as *Pigamist*, then I can forget about that."

"Plays are the bacon of the literary world." Dreden replied, matching his friend's grin. "They might taste really good, but too much of them are unhealthy for a long-term intellectual diet."

"I just hope one of them is better than *Pigamist*." Chanin said, unable to keep a straight face at the name. "Okay. I'll give you that one. If the names of all his plays are as funny as that one, this Winds Wilk character is probably funny."

Gerrika tucked the small booklets into his jacket. "Thank you, Chanin. I'm glad one of you sees it my way. Anyway, I need to get home."

"Same here." Dreden said. "See you guys tomorrow. Breakfast again?"

"Maybe." Chanin nodded. "I think my parents want to take me out to lunch tomorrow, but I'll come to your place before eleven to tell you for sure."

"Cool. Goodnight, Chanin. Enjoy your new literature, Gerrika."

"I *will*." He waved.

His father was at his desk again when Dreden arrived home from the play. The professor turned his attention from his books when he came in.

"Have fun tonight, son?"

"It was alright," he replied, tossing his coat onto his bed. "The play was a bit dumb in some parts, but it was a good time."

"Good. Good." His father said those words as if he weren't listening, as if he would have said them regardless of what Dreden said.

His son noticed. "Is everything alright? Since this morning, I've had a feeling that there was something you've been wanting to tell me."

His father couldn't, or wouldn't, meet him in the eyes. Dreden felt a weight go down his spine. Whenever he was about to say something he knew Dreden didn't want to hear, his body language said it all. *Perhaps he cares for me too much*, Dreden thought.

"Son," he started, after a couple moments. "I know things haven't been easy for us, and the fact that Faeriebridge has fallen on harder times too hasn't helped at all."

"It's the Sea, isn't it?" Even though Dreden was the one mentioning it, he suddenly felt sick. He couldn't help remembering his scarring encounter with it.

"Correct," his father nodded. "it's expanding. Slowly, but still expanding. The natural philosophy department is starting to get money that would be going to my department. The university now feels that the preservation of Kroonsaed is a higher priority than having students who know how to critically read documents. I can't say that I don't agree with their decision."

"I guess you're going to be earning even less money next year?"

The professor shook his head. "No. That's not it. Dreden, I don't want you to worry too much, because it's not your problem. It's mine, and the administration said that as part of my severance you can still attend lectures for almost free."

"What are you talking about?"

"They're letting me go after the semester." He watched Dreden's mouth fall open, as he had to seat himself on his bed. "I'm just going to finish off the rest of the semester and that'll be it. The decision was finalized just a few short minutes ago."

Dreden's fingers tightened, grabbing his sheets for stability. His head lowered to his chest, as his head began to feel heavier. "How could they do that to you? After all the years you've been here? And your reputation!"

"Sadly, the issues of Kroonsaed supersede university politics." His father shook his head. "They've offered to help me find a place to live, that I could better afford, and be able to have a small lecturing position at another institution. The bad part is that it'll probably be many miles away, almost on the border of Angrell."

"Angrell!" Dreden stood up, now animated. "How do they expect us to live there? It's like they're making it impossible for me to still be a student."

"No. No. You misunderstand, Dreden. *I* will live close to Angrell. You will still be right here."

A knot formed in his son's throat. "They expect to separate us? They expect you to be exiled to the edge of town because they think they have no goddamn use for you?" Dreden's face grew hot.

"I wouldn't look at it that way, son. Considering the circumstances, it is very kind of Faeriebridge to be doing as much as they are."

"I won't give them the satisfaction! Maybe I'll drop out, then they'll have to find another way to give you a consolation prize."

His father got out of his seat, quickly enough for his chair to fall down behind him. "That would be a terrible idea. Dreden, you have to think about your own future. There is no shame in being as selfish as you can right now. You have your whole life ahead of you. Think about what you want to do with your life."

"What about *our* life?" he pleaded.

"It will be just fine." The professor approached his son, putting a hand on his shoulder. "You're more than halfway through your time at Faeriebridge. I know, I'll miss you very much, but if it has to be, let's not fight it. There are many university students that travel hundreds of miles to attend school, and they only see their parents in the summers."

Dreden shook his head. "But those people *choose* to leave. This is being forced upon us by a school that has the money to keep you but won't because they think what you teach isn't as valuable as playing with molecules and chemicals. Why couldn't they just give you a little less money? That way you could still teach, and you wouldn't have to move."

"It wouldn't be enough for both of us." His father sighed.

"Well, I'm going to have a word with them! If they won't listen to you, maybe-"

Neither of them could see it, but they sensed a tiny object penetrate the wall behind them, just as the sound of a blast followed.

From one blast came a second, and then a third. If Dreden hadn't already heard these same sounds just a day before, he wouldn't have known what was going on.

"Get down!"

In his panic he grabbed his father by the neck, hard enough to send him to the ground as Dreden fell to the side of his bed stand.

As they hit the floor, Dreden's eyes danced faster than a lightning bug. There was no blood on his father's clothes, and besides the shock and confusion from the assault, his father seemed alright.

But he had lost control of his breathing, as he fought for words. "Are...are these...?"

"The popping sticks? Yes." Dreden said.

Dreden remembered the three men from Heathback Caverns. Once their weapons had fired a shot, that was it. He had no idea how the things worked, but surely there was a whole other process that they had to do in order to set the weapons up again to fire their metal pellets.

Meaning that he might have enough time to get up and dash to find something to use a weapon.

In the next moment he was back on his feet. Considering his family's lack of possessions, there weren't many options. The deadliest things in his home were the bread knives, and to be able to do any damage, he was going to need to be in *close* range.

They were on the other side of the room. Dreden was too hopped up on adrenaline that he couldn't rationalize any of his decisions. His body belonged to his instincts now.

Ducking under the dinner table, he was within arm's reach of the knife drawer. *Come on. Come on. Let there be something better than a tiny bread knife in there. Please, for the sake of all fucking things holy, have something appear out of nothing for me to use the second I open the door.*

The fourth shot came through the window as his head was coming up. He felt the powerful little pellet graze through his hair.

Then came the crashing of the tiny thing against the wall. He could tell from the sound that his father had not been hit.

And the same went for the fifth, the six, and the seventh shots. They came in rapid succession. From what he observed of the strange men's weapons, there was no way they could have prepared them to fire again so quickly. That could only mean...

Risking his safety, Dreden's head came up, like a swimmer in need of air. To his relief, he could see the silhouettes of the assailants dashing away in the moonlight. But his darker suspicions were confirmed. There were no longer just three men.

Seven shadows grew smaller as they crossed the night's horizon.

There was no way of knowing for sure, but something deep inside Dreden knew where they were going. He was going to follow them, regardless of what it meant. *I'm putting an end to those bastards. They threaten my friends then they come to my home and threaten the life of my father. I don't care if I am as inept in combat as the most cowardly mouse. I am taking them out. And if I'm lucky, I'm not going to be doing it alone…*

For now, the danger was over. Dreden dug himself out from under the dinner table, then rushed back to his bed, slamming on his coat.

"Son!" his father shouted with a hoarse voice. "Where are you going? It's not safe!"

"It is for now. They're gone, dad."

"That doesn't answer my question. Where are you going?"

Dreden turned his back to his father, then opened the front door. "I'm going to Heathback, dad. I'm getting to the bottom of this shit."

He slammed the door behind him, instantly regretting it.

CHAPTER 7

Cipre's legs wobbled like rubber as she shoved herself out of bed. With the way she forced herself into bed lately, she could finally feel her legs getting back to use.

She needed breakfast. Willing herself out of her room and into the kitchen, she put a couple slices of bread on the stove and opened her jar of apple jam. When the smell of cooking bread and jam hit her nose, she remembered that it had been more than half a day since she'd last eaten. *In that case, maybe having four eggs with the bread won't be a bad idea*, she thought.

Once the bread was finished, she cracked open the eggs, stirring the yolks and the whites until they were scrambled. She usually had tea with her breakfast but, considering the day she was already having, today it would be coffee.

After finishing breakfast, Cipre just stared at the crumbs on her plate. She didn't know what to do with herself. She wasn't feeling numbed or fatigued anymore after the earthquake. Mirthinout wasn't going to resume business for at least a couple weeks until the building was once again deemed safe. She remembered the sight of the cause of the quake, how she was the only one to notice it. Seemingly no one had noticed the giant thing flying in the sky either, as she had during her meeting with Morell Edland. This whole thing was making her unique. *Could those two things have been connected?* she wondered. *Surely they must.*

A knock came from her front door. She shoved her plate out of the way as she got up and made for the door.

Opening it, an expected face greeted her.

"How are you feeling?" he asked.

"Better, Matry." she replied. "I just finished breakfast. If you had told me you would be coming over this early, I would have made you something."

He raised a palm. "Don't worry about it. I stopped for a pastry from the café around the corner. It's not my favorite one, but...well, my favorite one was eaten up by the earthquake."

"Sorry to hear."

"I'm sorry for the customers and the employees who were in there. I hear twelve are still in the hospital."

She grimaced. "That's what I meant."

"I know," he sighed with a resigned smile. "I guess I'm just the bearer of bad news today. Anything I could do to help take your mind off things? I need to get it off my mind as well."

"Want to go for a walk?"

"That sounds fun." Matry turned around, looking at the air around him. "It's supposed to be a nice day out today. Yes, I think some fresh air will do us both good."

She turned back, putting on a thin coat and closing the front door behind her. Surely Matry didn't suspect anything, but an idea had come to her. She didn't want to go on a walk just to get her mind off things.

It was exactly the opposite.

It was easy enough to pretend they weren't walking along the long line of destruction while on their stroll. The massive cracks in the earth were easy to follow, since for most of the length it was almost a straight line. Cipre didn't live far from ground zero. Only five blocks separated her front door from the massive gaping hole that almost swallowed her up along with all of Mirthinout. She and Matry zigzagged through the neighboring blocks, following the stone walkways, making sure they were never going *to* the damage, for their safety and in order to keep their minds off it.

After several streets, she almost *did* forget about the disaster. People were going about talking, walking, drinking, eating, as if nothing happened the previous day.

"What else could they do?" Matry said, after she told him what she was thinking. "Sure, everyone feels terrible, but you can't expect the average man or woman to turn their life upside down because the same happened to a stranger."

"I know. I know. That's part of what makes it even more sad. I'm sure if everyone did at least *some*thing, inconvenienced themselves slightly somehow every day until everything that could be done has been done, then I think we would be living in a better world. Because this...I understand, but it isn't perfect."

He didn't reply. She figured he sensed something in her tone that suggested she didn't want to hear a counterpoint from him. She didn't know how it would make her feel, but she was grateful for her friend's silence.

All the while, she kept her eyes on where they were going. They were getting closer to the source of the disaster. Matry, still having no idea about it, began whistling as they passed another street corner.

And hundreds of feet away, at the far corner of the block, her eyes caught the edge of the biggest crack in the city. It was getting smaller. *I think I'm getting closer*, she thought. *Whatever it was that broke the city, it went farther underground.*

She was already set on finding it.

She knew it didn't make sense, but she wanted to do it alone.

"Matry…" she started.

"Yes?"

They stopped their walking, as she paused in front of him. "I'm sorry, but I think I need to be alone for the rest of the day."

"Are you sure?"

"Yes. I hope you're not angry, but I want to continue the rest of the walk by myself. Just me and my thoughts."

He lowered his eyes, meeting hers as he put a hand on her shoulder. "I hope it wasn't what I said, Cipre. You know I wasn't being heartless."

"I've known you for a long time, Matry. I know that you're a good person." she smiled, showing him that she was fine and put her hands on his wrist.

"Thanks. Just be safe, won't you? Only go where everyone else goes."

"That'll be no problem." He turned around, making his way back to his corner of town. "Have a good day, Matry!"

They waved goodbye to each other. Once her friend had rounded the adjacent street corner, she turned around and continued her walk.

Part of her feared that other people might see her and grow too interested in what she was doing. She wanted to hide it for as long as she could. *Do I even know what I'm doing?* She wasn't sure.

Nor was she sure why she felt as if it were something that she had to do alone. Matry had always been a good friend to her, so it wasn't because she was sour with him. She knew there wasn't anyone she would want to come exploring the damage with her. It was as if she thought she had a *claim* to the answer because she was the one that caught a glimpse of the culprit, as if it entitled her to something.

Maybe I just want to do what's right. Maybe this is me just doing my civic duty. Besides, who would believe me if I told them that the fatal earthquake had really been caused by a subterranean behemoth?

The farther along the streets she went, the closer she got the damage. By now she had gone so far that anyone who suspected anything of her was long gone. Thirty minutes after saying goodbye to Matry, she was far enough through the end of Brunswald's central district that she had gotten within a hundred feet of the damage. Even though the reality of the disaster had already settled in her mind, she still had to blink twice. It was as if some god had cut through the city with a gigantic pair of rugged scissors. Rock and asphalt crumbled like a cheap dessert. She didn't want to get too close for fear of accidentally falling into the earth, but to her relief, it didn't look to be a long way down. She was far enough from the center of the damage.

She would be safe walking the rest of the way at her pace.

Another half an hour found her almost at the end. Looking in the direction she faced, there was no more evidence that a disaster had happened. That was it. This was what she was looking for.

The drop through the crack was no more than five feet down. Easily done, even by someone as unathletic as Cipre. She landed steadily on her feet. Now, from underground, she could see a small tunnel extending beyond the view from the above world. *Strange no one has seen this yet. Maybe it's like I thought. People would rather this not exist.*

She had to crouch down so her head wouldn't touch the dirt-coated ceiling. The farther ahead she went, the less she could see in front of her. The reach of the sun from under the city was fading as she went along.

Light returned to her in small doses after another ten minutes of walking. The presence of strange luminary stones surprised her. Cipre had no idea what they were, but she was grateful for them. It meant that she could see she wasn't about to fall into some abyss to the bowels of the planet.

The next thing that caught her senses was the smell. It wasn't exactly bad, but she couldn't decide how she felt about it. It was *different*. That was the only adjective she could think of.

Her senses were livid, looking for any new thing to take note of, but the only thing her body was telling her to do was run away as an ominous voice came from somewhere in the cavern:

"Oh? Hello there…"

The speech went better than he expected, which wasn't saying a whole lot. After the encounter with the Edlands, a nervous anger had washed over him. He thought he hid it well from the public.

The biggest surprise of all was their reception of his words.

They took his condolences with nodding heads and beaming eyes, and they applauded at the end. Part of him felt like he would be unable to sleep at night for what they would say about him in the papers this morning. But something in the way people accepted his words, the way he succeeded in making real tears roll down his cheeks, made him sure that he secured his high approval rating.

That included all the parts about the Edlands' new charity outreach.

"Still thinking about it, huh?"

He turned his head from the window where daylight was now in full swing. His wife, Venka, stood with a glass of water in their kitchen doorway.

"Yeah, not much else to think about. It seems that every time I look outside, I'm reminded of what happened and my place in it."

"I was talking more about how the Edlands made you adjust your speech plans."

Charles nodded, knowingly. "I thought easing it into my speech would be the best approach. Sprinkle a few hints in the beginning about how so many people lost their homes and jobs, and then present it as a healthy alternative, and by the end-"

"You were practically sending them there to the factories already."

"I wouldn't put it exactly that way," the Prime Minister returned a smile. "but yes."

A knock at the door stopped his wife's reply. Charles adjusted his collar before opening the door. It was a young woman, one of his new assistants. She didn't have the friendliest look on her face, and several loose strands of hair hovered over her face.

"Is the news really that bad, Jess?" Charles asked.

"No, I haven't looked at it." she shrugged. "Apologies, Mister Prime Minister, I think I'm falling under the weather."

He opened the door all the way, gesturing into the living room. "Don't worry. I think we still have some tea and honey left. Venka, please make this young woman a cup with extra honey."

Venka nodded, retreating from the kitchen doorway. Jess took a seat opposite Charles on the couch. The Prime Minister undid the strap on the newspaper. He didn't need to flip through the pages to find the story he was looking for. The main headline said it all: **PRIME MINISTER CHARLES DOWLEPOT PROVES ONCE AGAIN THAT THE PEOPLE WERE RIGHT IN ABOLOSHING THE MONARCHY.**

"That suddenly makes an awfully good start to my day."

When the pot finished boiling, his wife brought in the hot cup for Jess. She thanked her, taking a cautious sip before placing it on the coffee table.

Intrigued by the top headline, Charles decided to read the rest of the passage:

Not even ten minutes after the disaster struck, Prime Minister Dowlepot had engaged army and civilian medical relief to the hardest hit parts of Brunswald. His speech, though at parts seeming rushed, was heartfelt and human (with even a couple tears). One of the more notable and original portions of the speech dealt with the rising Edland business empire. It has long been suspected that the Edlands had hands as high up as the office of the commander of Skaltbard, and if it is so, Dowlepot is not trying to hide it. It is not for anyone to say as of yet, but what the Edlands propose could be a serious step forward in not only temporary emergency housing and relief, but the start of an innovative new method of employee/employer relations. It has been more than a hundred years since one typically lived in the same place that they worked, and perhaps that is an idea that could have some benefit in a return.

It went on, but he decided he had read enough. It was typical for the Brunswald Papers not to overtly take a side in a political issue, but he sensed a tone under there, and he didn't know what to think. Hell, he still didn't know what to think of the Edlands' plan. Wasn't keeping workers in housing in their factories a bit like slavery? Wasn't that something that went the way of monarchs, beliefs in magic, and gods?

He went down to another article to help take his mind off it. An article below discussed a popular event that everyone in Brunswald was familiar with:

Now a few weeks into spring, people from all around Skaltbard and even some neighboring nations are making trips to see the peak of one of the strangest wonders of the world: the Sunitian Sea. The strange, multicolored, enigmatic ocean of gas comes farthest to shore at the end of the first month of fall, and it attracts thousands and thousands of people every year. No illustration of it can do justice what one's own eyes can do, and from the way people talk about it in the outer cities, it is worth the trip over.

He turned his eyes from the page, wondering what the new disaster would do to tourism. The Sunitian Sea was a sight for sure, but people would be thinking twice about coming to visit while the city is rebuilding itself. More superstitious folk would probably be worried that another one would hit the city again. Or maybe they weren't superstitious, maybe scientists didn't know what they were talking about. Maybe it would happen again just as easily and fatally?

At least for now, he had made his appearance and given his speech and made sure help was sent where help was needed.

It was still early in the day. Perhaps he could take his wife and Jess out to lunch. His driver definitely knew a good place far away from the carnage.

CHAPTER 8

Gerrika had never read something so quickly before.

The first of Winds Wilk's plays that he read was *Pigamist*. Since he had just seen a performance of it, the play was still fresh in his mind. He wanted to know how reading the written play sat with him. After the first few pages, he found himself giggling at the same jokes that made Chanin and Dreden put their palms to their faces.

Now finished with *Pigamist*, the aveho got out of bed and placed the thin booklet into his desk drawer. He turned to the window. The moon was already noticeably farther west than it had been when he started reading. *Is this what it's like for Dreden and Chanin?* he wondered. *Being able to read and lose track of time? It's not that bad.*

Tomorrow was Sunday. The only thing he possibly would have to get up for was to get food with his friends again. He didn't need to be one hundred percent conscious during that. It wouldn't hurt to pull out another play and finish that one too.

In case he fell asleep while reading, which happened way too often with schoolwork for him to admit, he changed into his bed clothes. Gerrika kicked his boots to the corner of the room, pulling off his gray pants in exchange for more comfortable black ones. Since his feathers were so black, it often looked like he was naked when he just wore his sleeping pants, so he always coupled it with a white shirt. For as long as he could remember, there was a connection between him wearing day clothes to bed and nightmares. He didn't know why, but at least there was an easy way to avoid it.

The sound of his front door opening and closing stopped him in the center of his room. A panic struck him, and the memory of yesterday's near-death encounter with the strange men at Heathback almost made him tumble under his bed. Then he remembered his father said he was working late.

A knock came to his bedroom door. Based on the sound, the knock had come from some large creature with an arm thick enough to strangle a full-grown bear.

No worries then. It was his father.

"Come in, father." Gerrika said.

The doorknob turned, and Honja entered his son's room. The aveho that came in was most memorable for his bulk. While the species was not usually known for producing males with thick shoulders and upper bodies, Honja was a unique case. He wasn't obese, and he couldn't be, since most avehos had metabolisms that worked too quickly for that to be possible. One couldn't help but wonder how a creature that evolved from hollow bones could carry a frame with so much muscle.

Like the majority of aveho males, his father was dark colored. His body had the same black pattern of feathers from the tip of his head to his ankles. Instead of Gerrika's blue, he had brown around his collar and a large bushy red brow.

"You sound distressed," his father raised an eye.

Gerrika willed his heart to stop beating, but it persisted. "Yes. Sorry. I thought someone was breaking in. Then I remembered you said you wouldn't be back until after midnight."

Honja grunted. "I didn't see you after you came home last night, and I didn't see you before you left this morning. Everything good?"

"Yes, everything's good."

His son turned away from him, taking a seat back on his bed.

Gerrika caught his father eyeing his new collection of plays, now spread out on his sheets. He knew what Honja was thinking, and he knew that his son knew what he was thinking, so there was no use for words.

"It's late, son." Honja said, still standing in the same spot where he entered. "You can read and study while you're at the university."

Gerrika looked away from his father so he wouldn't see him rolling his eyes. "I've heard it before, father. This isn't even for school. It's just for fun, but that makes it worse for you, doesn't it?"

This wasn't the first argument they had had in the last week, and it wouldn't be the last. Especially when Gerrika had a tendency to end arguments with his father in the place where they would next be picked up.

Honja blinked, still processing his son's words. "I think weekends should be spent with just the both of us. You see your humans enough during the week. I think a little more time with your own species will be good for you. Perhaps your behavior will improve."

"If you say so, father." Gerrika crossed his arms under his chest. "Now, like you said, it's late. I need to get up early for an exam."

His father nodded and retreated out the door. Gerrika followed the sound of the wooden floor creaking under his father's weight until he couldn't hear anything. He was once again alone in his room, as it should be. He didn't care that he had just lied to his father about an exam.

Not wanting to incur another word from his father, Gerrika blew out the candles by his bed and put his head against his pillow. The words of Winds Wilk swirled in his head like a sea storm. He was never one for long texts, and novels never could hold his attention, as much as he wanted them to. Chanin enjoyed reading long books, but not as much as Dreden did. He knew Dreden surely always felt left out when he would try to engage them with the new thing he was reading. He and Chanin could keep the conversation going for a while, but it was a topic that didn't have a spark compared to normal university gossip. The idea of him finally having something like Wilk's plays to himself gave him an unquenchable urge to share them.

Beyond that, Winds Wilk had a way with comedy that made him want to laugh hard enough to lose his feathers. Yes, he knew that it wasn't the kind of literature they would teach in schools, but that didn't mean it couldn't be celebrated. And who was anyone to tell him that he should be spending time reading something else? Dreden? His own father?

He was having enough of his father. The aveho was a traditionalist in a strange sense and didn't like any form of human culture taking shape in his life, so Gerrika knew it bothered him that he didn't have any friends that were his own species.

His father was supposed to work another long day tomorrow. Gerrika decided he would wait until morning to read his next play, probably *Astutedent*. It seemed that all the titles of Wilk's plays were puns. He could already hear how hard his friends *weren't* laughing at that one too.

He closed his eyes and put his bed sheet up to his torso. For a good ten minutes he was as still as a rock.

Then the sound of a large creature approaching forced him up.

With the lessons of his father programmed deep in his instincts, Gerrika sank himself as far as he would go behind his bed, leaving barely the top of his head visible from the corner of the window. Without the moonlight helping him, he wouldn't have seen the shadow approaching from a hundred yards away. Also with the moonlight, he could make out the identity of the approaching figure.

"This is strange…" he said to himself.

Easing himself away from his bed, he quietly opened the door to his room and stepped out. He was glad he remembered to take his boots off. Without them his footsteps were much softer on the wood.

He could hear the figure approaching the porch. Gerrika slowly opened the door, hoping to catch his friend before he made any more noise.

"Dreden?" Gerrika said. "What are you doing here?"

He didn't notice it before, but Dreden was carrying a long, thick tree branch over his shoulder. "It happened again."

The way his friend spoke coupled with his steady, wide eyes sent a nervous chill down his neck. "What do you mean? What happened again?"

"Those crazy bastards with their blow tools. They came to my home and shot it up."

"Oh my!" Gerrika immediately shut himself up. His father was probably still awake. "Wait. Wait." He continued, now in a hushed volume. "They didn't hit you anywhere did they? Or your father?"

Dreden shook his head. "We're both fine, but that doesn't change what we need to do." He loosened the tree branch from his neck, slapping it against the palm of his other hand. "We need to get these fuckers at the source. We need to go back to Heathback."

"Dreden, I can only try to imagine what you must be feeling now, but we need to put our heads together. What can the three of us do that the City Guards can't?"

"For one, we seem to be the only people around here who have been targeted by these people. And… I've been overcome with this feeling that there is a mystery here no one with experience in crime solving can possibly wrap their minds around."

"I've been having strange feelings too. Come, let's go take a walk. You know my father has a strict policy about humans on the property."

His friend nodded, knowing.

They took a short stroll two hundred feet away, under the shadiest tree that kept them shied away from even the moonlight.

"What's the plan?" Gerrika asked, now that they were seated. "What? Are we supposed to lure them back into the city to be caught?"

"I don't think that'll do. And neither will this stupid thing." Dreden chucked his tree branch away. "I just picked that up in case I encountered them while coming to get you. We're going to need something deadlier than a wooden club."

"I see." Gerrika looked back over to his front door, making sure his father hadn't caught them yet. "Besides, there is the chance they'll go back into the Sunitian Sea again. Are you sure it was the same three people that attacked us yesterday?"

"I didn't get a good look at any of them, but the fact they still had those weapons was telling. There weren't three of them this time. I counted seven."

Gerrika cursed, shaking his head. "You're right. They can't get away with this."

"That's what brings me to you right now. We're going to need real weapons for this."

Dreden locked eyes with the aveho. From the silence that followed, Gerrika knew what Dreden was really trying to say.

"No." Gerrika frantically shook a talon-hand. "Absolutely not! I'm not stealing weapons from my father. In all my life, he has never let me lay a claw on them without his supervision."

"One of us could die next time we encounter them, Gerrika. Are you sure that you're willing to risk that on account of your fear of what your father would do?"

Gerrika felt like burying his head in the ground. Neither option was pleasant. He didn't want to betray his father, but he and his friends were in danger from the strange men. And it might not just be them. Many others could also be having deadly encounters with the same men.

His father wouldn't like it. Then again, Gerrika didn't remember the last time he did anything his father approved of.

"Very well," Gerrika sighed. "but we have to be really careful with them, and we need to make sure we have them all back by morning. I don't know for sure if my father counts his arrows every night, but even if he does, he might not suspect me."

"Great." Dreden smiled, giving his friend a pat on the shoulder. "I'm thinking a sword for each of the three of us-"

"Three?"

"We're getting Chanin next, of course. I might not have a ton of bow and arrow experience, but I think one for each of us as well, and maybe twelve a piece?"

"How are you so sure my father has all that at the ready?"

"Your father is a professional hunter. That's like asking if *my* father has books lining all his shelves."

"Fair." Gerrika and Dreden stood back up, facing his home. "Okay. Just wait here. I'm going to get a coat and my boots on, then I'll get the stuff. Don't leave this tree. Got it?"

"Good luck."

Gerrika started back for his home, his yellow three-toed feet gripping the dirt nervously with each step.

Suddenly he found himself thinking about his own mortality. If those strange men were such a threat, odds are they wouldn't be able to take them all out with his father's comparatively simple weapons.

He thought about his last words to his father, and with all the waking adrenaline going through his veins, he couldn't care to remember what they were.

Chanin held a sword well enough. Gerrika didn't have to correct her posture much. Though by his own admission, Gerrika was not a skilled fighter. Or a fighter at all, so his instruction was held under scrutiny by the two humans, but what other choice did they have?

"Seven?" Chanin's jaw fell, as Dreden repeated his story to her. "There were *seven* of them this time?"

"There may have been more. Under the moonlight I could make out at least seven."

"Seven, eight, nine, twenty, I brought an armory to take any number of them out." Gerrika said, lagging slightly behind with the bag of bows, arrows, and daggers he was carrying over his shoulder. "Frankly, I'm impressed we got this far. I didn't think I would be able to weasel my way out of my home with all these without my father waking, and I certainly didn't think Chanin would be awake for this adventure. You're not exactly a light sleeper, my lady."

"Is that what I am now? 'My lady'?" she laughed. "Give a man any weapon and the old-world chivalry pops out. Human or aveho, a male is a male. I couldn't sleep, for your information. I was still on edge about our first encounter with these awful people."

"That's a mild way of talking about them." Dreden replied.

"I know, I guess I'm just trying not to think about it too much. Anyway, no matter what kind of sweet dreams I was having, I'm giving them up for a chance to stick it to them, especially since they just came back and attacked my best friend." Gerrika shot her a look from behind. "*One* of my best friends."

As they went along, their conversation seemingly went everywhere, with only a fraction of the time dealing with their most pressing issue. The three of them were terrified of a confrontation, and Dreden knew it.

None of us have a lick of a chance here, he thought. *I pray to God that this is for nothing. If those men are at the cave again, the three of us are going to die trying to fit our bows on the strings. Even Gerrika isn't going to last very long, with the little training he has. Despite my hotheadedness in running out on my father earlier, I still want to live. Doing shit like this isn't how one gets to keep living.*

After several more minutes, none of them wanted to talk anymore. The trio remained quiet, stuck in their own thoughts until the entrance to their little hangout at Heathback came into view.

"Here's our graveyard." Dreden said with a bite.

Chanin put her hand on his back. "Quiet. Let's stop here. Gerrika, Dreden, don't make a sound."

The three of them went down on their knees, then Dreden got down on his stomach like he was hiding from a lion. None of them moved more than an eyelash or feather for over a minute, but only were greeted by the sounds of field crickets and the occasional caw or hoot of a nocturnal bird. No sound of cladded footsteps, no sound of loud weapons, and not a sound of any men.

"Perhaps there's no one here." Gerrika said. "Maybe their threats against us were just bluffs."

"Maybe," Dreden replied. "or maybe we need to go somewhere else?"

"Where?"

Dreden looked ahead. "To the cavern. To our little spot."

"You think that's going to make a difference?" Chanin asked.

"It's worth a try. Remember, we didn't hear those people coming last time until they were in immediate range of us. It's like they had just been birthed from thin air. It might be strange, and kind of anti-academic, but there is something greater going on here than we know. The three of us might have to play by certain rules, and if we can't catch them playing by our own, then we're going to have to confront them by playing by theirs."

Neither Chanin nor Gerrika had any comment. Without another word, Dreden turned to his friends, gesturing them forward with a turn of his neck.

They got to their feet and approached the mouth of the cavern. As their boots kicked against the tall grass of the unclaimed plain, the volume of wildlife activity ceased. Suddenly their feet and their own breathing were the only sounds.

It was so quiet that Dreden and Gerrika knew the second that Chanin paused.

"What is it?" Gerrika asked.

"It's so weird. I can't see the stars anymore."

She was right. Dreden couldn't see a single speck of light in the infinite above. Even the moon above them seemed to dim its lights like a dying candle. The cool winter wind they were used to ceased into an unnatural stillness.

Dreden felt sweat build on his palms.

He could feel it drip as they faced the mouth of the cave.

Nothing was there. It was just as they had left it, with the only hint of the men being the holes in the walls from the shots of their strange weapons.

"Wait," Gerrika raised an arm, reaching into his quiver with his other hand. "do you guys hear that?"

The two humans paused. It was still as quiet as the home of a hibernating bear.

"What is it?" Chanin asked.

"It's like…water. I think I can make out something like a waterfall. It's faint, but it's definitely there."

Dreden shook his head. "I can't hear anything."

They turned their focus back to the cave. Walking in, they were careful not to have their backs face the entrance, on the chance of being ambushed. Gerrika raised his bow up, arrow ready, as he guarded the backs of his friends.

"Oh shit!" Chanin's hand flew to her mouth. "Guys, take a look at this."

"Or not." The aveho stood still. "That rushing water sound is getting louder. I think we should get out of here. This isn't normal."

Dreden's only reply to Gerrika was a brush of his hand along his friend's shoulder. He approached Chanin and his mouth fell open at the sight of her focus. Ancient-looking images lined the cavern walls, all sprouting from the holes left by the projectile pellets of the men's weapons.

"What are those?" Dreden lowered his sword, gazing at the markings. "They look so old. They can't be more than a day old, because they sure as hell weren't here before."

Little human figures with round heads and stubby bodies were the stars of the story being told on the wall. Several figures held long sticks that looked just like the weapons that were oh so familiar. A couple leaned back, relaxing on a horseless carriage in another one. They went on and on, with the human-looking figures indulging in unfathomed technologies that Dreden could only visualize from reading fiction. They weren't exactly impressive art, since some looked more like toddler scribbles than glyphs.

The last one, and the most haunting one, gave mouths to the people. They were open in perfect ovals, paused in a speechless horror at the crumbling of the ground around them. Horseless carriages, like the ones presented earlier, were tumbling into an abyss, as did dozens of hapless people around it. They went crashing down, limbs flailing, as if into a fiery inferno.

And that was where the story ended.

"Holy…" Dreden felt his forehead for sweat. "Those men must have made these. Who else could it be?"

"No idea." Chanin took a step back to take in the full picture of the illustrations.

Gerrika grumbled, moving towards his friends who were mindlessly taken by the pictures with increasing reverence. "Guys! We have to get out of here! It's not water. It isn't a goddamn ocean. It's the Sunitian Sea. It's sweeping in!"

Then the humans heard it. Dreden wanted to kick his own hind for ignoring his friend. As if the increasing sound of the gas approaching weren't enough, the air around them suddenly became fleeting. To his left, Chanin began to choke. His own throat constricted, as if the air molecules were trapped in a shaking jar.

Oxygen was no more. No air was. Behind Dreden, Gerrika fell to his knees, unable to stand from the new weakness in his legs. Dreden followed suit, letting his arms hit the cold floor, as his spine felt as if it were shriveling.

He tried to scream. From Gerrika's open beak, he was trying too, but nothing came out.

And before the vacuum of space that had manifested in Heathback took his vision away, Dreden saw the bright green shade of the Sunitian Sea wash its tongue over them, claiming them like the men in red two days earlier.

CHAPTER 9

If it weren't for the deeply human feel she got from the whites of the creature's eyes, Cipre would have darted out of the tunnel like she was on fire.

Her level of terror was contained, even as the head that bore the eyes towered over her by almost ten feet. The creature was reptilian, that much was obvious from its lizard-like appearance along with the ruby-red scales that lined its body. It looked like something out of old mythology, but clearly it wasn't, or at least it wasn't any longer.

"I said 'Hello, there'," the creature repeated, this time with what Cipre recognized was annoyance. "Aren't you going to say hello to me too?"

"Hello…" Cipre's mouth was almost too dry to make a sound.

The giant reptile cocked its head. "You're a woman, aren't you? I've read about you in my books. There are pictures too, but none of them look as good as you do."

She fought a blush. "Thanks. If you know so much, then do you know how weird this encounter is for me?"

"I suppose I can only imagine. I've never spoken to a human before. I'm sorry if I seem overjoyed. I've never talked to a creature that can verbalize a response like we can."

Overjoyed was not anywhere near the word she would use to describe the beast's behavior so far. "Look, umm…do you have a name?"

"Minkompa."

"Okay, Minkompa, can you tell me just what you are?"

"I'm a dragon. Do I not look like one?"

"It's not that." Cipre began to feel dizzy and felt the cave wall for support. "It's just…well…"

"You look ill! Please take a seat. I can't have anything ruining our day *now!*"

She did as Minkompa told her. There were no chairs anywhere in the lair, so she just took a seat on the ground, leaning her back against the rocky wall.

"I'm sorry that I don't have any coffee or tea." the dragon said.

"No, that's okay. I'm not very thirsty anyway."

Minkompa blinked. "That's not what I meant. I meant that I'm sorry I don't have any coffee or tea for you to fix me. I read in my books that it's tradition for women to serve men beverages at the start of meetings. I hope you don't feel bad about it."

"That's a bit old fashioned." Cipre had to laugh. "That's not really done as much anymore. At least not like that." *Okay, so this dragon is a male*, she thought to herself. *Or perhaps more of a boy, he doesn't seem to have experience in the outside world, which would explain why everyone in the world except myself is still under the impression that these creatures are just folklore.*

"Good. Good. I would hate for you to be insulted."

"I'm not. I promise."

Cipre reminded herself why she was underground in the first place. She wanted to find the creature that destroyed her city. As strange as it was, there was no place where the behemoth could have gone. The road looked like it ended in Minkompa's cave.

"Minkompa," she started, slowly. "Do you live alone?"

"Yes. It's just me and my books, and the cave frogs, the insects, the bats and the rats. Why?"

"I don't know if you know anything about this-"

Minkompa brushed his claw against his chest. "I know a little about everything."

Cipre was back on her feet, feeling a surge of strength. "Then hopefully you can help me. You see, a powerful earthquake struck the city yesterday, and it left many dead, many injured, and many more without jobs or a home."

"I felt it too. That's horrible!" he cried.

"Truly. Before the disaster ended, I caught a glimpse of what really happened. It wasn't just any earthquake. It was caused by something massive. I could see a titanic creature crawling under the cracks causing the wreckage, and before that, I think I saw the same creature zoom past the city skyline."

"That's why you're here, isn't it?" Minkompa said, retreating his head. "You think I'm the one that did it."

"I don't!" Cipre raised a hand in the air, hoping the creature knew she was trying to keep him calm. "The thing I saw was at least four times bigger than you, a darker color, and probably not nearly as kind as you've been to me so far."

That seemed to work. The dragon relaxed himself, returning his composure. "Very good. I'm glad. I would hate anyone to think I've done anything so terrible."

"But that does beg the question," Cipre continued. "the monster came this way. I followed its trail all the way here. Are you sure you didn't hear anything come by? You didn't hear any loud burrowing?"

Now that she was once again as calm as she was before meeting Minkompa, she took a moment to take in his home. Massive bookshelves that would have been the envy of all libraries in Skaltbard lined the walls. Countless volumes, surely of every discipline, looked to be in perfect order. Beyond that, the cavern looked like it extended a long way back, giving the dragon a lot of wiggle room. There was a foul smell in the air, but she wasn't going to hold it against a creature that seemed to not get out for fresh air very often, or if he did at all.

"I'm sorry…and sorry again, since I don't believe I've gotten your name, woman."

"I'm Cipre." She smiled, catching herself about to extend her hand for a shake.

"I'm sorry, Cipre, I haven't heard any such thing. It is possible that the monster you're looking for managed to dig itself even farther underground, perhaps intending to use my home as a trick."

"It's certainly possible. Something that can cause so much destruction and keep its existence hidden is surely excellent at covering its tracks. Even getting this far was-"

The walls shook, and Cipre felt as if something had tackled her to the ground. As her back made contact with the rocky floor, the rest of the cavern room spun like a top.

It's happening again! She shot her arms out, trying to find anything to hold. *It's another earthquake!*

"I've got you!"

Minkompa fell to all fours, dashing with impressive stealth over to the human. A few pieces of the ceiling came loose, but the dragon's paw was there, shielding her from being crushed to death.

The dragon kept his paw over her until the shaking stopped. When it was clear that it was over, Minkompa backed up, laying down on his belly as Cipre rose and dusted herself off.

"I'm just no good at keeping out of trouble today." Cipre smiled. "Thank you so much."

"It was no problem." A twinkle flashed in the dragon's eye. Cipre felt that it was his version of a smile. "I can't have my first visitor in a long time die on me. It wouldn't make me look very good. So, you think that was caused by the thing you're pursuing?"

"Maybe. This one was different. I don't know. Maybe it's just because I'm underground instead of on the top floor of a building." A panic struck her, making her want to punch herself. "Crap! The city! This can't be good news for it! I'm sorry, but I need to go, and now."

"I understand." The dragon sat back up. "I hope everything is fine up there. You'll come back to see me, won't you?"

"No doubt about it. Something tells me we're going to have a lot to learn from each other, friend."

She darted into a sprint, rounding the corner and heading back up, as the slivers of sunlight seeping through the cracks grew bigger. She felt bad about leaving Minkompa that way, but what choice did she have? More of her home city might have been swallowed up by the earth. The titanic creature had tricked her, leaving her underground as it continued its rampage.

But this time there were no souls lost to the quake. Instead, three souls had just arrived.

The first thing Dreden felt was the quake. Then came the gasps. There were several unowned screams too, but they sounded like they came from even farther away. That was probably just his hearing sense being increased from the absence of his others. Another moment later, a bright light returned his vision like an active volcano.

His vision was the first to return. Chanin and Gerrika were standing up, but they were covering their eyes.

This isn't right. Dreden thought, looking around. *The sun is out. This is the day! We were knocked out all night!*

They sure weren't on the Heathback cave floor anymore. The ground under his boots wasn't covered in dirt, but looked like a giant rock. Dreden bent down to inspect it. It was like the kind of rocks that made impressive formations on beaches, or along the coast of giant lakes.

Looking up, several people stood along a metallic railing. Some were still on their backs because of the quaking. The sun was still in his eyes, so he couldn't see any of their faces, but Dreden felt their gaze on him and his friends. Their faceless bodies exchanged murmurs, and he was filled with sudden dread.

"Oh...God..." Gerrika slowly wiped his eyes, then dusted himself off. "What happened?"

He didn't see Chanin behind him. She let out a startled yip as he almost tripped over her.

"Sorry!" The aveho grabbed her arm and helped her up.

"Are you here, Dreden?" she asked. "I can't see anything."

Dreden grabbed her other arm, guiding her to the steadiest space on the rock. "It'll come back. I was blinded too."

"And so was I. Look there. Seems like there's a crowd forming to watch us."

The aveho was right. Since he last looked up at the sunny scene, more people had gathered along the top.

Dreden took a few steps forward on the rock. The sun was out of his way, shielded by the cliff and people above him. Men and women stared at him, with the occasional child stuck behind one of their legs. From their faces he looked down. The clothes they all wore were like something out of a play. Some of the men sported thin dark colors over their shirts, which were a milky white. Their thick coats looked like something one would need if they planned on sleeping all winter. And the hats that they wore extended well over their heads like spinning toys.

The women were much different. Some of them wore hats that were even bigger, and their clothing looked way more comfortable than the men's. With the thin, loose-looking fabrics that extended down to their feet, it looked like they were dressed for an entirely different season than the men.

Then Dreden noticed that there were only humans in the crowd. No avehos.

Hardly any of them were looking at him or Chanin. Most of their eyes were glued to Gerrika.

"Anybody want to help us out?" Gerrika asked the crowd, annoyed. "We've been knocked out all night here and none of you thought to see if we were okay? Wow. Kroonsaed is really starting to lose its wholesome reputation."

Dreden didn't want to move. He couldn't even bring himself to tell his friends what he was thinking. Gerrika was oblivious to everyone staring at him in awe, and he gave no mind to the strange clothes the people were wearing. Chanin looked only a bit more in-the-know, but her eyes were no longer on the crowd. She was watching something right behind Dreden.

"Hey, Dreden, those guys coming our way sure aren't the City Guard."

He turned around. Three men in black clothes and black hats were approaching them from the sides. One of them had a strange pair of dark glasses over his eyes. Dreden first thought the man must have been blind, but the way he moved his arms and legs suggested otherwise.

"Young people," the man with the black glasses smiled. "don't you realize that you're standing on government property? You're not allowed down here."

"What are you talking about?" Dreden replied. "Heathback isn't…" He stopped himself, remembering that they were no longer at the cave. "I mean, this isn't government property. No one owns these grounds. Right?"

"Wrong, son." The man snorted. "You three picked the wrong time to be delinquents. After what's happened with the earthquake, the government isn't taking any risks with tourist attractions."

"A tourist attraction?" Chanin asked.

One of the other men in black nodded. "That's right. You're standing on the grounds of the Sunitian Sea."

The three of them turned around. Dreden didn't know how he hadn't noticed it earlier or how he didn't *feel* the way the air grew thin around them.

Not more than twenty feet away from the ground they stood on was the sea of gas that everyone in Kroonsaed knew to stay clear from. In all its terrifying beauty, changing colors like a hiding chameleon from bright purple to lime green, was the Sunitian Sea.

His hand flew to his mouth. Chanin and Gerrika exchanged looks. Something was wrong. The air was fine. The Sea was quiet, and even worse, dozens of people were willingly standing around, looking like they were admiring it.

"How did you do it?" Gerrika asked the men. "How did you get the Sea to be so calm? Where is all the extra air coming from?"

The three officers paused, turning to each other, chuckling. "That's an impressive costume. What is it made of? Peacock and raven feathers?"

"No… They're my natural colors."

"And that mask." The third man pointed. "How did you connect the beak with your mouth? It looks like it's saying exactly what your lips are doing."

The aveho cocked his head, scratching the side of his neck. "Keep your day jobs, guys. You're not very good comedians."

The main, glasses-wearing officer let out a sigh. "Okay. I've had enough of this. Come on. Come with us. Hopefully your parents can pay the fines for you."

Chanin backed away. "Fines? I'm not convinced we've done anything wrong. Where's the City Guard? I think they'll have a lot to say to you about your stupid fines."

The next thing Dreden felt were cold shackles being strapped to his wrists. One of the other men grabbed his free arm and shoved it behind his back. He clapped the other metal shackle around the other, and now his arms were locked.

"Let me go!" Dreden shouted. He tried prying himself free, but it wouldn't work. Also, his captor seemed to be amused by his attempts.

Chanin caught the look on her friend's face. She followed his lead, letting the officer clamp the small metal cuffs behind her back. Upon seeing his two friends give up, Gerrika didn't see a reason to continue. He turned his back to the approaching lead officer, putting his arms out for the cuffs.

"They seriously look so *real*. You even put a little feathery tail on your costume! You must be a great actor, son." He clamped the cuffs on the aveho's wrist with a click. "What do you do to your hands to make them so talon-like? You know, some lotion could really help with this."

"I'm an aveho, smart-ass." Gerrika spat. "These jokes haven't been funny for at least hundreds of years."

The man waved him off, now looking bored of the encounter. He and the two other officers ushered the trio off the rock, leaving the calm Sunitian Sea and the still awestruck crowd behind them.

CHAPTER 10

Now the three of them were stuck in a room, alone. The room was warm, windowless. All that was there was a table big enough for three on each side. The trio was on one side, while the other had one lone empty seat.

Dreden had been shoved into the seat on the farthest right, while Chanin was put in the middle and Gerrika on the left. None of them had anything to say. There were way too many questions that didn't have answers.

On the way over to the police station, as it had been called, Dreden watched the city passing by on the back of the carriage. Despite his current situation: being trapped in some mystery city that existed outside of time with no way of getting back home, he had to give respects to the architectural marvels that lined the city's skyline. Buildings taller than anything he had seen before were as plentiful as the people inhabiting them. Only the churches of Kroonsaed had the potential to rival any of these buildings, which ranged from an ancient pyramid build to some that looked more like metallic trees.

Civilization advanced to return mankind to the jungle here, Dreden told himself along the ride. They huddled in hovels of fire-cooking bread and meat and dared their mammalian instincts all the way to the top of the skies, where no wingless creature had any business. The roads were all smooth and put together like a mosaic, making the civilized animals into considerate beings, like little ducklings careful to keep a straight path clear behind their mother, and in this case, the mother was a tall carriage peopled with citizens who were good looking yet didn't know what any of it was for.

He wanted to get to know the new strange place more, but no doubt his father was panicking from his absence.

"Was it just me," Gerrika cleared the silence in the room. "or were there absolutely no avehos anywhere in the city to be seen?"

"I thought it was weird enough that there weren't any outside by the Sunitian Sea." Dreden said. "I probably wouldn't have noticed if not for the fact that they were all staring at you as if you'd grown a second head."

"Is it too weird to think that in this city they've never even heard of us? You heard how that officer was talking to me. I think he was completely unbelieving that I exist."

Chanin frowned. "And no one in our City Guard would get away with talking to you like that. They've too much humility for any crap like that. I wanted to knock those stupid spectacles right off his square face."

"You humans really need to learn your place." Gerrika turned to his friends, smirking. "Avehos learned to walk upright before monkeys existed. All this stuff, culture, architecture, religion, technology…we had it first."

"Yet it occurs to me that we're on the same plane of civilization right now. What happened then? And you…" Dreden caught himself, remembering what his father had told him about the most recent incident of an aveho killing a human. So he changed his point with a convincing smile, "Or maybe that's why this place has rude police. They don't have the influence of aveho manners."

"Only explanation. Only explanation."

It wasn't until almost another ten minutes before someone finally came into the room. It was a gentleman who was older than any of the others they had seen. He had short hair under his hat and a coffee-colored mustache under his nose, which showed signs of a lifetime of drinking. His face had enough of a hint of youth that made Dreden wonder how he ended up in his rough profession.

"Sorry to keep you all." the man told them, fixing the chair in front of them for himself. "It is not a good time at all to have my job. Then again, when is it?"

He sat himself down, opening a little brown folder. His fingers flipped through the pages that made up the report, then closed it, looking around at each of them with a smile.

"I understand you three are fans of pranks. Don't worry. I understand. I was young once. When can I expect your parents to come?"

"I really don't think they'll be coming, sir." Chanin told him. "Does your report say anything about what we tried to tell your men?"

He gave the report another quick look. "No...not your literal quotes. It's written that you weren't being very cooperative. It says you were making up stories."

"We weren't." Dreden crossed his arms. "Everything we tried to tell them was true. Think about it, how would the three of us have been able to get down there without being seen? And how do you explain the earthquake right as everyone first noticed us?"

"That's the thing, young man-"

"I'm Dreden, just so you know our names. This is Chanin," she gave the officer an awkward wave. "and that's Gerrika, the one your officers were being especially rude to."

"I'm Chief Milbrey." He gave his cap a friendly tip. "I apologize for the behavior of those men, but if your friend is going to dress like a joke, then you can't be surprised if he is treated like one."

The aveho kicked the bottom of the table. "I'm not a human. I'm getting tired of saying this. How the hell don't you know what avehos are?"

"Probably the same reason I don't know what a reliable parcel service is. It's because it doesn't exist."

None of the three gave his joke any recognition. "I'm serious, sir," Gerrika continued. "I'm an aveho, and believe it or not, we were the first bipedal creatures to live in what you would call civilization."

"Son, I really don't want to have to rip that costume off you, feather by feather, because I assume you had many sleepless nights putting it together, but I don't want to be here more than I have to." Now even Chief Milbrey's mustache looked like it was frowning. "First, hundreds of citizens become convinced that they saw a giant monster in the sky, then the worst natural disaster in the history of Brunswald occurs. People are dead, hurt, unemployed, homeless, and it is the perfect breeding ground for crime, and now an aftershock happens and people are losing control all over again."

Chanin looked away. "I think you're missing-"

"I'm not done!" He raised a finger to her. "I'm chief of police in this now godless city, and I've never been so damn exhausted as I am now, in all my years, so forgive me if I have no patience for juvenile games. It's a courtesy that I'm even giving you a visit, instead of automatically having you spend the night in jail."

The chief paused, staring the three of them down in silence. Dreden couldn't meet the man in the eyes, and neither could his two friends. He knew they had nothing to be ashamed of or sorry for, since coming into the new city wasn't their choice, but that didn't stop him from feeling bad.

"Now, I'm sorry about this, but it's the way it must be, children. Unless you can get your parents here to pay the fines that you owe, I'm afraid you will be spending the night in a cell."

"What was so bad about where we were anyway?" Chanin asked.

"Ordinarily, not that much." The chief scratched his facial hair. "Since the earthquake, the big one, the government has been doing everything it can to maintain its special interests from any threat. The Sunitian Sea is how we get our biggest revenue from tourists. If we don't get that money this year, we'll be in this pit longer than anyone can stomach. We can't have-"

The door burst open. A young officer with a neat trim and a tie rushed in.

"Chief," he took a moment to regain his breath, and wiped the sweat from his brow. "there's too many of them. There's too many of them to contain."

The chief dashed to his feet. "What are you talking about?"

"We're being flooded with witnesses. It looks like everyone who was at the Sunitian Sea when these three were arrested is here to be heard. Sir, believe it or not, they're all saying that these three did nothing wrong. They say they weren't trespassing. Everyone says they saw these three simply *manifest* from out of the Sea, followed by the aftershock."

"But that can't be!"

"Hundreds of people out there all claiming the same thing are probably not incorrect, sir," The chief offered the young officer a glass of water. "Thank you. Sir, you've got to believe whatever these people are saying, even though the public can hardly believe their own eyes."

Chief Milbrey turned back to Dreden and his friends. This time all the former malice was gone, and the chief looked as if he were about to find out who the murderer was in a classic case. "Okay. I'm all ears. Tell me your story."

The three of them each took turns, explaining their personal history, along with the events leading up to their appearance in the strange city. They told them about Faeriebridge University, about Kroonsaed, about the difference in technology between the two cities.

"There is no such place as Kroonsaed on this planet." said the chief.

"And there is no such country as Skaltbard where we come from." replied Chanin.

Dreden shook his head. "Or any city called Brunswald."

As their tales went on, the chief took more of an interest in Gerrika's story. He wanted to know more about avehos. How many were there where he came from? As many as humans? Did they outnumber humans? To which Gerrika replied: millions, roughly, and probably not.

"Right hand to God, boy, you are really a crow-man?" asked the chief. That youthful gleam Dreden got from him earlier had returned.

"Yes, if it helps you understand." Gerrika smiled and pulled down his collar, showing black and blue feathers. "But not all of us have dark colors. Like humans, we can come in a spectrum of color."

"A whole other world..." The chief paused, as if trying to see his own words coming out of his mouth. "A place where our God may not have jurisdiction. Where a whole other race of men scatters the plains in search of a whole different meaning, a whole different morality, and one where your God may be even more silent than ours..."

"What?" Dreden asked.

"Sorry, just thinking out loud. Could it be? Is it possible? A parallel universe?"

"As strange as it is, I see no other explanation than that." Chanin said. "Despite all the wonder, sir, we have people back at home who are definitely worried about us. We're going to need to leave. Let us back to the Sea."

"That'll be tough. You see, you guys came in at high tide. I'm not just talking about the daily tide. It was high tide for the whole month."

"Okay," Gerrika said. "then we'll just walk the rest of the way till we get to the Sea. Easy."

"Maybe. Maybe not." replied the chief. "High tide is when the Sunitian Sea is at its most active. It is most vigorous. Sometimes it's strong enough that the people living in the streets nearby think an earthquake is happening. I'm no expert, since all this just happened for the first time, but I'm thinking that the reason you were able to come in through the Sea in your world was because of the activity." Milbrey dragged a palm down his face. "Our scientists have been trying to crack the mystery of the Sea for about a hundred years when it first appeared. I think this is only going to feed into even more cluelessness."

Chanin cleared her throat. "What are we supposed to do until then?"

"Apologies. It won't be as strong tomorrow, but around noon will be your best shot at getting back to your home. And, well...until then," Milbrey stood up, fixing his jacket and giving the trio a large mustached smile. "enjoy our city. Maybe you can learn a thing or two. Get a few souvenirs why don't you? This may be the only time we ever get visitors from another world, so I'm sure everyone in town will want to make a good impression. Oh my, summer has truly come early for scholars and creatives alike! You three will be eaten up."

With a parting wave, the chief left the room. The young officer who had come in out of breath held the door open for him, then looked over to Dreden and his friends, waiting for them to get up and go as well.

"We're going to be here for an entire day, guys." Dreden sighed. "That clock over there says it's just after four. Twenty hours. What are we supposed to do?"

Chanin exhaled. "You guys don't suppose this place has beer?"

First Interlude
The Greens
Home of the Bellsignor, the King of Andayt. Capital city, Nindeck.

"That is a ridiculous idea." Alad scowled as he addressed his fellow senator.

His fellow senator, an older woman named Ennry Halan, returned his distaste. "You're not thinking this through. Who could have ever predicted that we would have this kind of chance?"

"It isn't right, Madame Halan. I don't mean to sound hypocritical, because in the current era, every politician is in the business of war, but I am not going to urge the Bellsignor to be the first to strike. It'll be like kicking a small child in the head."

"I think of it more as kicking an elderly invalid, Mister Tich. When you have the kind of history that Skaltbard does, you don't get to pretend to be a hurt child."

Alad could feel the sweat building on the back of his neck. He didn't want to wipe it, since that would let Ennry know he was nervous. He just adjusted his collar, fixing his velvet jacket. It was a hot day. Summer was not far away.

Walking in The Greens used to make him feel like a child at the circus. Alad was one of the youngest people in the Andaytian high senate. At twenty-five, he had accomplished more than most had when they were thirty. His background in the history of war along with his status as a scholar of the greatest generals of Andayt, Skaltbard, and Borgetta of the last hundred years meant that his mind was one that begged for even the politics of a breakfast of sausage and toast. He often felt condemned with his knowledge. He had passion, but in times like these, there was nothing very morally fulfilling one could do with political expertise. If he were lucky, it would only be another couple decades until he saw the joys of his job come to fruition. For that to happen, many people had to die, as were the ways of war. With the rise of greater artillery, ammunition, guns that could shoot more than one round a minute, the business of politics was getting bloodier.

No doubt he had contributed to policies that resulted in the deaths of innocents, but starting an invasion against Skaltbard, whose capital city, Brunswald, had just become victim to the biggest natural disaster in more than a century, was not something he was going to recommend the Bellsignor do.

"Just because it's not our people in such trouble doesn't mean we have to ignore them." Alad told her. "I'm not inherently opposed to an invasion of Skaltbard, but it'll have to wait. It'll have to be when I believe the people of the country would actually benefit from our presence."

"And, Mister Tich," They paused their stroll through the halls of The Greens, as she finally showed him a smile. "do you think the Bellsignor will take sympathy on your position because you are young and completely alone in holding it?"

"The answer to that is neither here nor there. Besides, I think my reputation will speak for itself, as will my words. The high senate needs to get it in their steel skulls that simply because a young man has a new idea doesn't mean that it is a 'young' idea." He returned her smile, knowing that she meant no bark from her words. "It would be better if we all wore cloths over our faces in the senate and passed our ideas down in anonymous handwriting. That way we don't have to waste time wondering what kind of ulterior motives our senators have. We can take them at face value, so to speak."

"Then you'll never know who not to trust. It is a mistake of yours, young man, if I may refer to you as such, that you think government is only ever about doing what is right for the country and its people. Ever been to a ball? It's all make-believe theatrics for people with too much money and time, and too often politics is the same. Our egos will never allow us to give our voices and never let anyone know who owns them."

As they continued down the halls of the castle, Alad admired the massive paintings that lined the walls. Some of them weren't even contained to one room or hallway, and they continued around the corner or through the opening of a door. Starting from the main entrance, the art sprouted in every direction, telling the story of the formation of Andayt. Once hundreds of city-states that had intermittently been at war for almost a thousand years, the rise of machines, increased automation, and faster travel around the world eventually informed them that their little wars were a lot smaller than they realized.

The advancement of warfare technology created more destruction than they could handle. Alad wanted to turn away from some of the more gruesome images on the walls, but the Bellsignor thought they were necessary. It was important to always be reminded of where you once were, to show how far one had finally come. Alad agreed, but that didn't mean he had to enjoy looking at paintings of civilians getting chopped down, then gunned down, as the future of warfare gave.

When the governors of the city-states realized their modes were unsustainable, they managed to set aside their histories for a future. Alad couldn't imagine modern politicians ever coming to a decision so peaceful and monumental. He thought it was because war had gotten too easy. It was one thing to shudder at gruesome art of an unpleasant past, but how good were reminders like that if war had become so easy? It wasn't in the cities so much anymore. It was somewhere far away where it couldn't be seen. It was out *there*. The world might have gotten smaller from faster travel, but that also meant it was easy to dump what you didn't want somewhere else. A generation of men and women had not witnessed violence in the streets. They didn't know how the screams and the gunfire stayed in your ears long after the last ounce of blood dripped from a wound. Alad felt guilty that he was a part of that generation.

The rushing of someone from behind them stopped his thinking. He and Ennry turned around. From around the painted corner, a woman in her red senator cloak with her hair everywhere in her face ran to them. Alad recognized her as Iza Minz, one of the Bellsignor's closest friends in the high senate.

"What's the matter?" Alad asked.

Iza took a second to recover herself and wipe the hair out of her eyes. "You haven't seen him, have you?"

"Who?" Ennry asked.

"The Bellsignor! Apologies for shouting, Madame Halan, but this is cause for emergency."

Alad put his hand on her shoulder. "Did you check his quarters?"

"No, I couldn't. I don't have an invitation. Alad, Ennry, he didn't attend any of his meetings this morning, and he didn't show up to the meeting he was to have with me just half an hour ago."

"Surely there's no cause for alarm, Madame Minz," Ennry shifted her gaze back and forth between the two younger senators. "He's done this kind of thing before."

Iza had started digging into her bag before Ennry finished talking. A folded-up note appeared in her hand. She unraveled it, accidentally tearing the sides in her panic.

"Has he ever done *this* before?" she asked.

Alad took the note out of her hand. Ennry sidled up to him so she could read what the note said.

It was just three words, and the two of them instantly understood her panic.

I'm being held, it said.

"Damnit, girl!" cried Ennry. "When were you going to tell anyone about this?"

"I just got it! One of his carrier ravens pecked at my window and gave it to me. The first thing I did was rush over here."

"This isn't a job for someone like you, Madame Minz," the senior senator regained her composure, with regained politeness. "This is for his private guards to deal with. Surely it's a prank. How could anyone get by-"

Alad noticed it the same time as Ennry. The entrance to the Bellsignor's quarters was just ahead. Always, at every point of the day, there were at least three guards stationed in front of the door. Now, before them, the front door was as vacant as a tavern in the morning.

"This is no joke..." Alad said. In his next breath he was in a sprint, tossing away his heavy senator's cloak and gaining speed.

"Alad, come back!"

Iza was at his heels, following his lead. Once she was left behind, Ennry darted after them.

Ennry was still half the length of the corridor away when Alad opened the door to the Bellsignor's chambers.

"Sire?" he shouted. "Are you in here? What is the meaning of your message?"

Alad pulled the chain for the electricity, and the room was bathed in light. It looked exactly the same. Everything in place, nothing broken, no sign that any fight had occurred.

Then he saw him. The Bellsignor was standing in the corner of the room with his back to the door. His silhouette was swallowed by the ceiling-high window he was facing. From the doorway, Alad could see what the king was seeing outside. It was an active world, and the sun was showing its first signs of shying away for the day. Electric lights lined the sidewalks where pedestrians and the click-clack of horse-drawn carriages gave the Bellsignor the illusion that he was not always so alone in his quarters.

"Sire? What was the meaning of your letter? Where are your guards?"

"That note?" the figure laughed. "You're duller than I imagined. You've been reading the Bellsignor's writing for years and you can't tell when someone else writes?"

Alad tightened his grip on the doorknob. Even before the man finished his sentence, he realized the man standing at the window was not the King of Andayt. It was the same height as the Bellsignor, he knew that much, but the glare from the window kept the rest of its features in shadow.

The man turned. Alad followed the movement of his body. His jaw dropped as he caught something hanging from the man's rear.

He had a tail.

The speaker was staring him in the eyes. Alad could feel the presence of Iza and Ennry behind him. He kept his arm on the door, stopping them from entering.

"Who are you?" Alad asked.

"It depends on my mood." The thing shrugged. It moved closer into the light of the electric lamps. From the fluffy tail that was sticking out of its pants, Alad wasn't expecting the thing to look like a man, but he was still surprised. Smirking the trio down was a grey and white snout, with a round sun hat that was covering a pair of ears.

"Holy…" Ennry backed away. "Alad…that's a dog."

Alad gulped. "What have you done with the Bellsignor? You mean you pretended he was being held captive?"

"*Was* is the key word there, people. I think you'll find that that's no longer his main problem."

The dogman picked something off the floor and tossed it over to Alad's feet. He knew it couldn't be real. He knew it was impossible. No one could get away with doing what he and the other two senators were looking at.

The head bounced like a stone, spinning around on one side like a teapot.

The late king's eyes were open as if he were staring out into an endless sea.

"It was really quick, I promise you." The dogman said. "I see no need to be unnecessarily cruel, even if it would have been fun."

Iza screamed. Alad fought the pain in his shoulder as she grabbed it in terror. Behind him, he heard Ennry hit the ground, fainted.

"Why…" The young man couldn't bring himself to cry. He was fighting a headache that a quick shot of new reality had given him. "Why did you do that? Who the fuck are you?"

"I'm what could have been. Oh, what a joy it is to be something that never existed." The dogman walked toward him, now completely out of the window's gaze. "Philosophers have asked that question for hundreds of years. Why is the universe as it is? Are we living in one of infinite possibilities because of the chaos of entropy and the rise of free will? Or is the universe the way it is because it is the *only* way it could be. If the latter is true, I can't possibly exist, right? Good good. If I don't exist, then none of my actions have consequences. Can we agree on that?"

Alad couldn't reply. None of them could. Iza's grip on him laxed, and she began to fight a sob.

"If that's the case, then your precious Bellsignor is still alive. I was never here. His head was never scythed like a field, and your lovely Nindeck never went the way of Brunswald. Gee, I wonder who will think about invading *you* now."

With a smile, the dogman sped for the window, taking a leap as if ready to pounce a doomed deer.

Alad rushed forward. He knew it made no sense to try to go the way of the dogman. The Bellsignor's quarters were on the third floor of The Greens. The humanoid canine surely had a rough landing, and he would too if he tried to pursue.

A shape shot up from the ground. From behind, Alad knew it was the dogman from the tail that was now tattooed in his memory, but the shape appeared to be in flux. It was getting bigger. It was getting darker, and it was beginning to sprout wings.

In less than a minute Alad and the rest of the senators would be dead, crushed to death by what was left of The Greens. But before that, Alad Tich couldn't will himself to turn away.

Above him, and above the living city that was now paused to look at what was peeking from the sky, was a behemoth that no shadowed recess of the human mind could describe.

It rushed down, and with one grand flick of a wing and a tail, the entire street was leveled.

Claws first, it burrowed into the ground that was once The Greens.

CHAPTER 11

"This doesn't look like too bad a place, you guys." Dreden said.

The noise in the bar made the roaring Sunitian Sea sound like a puppy. Chanin wanted to cover her ears. "I guess so. It's really crowded. That does give us a lot more privacy."

They didn't have any idea where to go once they were let go from the police station. The only glimpse of the city any of them had gotten was looking at it from out the window of a carriage, and there was so much more that they never got to see. One of the locations Dreden remembered seeing was a place called Keethkay's Tavern. He figured any place that called itself a tavern in any universe was a place where they could grab a pint.

"I must say," Gerrika started. "it isn't a comfortable transition, coming here after getting away from the swarms of humans outside the station. They're going to be staring at us the entire time we're here."

"They let Dreden and I out easy enough," Chanin smiled. "I guess we're not so remarkable in their eyes. No avehos in this entire city…this must be one strange world."

Dreden ushered his friends forward. The bar was completely occupied, with no stool left for them to sit on. From his place, he could see only two bartenders. It was going to be hard to get either one's attention from all the people and all the conversations, so he tried slipping them farther into the corner.

"You think we'll be fine down here?"

"I think so, Chanin," Dreden stood on the tips of his toes, trying to get the attention of a server. "Better than nothing. You think the beer in this place is any good?"

"I've been eyeing what everyone else is drinking." Chanin replied. "It looks to me that most people are drinking beer that's a golden amber color."

"Doesn't really help us at all." Gerrika's eyes fell, and he gave the sides of his pants a check. "Crap. Guys, we're not going to be able to get anything here. We don't have any money!"

Dreden and Chanin threw their heads back, kicking the floor under their feet. "Shit. That's a very good point." Chanin bit her lip. "What are we going to do about that? We have to eat while we're here. Surely Chief Milbrey knew about that."

The aveho looked around at all the busy barstools and dining tables. "You think maybe we can get away with not paying? Maybe in this place they serve us first and then we pay them afterwards?"

"The last thing we need is to become *intentional* criminals in a place we intend to leave tomorrow." Dreden said.

"Maybe Milbrey would be nice enough to give us a little bit of money?" Chanin asked.

"You think he'd do that?"

"He seemed like a nice enough guy once he started believing our story."

"Great," Gerrika let out a breath. "let's go."

"I think one of us should stay here and save our seats." Dreden replied. "You guys can go. I'll stay right here."

"Why are you the one that gets to stay?" Chanin asked.

"I think I was the one the Chief liked the least. Besides, he was most stricken by Gerrika so he should be the one to go."

"Don't make me go back." The aveho whined. "Chanin, if I'm going to be the one going can you at least come with me? The people in this city give me the creeps and I don't want to have to deal with them by myself."

Chanin grabbed Gerrika's hand. "Alright. If the little baby bird needs me, then I'll go with him." She wrapped her arm around his shoulder as she started back for the door. "You better still be here when we get back, Dreden, *with* our seats."

"I'll keep an eye out for anything to open up." He waved them goodbye. "Look for me at the dining tables too!"

Chanin said they would, as the pair traversed the crowded bar area. Even after his friends were no longer in sight, he could see the reactions of the patrons who had finally noticed them. Gerrika especially. Murmurs swept the tables and counters. People turned to each other, spilling their drinks on their shirts and ties trying to get a view of the new strange creature. Some of them followed his friends out the door, pausing outside the entrance to watch them walk down the street before turning the corner for the police station.

Dreden clenched his teeth. The whole thing made him nervous. At least he looked like everyone else in the city. There was nothing Gerrika could do without having to be bothered every second by some new person who wanted to get a look at the exotic creature that had come out of the Sunitian Sea. Considering the crowds that formed outside the Sea, the police station, and now, surely, Keethkay's Tavern, there was no one left in the new city that didn't know about them.

He didn't want to forget about why they were here. They needed to get the men that tried to kill them and his father. Every moment spent in this jolly little hell was a moment gone from the fight.

Lost in his thoughts, Dreden had his back against the wall. Neither of the bartenders noticed him yet. His eyes were surveying the gaps of the human hive. Finding a spot for his friends to relax would be the least he could do.

"You look lost."

In his trance, Dreden hadn't heard approaching leather shoes on hardwood. To his right, a young man stood alone, as if he had the power to part the crowds like a wizard from a fable. He couldn't have been more than three years older than himself, though looking an ounce more mature from the way he wielded the glass of whisky in his hand. The man's green eyes were meeting his own, as if he didn't need to see anything more from Dreden.

He flashed him a smile with some teeth, and in that moment, Dreden could only try to replicate it.

"Is it that obvious?"

"Yes, my man. I have an eye for things like this. Also, I was at the viewing port of the Sunitian Sea when you and your two friends appeared."

"Oh." Dreden cleared his throat, trying to keep a grin. "I assume you probably have a lot of questions to ask me?"

"Can you blame me?" the man took a sip of his drink. "But I won't bother you with them. I doubt that's what you want. From the way you and your friends were acting before the police got you, you don't want to be here."

The man was right, and Dreden's face couldn't hide it. "I don't. We don't. The only reason I'm here at all is because Chief Milbrey says it's the end of high tide, and there's no way the Sea is going to do anything. That and he'll probably arrest us for good if we disobey him."

The young man laughed, hunching over and clutching his drink against his cravat-covered chest. His thick black hair was combed to the right, and he adjusted it as a few rogue strands drooped over his eyes. "Chief Milbrey is a required taste, my man. My family has known him for so long I can hardly remember the time we were first introduced. He's stern, but a chimp once you get a couple ounces of Magill's in him."

"Magill's?"

"Right." he laughed again. "You're not from around here, so no way you would know what the finest whiskey in Brunswald is called. You're going to need to try it."

"I don't think my friends and I can afford drinking like that." Dreden said. "All our currency is pointless here, and I doubt Chief Milbrey will give us the money for good alcohol."

"Nonsense. It's my treat." He extended his free hand to Dreden, showing his teeth again in a smile. "Morell Edland."

Dreden was struck again. He returned the smile and took the young man's hand. "Dreden Sharpstand."

"And your friends? The girl and the bird?"

"Chanin Adderfoth and Gerrika, respectively."

"Strange names," Morell paused. "but I'm sure the names you'll find in this place will be just as alien to you. I can show you around if you'd like."

"Why do I get the feeling you're a big deal around here?"

Morell wrapped his glass-carrying arm around Dreden's neck. "I'm afraid I'm humble in words and friends alone, Dreden, but if I'm in Keethkay's for too long, I suppose the truth has a way of getting out of me. Oh, Stavans!"

The bartender instantly turned to them, stopping his shaking of a cocktail.

"I'm going to add another man to my tab, Stavans!" He gestured Dreden forth.

"Umm…I'll have whatever beer you recommend the most."

"No," Morell shook a finger. "he'll have a whiskey. Get him a glass of Magill's, neat, and another one for me."

The one called Stavans smiled and shook his head, finishing up what he was doing in a hurry and started on Morell and Dreden's order.

"You must be a regular here."

"Being a social drinker and a lone, pensive drunk is an expensive lifestyle." Morell downed the rest of his Magill's and brushed his mouth with a napkin.

"Why the dual life, Morell?"

Dreden couldn't recall if he had stopped smiling at Morell for a moment. From the way he had navigated his way to him, parting the paths with his very aura and the way he talked to people made him wonder if this world was full of such charming men. In his more than two decades of life he couldn't recall someone talking to him and using the body language that Morell showed him. It made him feel like his veins were being flushed.

"There's good reason. I promise I'm not your sad little tattered tavern tick. When I drink alone, it's because I'm writing."

"What do you write?"

The bartender came from around the bar counter and handed the glasses to Dreden and Morell. Dreden raised the glass to his head, giving it a quick sniff as Stavans took Morell's empty glass away.

"Thanks, Stavans. I'm a writer. A novelist, to be more specific. Well, I *was* a novelist. Have you heard about the earthquake that happened here?"

Dreden nodded. "It's come up a few times. How bad was it?"

"The worst in recent memory." Morell sighed. "Truly terrible. I can't imagine what some people must be going through right now. My printing company, Mirthinout, took a big hit from the quake. Business is going to be out for weeks, months potentially. I hear no one will be let in until they know for sure the earth beneath it can once again contain the weight of all those people bustling around the office." The young man chuckled, covering his mouth with his glass. "I'm sorry. I've been talking your ear off. Please try Magill's."

Dreden didn't argue. He wouldn't have been able to find the will to fight the crisp baritone of Morell Edland's command.

The first sip stung his tongue. It was not at all what he was used to in booze, since it wasn't beer or wine. It was sweet and tasted like something that had wisdom Dreden would never be mature enough to fathom, and the oak aftertaste sent his mind back in time to when the plants ruled the earth. And then a warmth fell down to his toes with nourishing energy.

"My God..."

"God?" Morell smiled. "Do they believe in only one where you come from? You shouldn't have too much trouble with the local clergy then."

"How much does a glass of this cost?" he asked, sucking the taste off his lips.

"Dreden, you let me worry about that." He winked. "You were right. I'm very well known around here. My parents are the biggest businesspeople in the country.

Lately they've become more popular with all their humanitarian work with the earthquake."

The buzzing in the colony that was Keethkay's Tavern paused again, with everyone turning back to face the entrance. Twin pairs of footsteps clapped against the hardwood floor. It was the one thing familiar to him in the crowd.

"Okay, we're back." Chanin said, as her chest rose and fell like a lever.

"You guys alright?" Dreden asked. "You didn't run into any trouble, did you?"

"Not too much. You were right. Chief Milbrey was more than happy to loan us a little bit of money. We just had to rush back here because a stampede was starting to follow us, but I think we lost them."

Gerrika paused, paying no mind to the dozens of pairs of eyes that were stuck to him like sap. "I wouldn't be too sure. The station isn't far away."

"I say let them come," Morell said, nudging Dreden's elbow. "the more the merrier. You must be Chanin and you must be Gerrika. Dreden has told me about you."

"Is that right? You, sir, seem like a calm change of pace for us." Gerrika extended his talon hand, and the human took it. "Good to meet you."

"Likewise, and I can't forget you, dear," They exchanged hands and Chanin returned his hello. "I would love to know about where you three come from."

Dreden smiled at his friends, partially hiding his mouth as he sipped his whiskey. "I'm sure I speak for the three of us when I say we feel the same."

"Then you're in the right place. I can't remember who said it, but there is a good quote about how bars are the nucleus of a culture. Every important idea always started from a moment in a tavern. I happen to believe it's true."

"I don't know…" Chanin paused. "We were just hoping for quiet drinks here, but now I think we've brought too much attention to ourselves. I think we should go."

"Don't be such a sourpuss, Chanin." Dreden teased.

"You have never once used that word before."

Dreden's face lit with color. "The point is still the same, guys. Come on, we're never going to have this chance again. I say we just enjoy our time here."

Neither Chanin nor Gerrika looked convinced. Dreden could see it, but it was Morell to the rescue.

"If you were in any other company, I'd tell you three to forget about it, but they happen to love me here, and not without reason." He dug into his pocket, palming a tight cluster of bills. "Save the money Milbrey gave you for souvenirs.

Tonight's on me. Come on, just enjoy yourselves. The owner owes me a favor. I can get us the party room, if you're worried about privacy."

The aveho shrugged. "I'm not going to say no to free alcohol and a party room."

Chanin didn't say anything, but after Gerrika gave in, a life returned to her face.

"Great!" Dreden raised his glass above his head. "I think we'll enjoy this. Let's be honest, this place makes the Faeriebridge campus bar look like a stable."

Morell turned around, pointing the way he had come before first greeting Dreden. The stairway to the second floor cleared away, as if it were an old rock structure fighting the curse of rising water levels. The people dispersed, and upon seeing Morell their smiles turned into sheaths for their sharpest tongues. He passingly held their hands in his, giving kisses on the cheeks of men and women alike.

And Dreden followed him like a shark to blood.

Suddenly the discovery of a living breathing dragon was no longer the biggest story of the day. At least not for Cipre, since she had yet to tell anyone about her new scaly acquaintance.

"Visitors from another world!" A man shouted, darting into a crowded street and almost getting trampled by horses of four different carriages. "The chief of police confirms it! The story is real!"

Cipre watched the man retreat into the doorway of the Brunswald Herald building. Apparently, he was a journalist, wanting to be the first to get the story in print for the following morning.

Other than the fact that her dragon story would be obsolete by the time the news of whatever "visitors" had come to the city, she noticed that there was no residual damage from the aftershock she felt in Minkompa's company. Chunks the size of horse heads crumbled from the cavern ceiling, and she wouldn't have made it out if the dragon hadn't protected her.

A dragon protected me…

Saying it in her head didn't make it any more believable.

I need to know more about this "visitors" story. If I'm not going to be working as much since Mirthinout is under evaluation, I'm going to need something to occupy my time.

This could be what I'm looking for.

She knew she had been waiting for months and months for a great story to appear on her desk for her to review. Since she was in the fiction business, she always assumed it would come from the imagination of an upcoming cultural icon, but it seemed that fate was becoming the storyteller she had been looking for the whole time.

Upon approaching her home, a familiar figure was sitting along the bricks on her porch, wearing a short cap while nose deep in a book cupped at his breast.

"What are you doing here, Matry?" she asked.

"Cipre," he stumbled back on his feet and folded the book under his arm. "I just wanted to make sure you were alright. You still seemed dazed when I left you."

"I'm fine. I'm fine." She stopped at her door to face him. "I've had an interesting day myself. My head is half in reality and half in a story, and I think that's really relaxing me."

"I take it you've heard the big news?"

"I've heard bits while walking back here." she said. "Can you fill me in?"

She sensed they were going to be talking for more than a few minutes, so she unlocked her front door and they made themselves comfortable in her living room. After the walk all the way from the cave, she was both hungry and parched. She poured herself a glass of water, offering Matry an assortment of olives and cheese as he told her everything he knew.

"Did you see any of them?" she asked, shoving an olive in her mouth.

"No, but Pillings from advertising saw them in passing a block away from the police station." He cut a sliver of soft cheese, stuffing it in a green olive. "The chief was leaving for the evening, and a crowd of people wouldn't leave him alone. The only way he could calm them was to tell them what he knew."

"Is that even legal?"

"I mean, the three visitors aren't really criminals. Apparently, they're not doing much to hide themselves, so I think Chief Milbrey assumed it was fine to tell everyone."

"What did they look like?" She took a sip of water. "You said two of them were humans, and the other was a birdman?"

Matry wiped juice off his lips. "That's what they say. They say he, if he is a 'he', kind of looks like a crow or raven with some blue on its feathers. The two humans look pretty much like us, with the boy being bit darker than the other. On my way over here I bumped into Najelle, the office assistant, and she said they're at Keethkay's on Forging Street. Want to go see if we can catch a look?"

"Won't there be a lot of people trying to get through the door?"

"Probably. Maybe that's what everyone is thinking, and therefore no one is going there."

"I don't know. After the day I've had, I think I just want to stay inside under a loose blanket with a cup of tea."

"Got a good book to read tonight?" Matry asked.

"I don't really like to read while I'm at home." she said. "It reminds me too much of work."

"That, Cipre, is perfectly understandable." Matry rose from his seat, picking up his coat and throwing it over his shoulder. "It's too early to call it quits for me. I think I'll grab a beer from Heppler's. If I get drunk enough, maybe I'll actually try to meet our little visitors and offer them a book deal." He chuckled, slipping his arms through the coat's sleeves. "Goodnight, my friend, maybe I'll see you tomorrow."

She hugged him goodbye and saw him to the door and stayed there until his shadow from the setting sun had rounded the corner and was gone for the night. No doubt Matry could tell there was something she wasn't telling him, or at least that she was still off from earlier in the day.

I need to focus myself. It never works out for me when I'm trying to do a hundred things at once. Minkompa is my story. I'm the one that discovered him. No one is going to take him from me.

As interested as she was in the story of the three visitors, they were the thing that was on everyone's mind. When news grabbed the public that quickly and manically, the fervor tended to die before it could reach its full potential. It dispersed like a sandcastle in the water, and the best thing to do to keep it fresh would be to only write the facts. The truth. Only what could be verified. Cipre's intellectual curiosity prayed that they didn't make any mistakes with the visitors, but the story manager inside her wanted people to be disappointed with what they got from the two humans and the bird.

Minkompa would be the one that stuck. She would see to it. She was not done with him.

CHAPTER 12

"Can you fly?"

Morell's question almost made Dreden choke on his cocktail. It was valid, but it was a question no human over the age of three would be caught asking in Kroonsaed.

"No," Gerrika shook his head, not hiding the amusement on his beak. "It's unclear if our evolutionary ancestors had wings themselves. The best assumption natural philosophers have is that we broke away from winged birds about fifty million years ago."

"Natural philosophers? That's a bit ancient to us." Morell replied. "We call them scientists here."

"That word makes sense." Chanin had a beer in one hand, and a glass of mead twice as big as the beer in her other. "The word 'science' does exist where we come from, but it's typically not used in academic settings."

"I'll bet pastries to pennies that we'll all be hearing a lot more of that word since you guys appeared. Though I haven't yet decided if I think the genre of science fiction will bloom or rot now because of this sudden development." Morell turned to Dreden, clinking his glass against his. "I take it you don't know what science fiction is?"

A splotch of whisky landed on his sleeve from Morell's shove, but Dreden was too inebriated to care. "I assume from its name it deals with the creation of alternate natur-...science in order to create a compelling narrative."

"Exactly right." Morell said. "It'll be interesting to see. Either way, thank God I don't write science fiction. I keep the form of traditional literature, with some subversions here and there."

"What's your book about?" Dreden asked.

"Excuse me...pardon...move please!"

A chorus of apologies and irritated gasps sounded from the doorway. A stampede of people rushing across the bar towards the party room forced everyone to turn their heads. The approaching group had their heads ducked down and they were carrying equipment that was just as tall as they were. Despite their efforts, their gear kept prodding people on the shoulders.

"What's going on?" Chanin asked.

Morell shook his head. "Looks like your privacy is over."

"Visitors! Visitors!"

There were eight men and two women in total. Half of them had notepads flipped open with pens uncapped and ready, while the others put their strange three-legged equipment on the floor and adjusted them to an easier height. A black cloth fell down the back of the machine like a cape. The men and women with the devices lowered themselves under the cloth, using an unsheltered hand to adjust something on the side of the machine's head.

"Visitors!" repeated the same man. He was middle-aged, with white stubble for facial hair and for his hairline. "Can we get the three of you more in focus please? I'm Alemy Mewws from the Brunswald Herald. We need a picture for the morning paper."

"Picture?" Dreden asked.

A flash of light swallowed them up, followed by a clicking and a 'winding up' sound that reminded Dreden of something a child's toy would make. He grunted, and in his confusion he saw Chanin wiping her eyes of the light and Gerrika rubbing his temples.

"Do you mind?" Morell shouted. Only the one who introduced himself as Alemy Mewws heard him. All the others were still toying with their equipment.

"Apologies, Mister Edland, but we're not going to let the biggest thing to happen to our city come and go without making the front-page tomorrow."

"What the hell was that?" Chanin asked, shooting daggered eyes at the crowd.

"Those are cameras." Morell explained, looking around at the three friends. "They're still new around here. Wonderful devices they are, when they're *called* for. They're like real-life illustrations. When the light flashes, it captures what it sees in a still-frame."

Gerrika snorted. "I hope we all look pretty."

Dreden finished blinking. "Do you know them?"

"A little." Morell said. "I've met most of them when they've covered stories about my parents."

"Mind telling them to leave us alone?" Dreden turned away, heading back into the private room. "We're not going to be here much longer anyway."

Chanin and Gerrika followed their friend back into the lounge. Morell and some of his friends held up the reporters, trying to shoo them away, but that didn't stop several more flashes from going off, making Dreden recoil again.

The retorts and complaints from outside turned into buzzing as Dreden shut the door, and he raised his drink back to his lips.

The lounge itself was nicer than any little commodity Faeriebridge offered its students. A sharp red rug lined the floors of the room, and an old bearded gentleman played the piano in the corner. Dreden didn't recognize the music, but it was pretty and had an up-and-up beat to it that only old love songs tended to have back in Kroonsaed.

And it was getting harder and harder for him to walk in a straight line. That was something that hadn't happened in a long time.

If Gerrika and Chanin were faring the same way, they probably did a better job of hiding it, or perhaps that was just his perception being distorted from all the Magill's.

The door opened again. Morell and his friends came back into the room shaking their heads.

"Sorry about that, friends. Sometimes reporters can be leeches. I think I gave them enough to satisfy them for now, but don't be surprised if they're waiting for you by the Sea tomorrow."

"That's fine." Dreden smiled. "I'm sure you did all you could. Also, we weren't done with our conversation."

Morell threw his head back slightly, brushing his hair again. "Right! Right, yes, I was going to brag to you about my book."

"Bragging or not, I'd like to hear about it."

"Mmm," Morell cleared his throat before taking another sip of whisky. "It's called A Mad Past."

"And just how angry is that past?"

"Quite." He turned from Dreden, unable to hide a twinkle in his eye from his enjoyment of him. "It's about a woman. She's…how should I say… a victim of her present. She's the kind of person that is suffocated by the weight of all the lives she's not living, the lives she *could* be living, but is instead bound too much by her class. She's adopted, and her family is very well-to-do.

"Anyway, her desire to live finds her across the world. She meets all kinds of characters from everywhere: all cultures, creeds, colors. Then she decides that it would be selfish of her to try to keep the whole experience to herself, so she writes a book about it."

"A book *within* a book?" Dreden asked. "Did you write that one too?"

"A lot of it, anyway, eventually it gets to the Prime Minister and even he reads it-"

All the drink was instantly drained from Dreden's blood. "What did you say?"

"I said I kind of wrote that book too," Morell blinked. "and eventually the Prime Minister reads it."

"How do you know those words?"

Morell smiled awkwardly. "Dreden, everyone knows who the Prime Minister is. The real question is: how do *you* know what the Prime Minister is? Do you have one where you come from?"

Dreden explained everything to him. He went over the encounter at Heathback, telling him about the strange weapons that the men were using. They claimed to work for someone called the Prime Minister, and he told Morell about how their second attack on his home was what flamed him up enough to take them back to the caverns.

"That was what we were doing when we got here." Dreden's voice began cracking. "No...no no no, I can't believe what I'm doing. They're still out there!"

"My friend, I don't think that Charles Dowlepot has any intergalactic beef with where you come from. No way he would even know about the place you come from without secrets getting out. Believe me, he's nice and competent enough, but he and his men are certainly not qualified to keep a secret of that magnitude."

"But it can't be a coincidence, can it?" Dreden felt the sweat start to fall from his brow. He put his glass of whisky on a nearby counter. "Seriously, this is too unlikely. Me and my friends ending up in a place that has the same language, same species, except for avehos...no, I've got to get back home!"

Dreden started to dart away. The rushing of his feet caused all eyes to come to him, but Morell grabbed his upper arm.

"Dreden. Dreden Dreden Dreden," he said soothingly, putting his other hand on Dreden's back. "There is nothing to worry about, and you're certainly not going to get anywhere with how much you've been drinking tonight. Your story disturbs me. A good man like you shouldn't have to go through that. I'll see to it that there'll be an investigation. My parents have enough pull for that to happen. The best thing for you to do right now is to just enjoy yourself."

He wanted to argue. Thinking about his father all alone in their tiny home worried about what had become of his son was something that made his eyes water, but whether it was the whisky or the way Morell Edland's eyes sucked his soul from his heart to his irises, fighting his pain became second nature.

"You good now, man?" Morell asked, putting his hand on Dreden's chest.

"Yes," he coughed, wiping the corner of his eye. "you're right. I'll be fine."

Morell picked his glass of Magill's off the counter, returning it to Dreden's grasp. "I'm glad. I'm not going to let a friend of mine not enjoy his first night at Keethkay's. I'm going to catch up with a couple friends, but hey, I'll see you again in half an hour." Morell smiled at him, winking before passing through the center of the room, joining a group by the piano.

Now he was left in the corner, only his drink to keep him company. Chanin caught wind of it a few seconds later, and she joined him at his side.

Dreden didn't want to meet her eyes. He looked down the other way, scratching the back of his neck.

"You two okay?" she asked.

"Yeah. Yeah." Dreden nodded. "I'm so damn drunk, Chanin."

"Glad I'm not the only one. Morell seems like a nice guy. Seems to like *you* a lot."

"I told him about how we got here. I told him about the strange men in red."

Chanin didn't find the coincidence any less unsettling than he did. After explaining their conversation to her, Chanin took a few more sips of beer out of her glass.

"I'm worried too. I can't say that that hasn't been on my mind this whole time." She turned from her friend, surveying the crowd. Young men and women in nicer, sharper clothes than they had ever seen conversed as the piano man did his thing. It was like they were part of the song, that if the song wouldn't be playing, they would all evaporate, and without the song, the people had no reason to evade loneliness.

And at its nexus, Dreden caught Morell Edland again. Laughing and throwing his head back at something another one of his pretty friends said. He was a writer, he said. Nothing like any writer Dreden knew at the university. He had the kind of attitude about his life and his work that Dreden could only fantasize about. Any attempt at pursuing something creative would put him in the same position as his father, probably worse, and Morell was so comfortable with it, as if in the nature of his own explanations, he challenged all criticism, welcomed it, and relished in it to make it something better. The way the man moved from person to person like a snapping lobster presented Dreden with an image of him that was both too mundane and too story-like to be anything but true.

"Not just that, Chanin. I am an absolute serpent for even enjoying my time here."

"I can't say I blame you. You love your father." She brushed her hair over her ear. "That's a problem I currently don't have with either of my parents."

Dreden shook his head. "I know about that. I'm sorry."

"Don't worry. You're the one with the bigger problem now. I want to hear about it."

"Beyond my father," he continued, casting another look at Morell as the man was swallowed up by a group of drunk friends. "I've felt lost…for a very long time. And Morell…a part of me-"

"You're a homosexual."

Dreden coughed, drunkenly wiping his mouth in surprise. "Where did you get that from?"

"First of all, I've never met anyone heterosexual who *ever* referred to themselves as an 'absolute serpent'," she smirked. "and I've had the idea for a while. I've seen the way that you look at other men, and your two best friends are a woman and a male of another species."

"The last part isn't a giveaway. I could say the same about you."

"Fair enough." She laughed, taking a few more gulps of beer. "In seriousness, Dreden, I think that it's important for you to stop hiding yourself that way. Kroonsaed isn't the backwards place it was a hundred years ago, and this place seems the same, if not better. I think you should learn from this. Remember how being right here in this room makes you feel. Take it back with you to the worst parts of your life. No matter how much time and pain go by, this was always real."

"I think I can," Dreden bit the inside of his mouth, emotional. "Thank you, Chanin."

"Guys! Guys!" Gerrika came running back from the corner of the room, dropping his glass of rum on the floor. "Guys! Wait, what's wrong?"

"It's nothing." Dreden said. "The two of us were just having a moment. What's the matter?"

"This song. The song that the man at the piano is playing!"

Dreden stopped, listening to the tune being played. He hadn't noticed that it was any different than what had always been playing.

"What about the song?"

"I recognize it! It's called Sky Man. It's a song that my mother would sing to me as a child." The aveho closed his eyes, tightening his talons into fists. "Yes. Yes. No doubt about it."

"How is that possible?" Chanin asked. "There are no avehos here."

Gerrika began humming it. "Mmm *HMMMM* mmmmm *HMMMM* Mhmmmmmm. I don't know, but nevertheless, someone's got to sing this. Mmhmm. Yes, we need a voice for this," Gerrika extended his arm and shoved Dreden's shoulder with a talon finger. "and I don't care what *you* have to say about it."

Humming it louder by the second, Gerrika turned away from them, speed-walking back to the piano.

"Why did he say that to me?" Dreden asked.

Chanin shrugged. "He's drunk. Don't think about it."

In the next second, all chatter from the corner of the room ceased, spreading like a spill through the room. The piano got louder, or, as Dreden realized, he was able to hear it clearer now that everyone was silent, and a singular set of lungs took their place.

When all the shadows are the night
And the moon can't cough another light
There's one thing no one knows,
I won't mind. I won't mind.

I can run without sound
I can fly without sight
And when there is no one around,
I will fall to the ground.

My god took my eyes
My god took my voice
And took them above the clouds
And left the rest to the flies

I won't mind. I won't mind.
They saw my eyes and heard my voice
In the clouds, and I sang my choice
And the world was never so kind.

An eruption of applause followed. The piano man jumped from his seat to join the whistling men and women, but Dreden and Chanin were too stunned to move.

"My boy," the musician's hand flew to his breast. "how ever did you learn to sing like that?"

"Oh, I've always." The aveho tapped his throat. "It comes from an evolutionary trait. We don't have teeth, so we have to swallow food whole sometimes and expand our throats. It works wonders when you're trying to get those high and low ranges."

Indecipherable chatter resumed through the room as everyone crowded Gerrika. They didn't like the look of it, so Dreden and Chanin rushed through the crowd. Some people tried to keep their feet planted, but upon seeing who it was trying to get through, they let the two strangers pass.

"Gerrika, oh my *God*!" Dreden exclaimed. "I always imagined you could sing, but that was one of the best things I've ever heard."

"I guess you wouldn't." Gerrika said shyly. "It's not something many avehos like to do."

"*That's* a song your mother would sing?" Chanin asked.

"Yeah. It's pretty."

"It's also a total downer. I'm surprised *my* parents didn't try it on me."

Morell came out of the crowd. His face was flushed red, but Dreden couldn't tell if it was from drinking or all the smiling. "You people are just full of surprises, aren't you?" He slapped his hands on Gerrika's shoulders. "Those are quite the lyrics you came up with."

"No." the aveho shook his head. "I didn't write them. It's an aveho song. Sky Man."

"Not here it isn't. It doesn't even have lyrics. It's called 'Drink on Me', and you'll never find a musician in a tavern who doesn't know how to play it."

"I'm just happy to be having such a good time here," Gerrika smiled, struggling to balance his large feet on the floor. "Ooof, we're going to need a place to stay tonight."

"That'll be no trouble." Morell told them. "Believe me, friends, this has been one of the best nights of the year for me. I'll say, the three of you can really make a guy forget his troubles. Once you're gone, I hope you tell all your friends about how good of a time Morell Edland showed you."

Giving each of them a quick hug, he went back to his friends, topping himself off with the rest of the whisky from the communal bottle.

In the passing minutes it became clear that Gerrika's song had marked a decline in the party. As people left, they returned to the aveho to praise him one last time before giving their farewell, likely not to see him again. Gerrika was reveling in the attention, and Dreden couldn't blame him. He didn't just want to have those people smile at him and give him pats on the back. He wanted Morell's eyes on him.

In the last hour of the party, every time Dreden was meeting new people or speaking with his friends, he didn't go a minute without turning to see where in the room Morell was. Half the time he caught Morell looking at him, and he had to fight the blushing in his face along with the urge to look away.

At the end of the night, when Morell put the three of them in lodging right above Keethkay's, Dreden wanted to refuse, telling him that he would only go where Morell went, but he was too drunk to manage that and would only come off as a fool and embarrass himself.

Whether or not Chanin or Gerrika were feeling the same, Dreden didn't care. His life in the strange city wasn't going to be over for good tomorrow.

CHAPTER 13

The story about the strangers coming in through the Sunitian Sea swept the news like butter on a pan. So much so that it wasn't until almost noon the next day when the citizens of Skaltbard knew about the disaster in Andayt.

Thousands were dead in what was already being considered the worst disaster in human history. Just *days* after the earthquake in central Brunswald, an even worse natural disaster strikes the heart of Andayt, the nation Skaltbard was on the cusp of war with? Charles Dowlepot shook his head. He wasn't a religious man or much of a believer in fate, but if he didn't know any better, he would say that it looked like the planet itself was trying to get their attention and stop them from escalating their conflicts.

He laughed at the thought, but it wasn't entirely ludicrous. In the history of the universe, some awful things happened to the planet and the creatures who inhabited it. Disasters killed off the ancient amphibians and reptiles, and others hunted each other into extinction if they couldn't adapt quickly enough. His species was certainly guilty of the latter, but what was he supposed to do? It wasn't prudent to judge those who came before by modern standards of morality. Even then, humans had been warring with each other since they first crawled out of their caves. What would make *this* conflict any worse than the ones that came before? Just people being people. Unless they had any chance of adapting out of it, that was going to be the way of things forever.

As the Prime Minister saw it, that was okay.

He needed some fresh air. "But more importantly," he said to his wife Venka as he stepped out the front door. "I need to keep a sharp mind."

"To the library?" she asked.

He nodded. "You know," she continued. "the taxpayers pay for people to get books for you. You don't need to go get your own books."

"That's the idea, hon. I'm under a lot of pressure right now. Anything to help me forget just for a second that I'm in charge of this messed up place is worth doing."

"I'll see you later." She turned around, heading back upstairs. "Don't forget that we're still on for dinner tonight at Palasol's. The Lommurs will be expecting us at seven-thirty."

"Got it. I'll have no trouble being back."

Putting on a thin black cap, Charles strode down Allistore Avenue, the hub of the Brunswald political wing, and headed for the library. The National Library was a convenient two blocks away. Venka always insisted on having a driver take him or just sending someone to go get the book he wanted, but she didn't understand the value of a walk or the humbling feeling of being surrounded by the whole history of the country. It was a mindset that he'd argue is vital to maintain if one wanted to be a figure for the people. Charles wasn't the son of an aristocrat, and his family was never very wealthy, but the countless hours he spent in the library disappearing from his friends and disobeying his parents were invaluable to who he had become. He now lived in a world where a child like that could grow up and become the leader of the strongest nation in the world.

As he approached the library, his mind went back to the destruction in Andayt. The Bellsignor was never a friend of the Prime Minister. Never. But thousands of people dead? The country experiencing turmoil that dwarfed the crisis in Brunswald? He felt for them, but there was nothing he could do. Skaltbard and Andayt were on the brink of war, and it wouldn't have been their first war.

The front librarian noticed him from the inside, as he saw Charles pull the doorknob through the glass doors.

"Mister Dowlepot!" cheered the librarian, a round man with thinning hair, the Prime Minister's age. "It always makes my day when you come into my business."

The Prime Minister smiled, taking off his cap and tucking it under his arm. "It's the state's business, Loid. You just happen to work here." Charles extended his hand and Loid shook it. "Having a good morning so far?"

"Not bad. They've got new jelly pastries at Enna's Bakery down the street. Not as good as Drew's over by Central, but you know what happened to that after the quake."

Charles put his hands over his lap. "I hope you know I've done everything I-"

"Of course." Loid waved him off. "I know it's an impossible situation. I read your speech in the papers. Hey, it's not every day that a longtime friend gets to clean up God's messes."

"Yes, I suppose I'm fate's custodian." Charles laughed. "Anything good come in here since last week?"

"Just some new plays. A few novels. What are you thinking for this week?"

"I assume you heard about the three strangers that visited the city yesterday?"

"Hell of a thing. I wouldn't have believed it if I didn't see the bird one myself. Can you imagine? A *real* other world out there?"

"I haven't made up my mind yet." replied the Prime Minister. "I will consider the facts as they come in. Anyway, seeing since everyone is saying that our biggest money-maker, the Sunitian Sea, is responsible for their transportation, I want everything you have on the Sea."

"*Everything?*"

"That's right. We're going to need all the money we can this summer, and I want nothing interfering with our promotion of the Sea. If there is a real mystery here, I want to help get to the bottom of it. I won't be a leader who lets everyone do things for him. I have a sharp mind and I intend to use it."

"Great words, my friend. Sit tight. I'll be back with everything you're looking for."

Loid scooted himself out from behind his desk, heading back into the jungle of bookshelves and book-suitors. Charles took a seat in one of the waiting chairs, shoving off his coat and resting it against the chair's back. He wasn't worried about being recognized. Even with the rise of photography, there were still enough people who had no idea what he looked like. And he was fine with that. They didn't need to care about those things, or him. That was part of the beauty of Skaltbard's political climate.

His attention returned at the sound of his old friend's familiar foot-dragging. Loid carried six books in his arms, creating a pyramid against his chest from biggest to smallest.

"This is all you have of the Sea?" asked Charles with a light laugh. Loid nodded, scrunching his face. "Wait, you're serious?"

"Yeah." He sighed, placing the books on the front table. "Remember, it might be the pride of the city, but we don't know much about it."

"I assumed there would be hundreds of books dedicated to how much we don't know about it." The Prime Minister approached the table, flipping through the titles of the books. "*Variation in Colors Through the Seasons, Effects on Migratory Birds During High Tide*, ah! Here it is, *The History of the Sunitian Sea*."

Charles flipped through the pages. It was the biggest volume of the six. The large pages were taken advantage of with the astonishing painted renditions of the Sea. Moving backwards, cupping the rear cover with his right hand, he slapped the clump of pages down to inspect the front of the book.

The first thing he noticed made his brow rise.

"This can't be correct."

"Why's that?" Loid asked.

"The publication date for this volume says that it was published in 1102."

He expected a response from the librarian, but he only returned his statement by standing still.

"That was eight years ago, Loid. How could the most comprehensive volume of the Sea's history only be eight years old?"

"A couple reasons, Charles." The librarian said. "Let me remind you of a little town history. Do you remember the main platform the very first Prime Minister of Skaltbard fought for?"

"That would have been Mick Jowns." Charles paused, remembering. "He wanted to get rid of every branch of royal propaganda."

"That's right. He believed that, even with the king and queen gone, that crown propaganda made its way through science, so he had a lot of scientific records purged from state and university libraries. Most had to do with physics, chemistry, hell, even biology, and the Sea was a victim of the purge too."

"That couldn't completely have been the case. No doubt we've lost valuable information."

Loid crossed his arms under his chest. "I suppose that's part of the price you pay for a better society."

"And what was the second reason there hasn't been any other information?"

"That's a much simpler one. It's because people don't care. Honestly, I don't blame them. The Sea has brought a lot of tourism to the city, but what is it? It's nothing. Just a giant cloud of pretty gas. There are more important things to fund in science. Like medicine and cures, or the air and the oceans."

"Maybe not anymore." Charles said. "Three strangers claimed to have been transported here from another world. People will probably want to know more about the Sea."

"Probably, but until then, if you want to spend your time reading this stuff, you're going to need to wait."

"Very well," the Prime Minister reorganized the books on the table, stacking them just as the librarian had done when he brought them forward. "I'll be going over these in my spare time."

Loid slipped out a large paper bag from under the table, helping the books inside. "If you leave now, I'll bet you can see the strangers before they try using the Sea to get back home."

"I saw their pictures in the paper this morning. I think I'm good." Charles tucked the bag at his side. "Where did they stay last night? You hear about that?"

"I heard they got chummy with the young Edland, and that he's the one who's escorting them back to the Sea."

"Oh my!" The Prime Minister's palm flew against his face. "Of course. Of *course* Morell Edland befriended them. That boy just *has* to be everywhere and know everyone. I guess it works out that it's him, considering who his family is. I'll see you the same time next week, Loid. Let me know if you get anything else about the Sea."

They said their goodbyes, and Charles Dowlepot was once again back on the street and taking the walk back to his home. Even with all the unsettling bits of news he was currently dealing with, it was the news of Morell Edland's new friendships that he couldn't shake. His mind returned to the encounter with the young man's elders in his office as he was preparing a speech. Whether he liked it or not, it seemed like his power was slowly becoming nothing compared to business dynasties like the Edlands. It was like he just realized there had been a race to meeting the strangers, and the Edlands won, leaving him as the loser.

Whether or not the strangers ever returned or if new ones were to come, the relationships that had just been made were like hairs on the head of a body that was looking less and less like the city he loved.

"How do you pass the time?" Cipre asked, pencil in hand and notebook on her lap.

"I read. When I've finished everything, I read again."

Minkompa was lying down on his belly, making their conversation easier since Cipre now felt that she was eye-to-eye with her subject.

"And...um, what do you eat?"

"Gold."

"Gold?"

The dragon blinked, shying his head slightly. "Is that weird?"

"It's just not what I was expecting." She looked down at her pad, taking note of his answers. "It's not what you think when you hear the stories about dragons."

"I must say, Cipre, that I disagree. I know the records and the history of things well. I think I fit the bill of what a dragon is supposed to be perfectly."

She didn't challenge him, simply returning to her notes. Not wanting to irritate her subject at all, she kept every other dragon question she had for him in the back.

"If you don't mind me asking-"

"You can ask me anything you want! I'm just happy to have someone to talk to."

She looked into his eyes. They had been what calmed her when she first encountered the dragon, but this was the closest she had gotten to them thus far. She didn't know how to describe the color. At first they were blue, then turned a dark grey the closer you got, and around the whites were sharp lines, as if a tiny dragon were trying to crawl out of his head.

"I take it that means you have a lot of gold here?" she asked.

"I do. Do you want to see it?"

He didn't wait for her answer. Minkompa shifted his body over to the side of the room. As he moved, his tail almost knocked over the far shelves, but Cipre assumed that after all the time living in the cave, he knew how to be careful.

After shifting some large rocks out of the way, the dragon grabbed a claw-full of gold pieces and dumped them at Cipre's feet. Her jaw dropped. The clinking, glowing pieces of metal scattered around her.

"Oh my God!" she sprang to her feet, dropping her notepad into the mess of riches. "You have had this much gold the whole time?"

"I have." The dragon cupped his head in his paw. "I have to survive, don't I?"

"Do you realize how much good this stuff could do? All the lives that it could improve?"

She caught a flash of annoyance in Minkompa's eyes. "That's not fair, is it? I shouldn't have to give up my property for something I have no part of."

At his response, Cipre sobered and picked her notepad back up. "Sorry, Minkompa, but would you mind if I questioned you more about that?"

The dragon scratched his chest. "Go ahead."

"If I may be honest: you seem extremely intelligent. In talking to you, I get that you have a moral compass. I know sometimes we humans have selective empathy. We choose to feel for other humans, and sometimes not others, like we empathize with animals like dogs or cats and reject others because of…usually human-centric selfish reasons. You read a lot, but how familiar are you with current events?"

"I try to be perfect, but it's hard when I don't have the books on it." Minkompa replied. "I've been trying to listen for things. I know Charles Dowlepot is Prime Minister, and, of course, there was a massive earthquake."

"That brings more questions than answers." Cipre wrote his words down. "In that case, you know that after the earthquake people need help, and that *you* can help them. Why don't you?"

Minkompa's raised his neck, looking down at her from farther away. "I owe no one anything. It's not my fault I have to consume gold to live, and it's not my fault I was born down here. I know all of human history. They've never gotten along with themselves, and there's certainly no chance they'll get along with me. I feel bad, Cipre, but understand. I'd rather be an observer of stories than become some character in a human's story. That's not to say I hate humans. Not at all. I simply am aware of my rightful place here."

He paused. Cipre wasn't sure if he was done with his answer or if he was giving her time to finish writing down his words. If he had more to say, she figured that it would come later. She had a bigger question that she wanted to pose to him again.

"Minkompa, I know I asked you this yesterday," she rubbed her fingers over her eyes nervously. "but…I know what I saw the day of the earthquake. I *know* that I saw some giant monster in between the cracks in the ground, and I *know* that it ended up around here. I'm not accusing you of anything, but are you absolutely sure you didn't see or hear anything come this way?"

The dragon didn't reply. For a second Cipre thought he had lost focus and was looking at something in the far wall behind her, but his eyes were locked on hers, as they had always been.

Softly, he lowered his head back to the ground, tucking his snout against his arms like a giant puppy. "Do you promise you won't tell anyone?"

The human gulped, returning her hand to her pen. "Yes. I promise. What is it?"

"I hear things. Things that I don't think any living creature deserves to hear. They're..." the dragon sniffed, turning his eyes to her right. "I don't know how to describe them. It's like something's cooking...burning, popping like bones. Every time they come, I hear a giant gurgling sound come from the walls, over me and under me. It's like it gets in my head and I just want to put a blanket over my head like a scared hatchling..." His breathing became harder, his massive chest rising and falling like a tent in a storm. "It's been happening more and more often. It's why I've largely confided myself to this room. I used to be freer. I used to have all the caves under the city for my home, but now I'm too scared to wander far off. After the earthquake, whatever it was came back stronger than ever before."

Cipre had only gotten his first two sentences before stopping. He was confiding something in her, and she didn't want it all in writing.

"I'm so sorry, Minkompa." She told him. "I can tell that it's been a long time since you've trusted anyone. I hope that my coming here has made you feel better."

"It has. Believe me." His voice returned, losing its emotional anchor. "I think making friends will be good for me. Feel free to bring more people here. I'd like to meet more humans."

"I think that would be a wonderful idea." Cipre smiled, as the dragon's new look of delight sent a warm feeling to her heart. "I'm not doing anything tomorrow this time either. So, I'll see you then?"

"I hope so!" he cheered.

Cipre turned around, tucking her notebook into her bag. Behind her, Minkompa shifted all the way around. The sound of him throwing his weight made her look back up.

"Something wrong?" she asked.

"No! I...um...want to share one more thing with you, if you don't mind."

He turned all the way back around in one move. Cipre had to fight the urge to back away, afraid of him accidentally squashing her.

Lowering himself back to her level, he let a thick leather-bound book slip out of his claws and into her hands.

"What is it?" she asked, wiping dust off the cover.

Minkompa flashed some teeth. "It's my book."

"You have thousands of books here. What's special about this one?"

"Because it's *mine*," the dragon replied. "That's the book I wrote."

"*You* wrote a book?"

"I did. I don't know if it's any good," Minkompa paused. "but I've been reading about humans all my life, and I've been fond of stories just as long. I think that I could use my knowledge to tell a good story. I figured it's time I share it with someone. I want to share it with you."

Cipre's smile grew a mile long, as she flipped the book over. There looked to be nothing special about it, except for seeming a bit neglected. Opening it up, the text was all in black ink with writing that Cipre knew could pass for professional penmanship.

"I'm sure writing in such comparatively small pages was a challenge." she said.

"It was, but it was worth it. It was fun to do."

Strapping her bag back over her shoulder and tucking the dragon's book at her side, the two gave their goodbyes and Cipre was off back into the surface world. He was too big to give a hug to, so she had to settle for giving a shake to one of his claws.

Cipre didn't want to seem like she was treating the dragon any differently than anyone else, but the fact that he had written a book that was now in her possession inspired a lot of possibilities. She had never told Minkompa that reading stories was her job. He had just given her his book as a gesture of trust. Of friendship. She didn't want to betray that trust, but having a book written by a supposed mythological beast was not something she could pass off in her professional conscience.

As the sunlight returned to her eyes, she realized that she hadn't asked the dragon how he knew about Charles Dowlepot. Could one really learn so much from hearing people talk while confined underground? What else could he know?

Did he know about the three strangers as well?

CHAPTER 14

It worked.

Dreden had been anxious all morning that nothing would happen when the three of them went back to the Sea. Morell didn't want to send them off with empty stomachs, so he took them to a bakery across the street from Keethkay's for breakfast. He had to force himself to eat the food even though it was excellent. His anxiety about being stuck in the strange city both made him want to hurry up and get it over with and keep it off as long as possible so he wouldn't yet know if they were stuck there or not.

And it gave him a couple extra hours with Morell.

He didn't say anything. He didn't know *what* he would say. He had never been in such a position before. What was the point? Who knew if he would ever be coming back?

Dreden's head felt heavy all morning. Could that mean the end of the soldiers who tried to kill him as well? If that were the case, then sacrificing getting to know Morell better was a simple price to pay.

After being allowed back onto the rocky shore by Chief Milbrey, the trio had climbed down the massive rock formations and back to where they had appeared almost a day before. Dreden was shaking. Chanin and Gerrika were too. They didn't know for sure it would work. Even if it did, what if they ended up in some *other* new place? They got lucky that the people of Brunswald were accommodating, but there were surely many other places that weren't.

As the Sea returned, bringing with it flashes of green and purple bright enough to return sight to the blind, Dreden cast a final look at the crowd. They stood just as speechless as they had when they arrived, with a murmur here and there. Morell

Edland had his head tilted forward, eyes on the Sea as if it were an approaching predator. As he saw Dreden begin to fade away, he gave him a thumbs-up.

And then they were back at Heathback Caverns.

Their weapons were still on the ground, untouched.

"I guess we're back." Gerrika said, looking around at the caverns like they were an ancient artifact.

"I never thought I'd be so happy to see this place again." Dreden sighed.

"What time do you think it is?" Chanin asked.

It was a good question. From their experience, more than a day had passed. They left Kroonsaed at around midnight and ended up in Brunswald in the afternoon, so it didn't seem like an exact transfer.

"Surely it didn't take us twelve hours to get there." Dreden said. "Probably just a different time over there."

"And depending which one is 'ahead', we either gained or lost a day." Chanin replied, circling Dreden and Gerrika as she gathered her thoughts.

Gerrika followed her actions, taking her by the hand and starting for the end of the forest. "There's only one way to know for sure. Classes shouldn't be in session now, so I think we should all go home."

"What are you going to tell your dad?" Chanin asked him.

"I bet he didn't notice I left." the aveho replied. "How about you?"

Chanin breathed a throaty laugh. "Please…"

Dreden didn't say anything, and his friends didn't ask what he was thinking. They all knew what was on his mind. Out of all of them, he by far had the best relationship with his parent.

He didn't want to wait. He gave his goodbyes to Chanin and Gerrika as he rushed ahead of them back to the city, leaving the pair to take their time getting back home.

The sound of the sliding classroom door opening was loud enough to wake up his father, if he were even asleep. Before the door had finished sliding all the way into its socket, Dreden heard his father bolt off his bed.

"Dreden!"

His father locked him in an embrace before he could say anything. Dreden felt his energy drain from him like a flood as the back of his neck became heavy from emotional stress.

"I'm so sorry. Dad, I'm back."

"Where have you been? You've had me thinking you were dead for almost a day!"

"It's a strange story." Dreden coughed, fighting the weight building in his head. "Me, Gerrika, and Chanin ended up on another world."

"Come on. Say something, father!"

Honja's eyes gave nothing away. Gerrika would have expected his father's eyes to widen and for him to have at least *one* question about the story he had just told. Based on his father's body language, Gerrika would have assumed that he had just told him something mundane, like he was heading out to class.

"You liked this world?" his father asked.

"Yes! Didn't you hear how I was describing it? The buildings were taller, the people were richer, the culture was like something out of some weird story, and the people we met were really interesting. And the technology, it was-"

His father rubbed the bottom of his beak. "And you say there were only humans?"

Gerrika could have kicked himself for not seeing that *that* was going to be the detail his father fixated on.

Honja sighed, walking over from the front room to the kitchen. He didn't feel that their discussion was over yet, so Gerrika followed him.

The scent of dried blood hit him as his father opened the kitchen door. Stained red rags lined the table, circling around the gutted body of a lion on the table. Honja grabbed a blade from the corner and sliced the side of the beast's stomach, down its left thigh. The wet sound of metal on flesh always made Gerrika wince. He always preferred not seeing where his meat came from.

His father grabbed the massive cat's foot, tugging it until the muscles and veins of the dead creature snapped apart. "Here, son. Don't let your lion get cold. Better eat. What I have to say to you might take a while."

Gerrika put his hands in his pockets. He didn't want to give his father the satisfaction in taking from his kill, especially since he suspected Honja was going to try giving him another lecture. "No thanks. My friends and I had a large meal before leaving Brunswald. Sorry, father, I don't think that anything you say will change my mind."

"I'm going to try, just so I can sleep tonight knowing this knowledge has been given to you." Honja raised the lion's leg to his beak and took a chomp off the side, fur and all, and swallowed. "There is an aspect of aveho and human history that modern institutions of learning have deemed too unsavory to teach. Regardless of what it is, I think it's important to not shove the parts of history you don't like under the bed. It should be all out there."

"What's past is past." His son frowned. "It seems stupid to me to fixate on problems our species had centuries ago. Sorry, I didn't mean to be so forward."

Honja took another bite of the thigh. "Always speak your mind forwardly no matter who you're talking to. I welcome the challenge as both your father and as someone with an opinion."

"That seems inconsistent with everything you've said to me for the last ten years."

"If that's the impression you got, then the blame must fall on me. I've never thought that a child should automatically respect their parents. It's the duty of a parent to *earn* their child's respect, and I sense that I haven't had yours for a long time."

His son shut his eyes. "No. Of course I respect you, father."

"Regardless," Honja wiped lion blood off his mouth with his sleeve. "continuing, the conflicts of our species are more recent than you realize. Not all of us are 'civilized'. There are some avehos who have decided that the forests and jungles are more appealing than streets and buildings. The largely *human* government doesn't like that. They have had to act in self-defense a number of times against them."

"I didn't know that." Gerrika slumped his shoulders. "I'm sorry, but what does that have to do with the other world?"

"*Everything*. It means they won."

"They *won*? It's not a competition."

His father shook his head. "It is."

"You realize that this other world has a completely different history than ours?" Gerrika asked. "You wouldn't be saying this if you had seen how they received me. It was honestly funny."

"Tell me how."

Gerrika paused, knowing that he was being put on the spot again. "First they thought I was some human in a costume. When they realized I wasn't, suddenly I was interesting. They all wanted to get to know me and all about where I came from. It was kind of wonderful."

His father huffed out a loud snort, almost a laugh.

"What? What is it?"

"They were fetishizing you." Honja said.

"Eww, no!"

His father rolled his eyes. "I mean they were giving you undeserved affection. Tell me, did you sing for them?"

"Umm, yeah. How did you know?"

"Because they just *loved* that, didn't they? Never mind *why* we have the vocals and range we have, just that it's pleasant to them." His father took another few bites out of the lion before tossing it back on the table, bored of eating. "They don't care about you. Not really. They just care about whatever's new, and when you can no longer amuse them, they'll toss you out the window. They would never love you."

"Forgive me for wanting at least *one* person to love me!" Gerrika shouted.

Honja backed up, surprised by his son's outburst. "Do I have to?"

"You're my father!" Gerrika was standing on the tips of his boots. "You must!"

"Have I not acted like a father all your life?" He shot back at his son. "Have I not fed you? Sheltered you? Allowed you to make your own life choices and attend university, even though your grades haven't been good? I've done everything a good father should have done. Why do you care if I love you?"

"What happened to you?" His son bit down on the corner of his beak, trying to keep his anger under control. "Were you always like this? That would explain why mother left you."

"Believe it or not, I was a lot like you when I was your age. But the real world got to me, and I adapted. I can't speak for why she left, but make no mistake. Your mother didn't just leave me. Your mother left you too."

Gerrika turned around and pounded his fist against the wall. The force of the blow was enough to chip off the weaker chunks of wood. He cried out in anger as the warm feeling of blood washed over his talon knuckles, leaving the rest to dry on the wall like paint.

Clutching his hand, Gerrika started for the door and picked up his shoulder satchel from the corner of the room.

"Where do you think you're going?" Honja asked.

"Away. This has been a very educational lesson from you." He went around his room, picking out everything he wanted to bring with him and shoving it all into the bag. "There are people who care about me. People who use that care to be good people." His little collection of plays by Winds Wilk was still on his shelf, just as he had left them. He put those on top of a blanket and spare clothes in his bag. "I'm sure I'll be back, eventually. Try to get along well without me."

Honja stood in the doorway between the front room and the kitchen, watching his son pack his things with the same look in his eyes that he had when he returned after a day of being missing. Gerrika wanted to give his father some final line, but instead he wiped the corner of his eye and opened the door, heading back into the night.

CHAPTER 15

Getting his father to finally calm down wasn't easy. The professor had a lot of questions, and as Dreden found out, he didn't have a lot of answers, even after being in the strange city for almost a day.

"It was not possible for us to try coming home after." he told him. "We were ambushed by their police before we could make sense of what happened."

"You couldn't have tried getting back afterwards?"

"The chief of police, Chief Milbrey was his name, said that nothing would happen. It was after high tide."

His father wiped his face, eyes drooping from stress. He took a seat back on his bed. Dreden felt the weight on his own shoulders of what he was telling him. "Are you sure that's what happened?"

"Yes. I remember it very clearly."

"You know that's not what I meant." he sighed. "That chief person didn't know any more about what happened than you did. Why would you listen to him?"

"But he *was* right. We're back now!" Dreden began pacing the room, unable to keep himself still.

"That may be, but it seems to me it was just a fluke that he was. Besides, you don't even know for sure that you couldn't have come back when the Sea retracted."

"Okay. I hear you. Dad, I'm sorry I didn't do everything I could to come back and let you know I was alright, but you wouldn't be so mad at me if you had seen what I had seen. The height of the city, the sound of different feet on different streets, the people..." Dreden remembered Morell, and the sinking feeling of the chance he would never see him again. "I'm so fucking sorry to have left you, but I had to pursue the men who tried to kill us."

"Did you learn anything?" insisted his father. "Did you find anything else about them? Get anywhere with that?"

Dreden shook his head. "No, no, and no."

"Well *I* did. Son, I have bad news. They've struck again."

He felt his heart stop. "Who? Where? Was it Gerrika's father? Chanin's parents?"

"A group of university students. You probably wouldn't know them. They're a couple years below you. They're all gravely wounded, Dreden. They're in the hospital now and might not make it. Also, a family living on the edge of town, not far from the main site of the invading Sea, claimed to see the men in red and hear their strange weapons. They say they saw them right before a neighbor's child was shot in the leg."

Dreden couldn't stand anymore. He tucked his arms against his waist, taking a seat on his own bed, facing his father. He groaned, planting his face into his palms. He could feel his father privately judging him.

"There's no way I could have known that would happen." He replied, after half a minute of silence.

"I'm not saying that you should have. I'm just hoping to get it in your head that this isn't about you. Yes, it seems like we were targeted, along with your friends, but clearly something else is happening too."

"The Prime Minister, the one who they claim to work for," Dreden continued, with new energy. "they exist in that world. A friend told me. So there, that's something I figured out."

"What do you think you're going to do? Dreden, I'm your father. In as small a home as we have, there aren't many places for you to hide your face from me. I know how unhappy you've been for years."

"That has nothing to do with this."

"It means that I can tell you're hiding something from me. Please, son, this will go a lot quicker if you just open up."

Dreden turned away, scratching his nose and audibly exhaling. "Last night I got more drunk than I've ever been, and I met some people."

Begrudgingly, Dreden told his father about meeting Morell Edland at the bar, along with all his intelligent, high-achieving and well-dressed friends. He told him about their conversations and about the wonderful exchange of culture that happened in that one room.

"Son, the way you're talking about these people makes it sound like you've never had a friend in your life. Need I remind you of Chanin and Gerrika?"

"You need not." Dreden rubbed his palms together, trying to keep calm. "I don't mean to sound ungrateful for all they've done for me as pals, but I've always felt...I mean...I don't think that they're *my* people."

"*Your* people?" His father laughed.

"Go ahead and amuse yourself. I know how I sound, and that doesn't change how I've felt. They're both great, but we don't have the same passions or many of the same interests. Morell and his friends... they were creatives and philosophers. I know I must sound a little awful, but I've never connected with anyone like I connected with Morell in just one day. You say I've been miserable? I have. I have for a fucking long time." Dreden got back to his feet, banging his fists against the sides of his legs.

"You have people who care about you, Dreden." replied his father, now with a bite.

"Don't give me that! If knowing that someone cared about me was enough, I would be the happiest person in town."

"Then what do you want from me?"

Dreden swallowed, fighting a breath. "I want you to understand! I want you to say you know how I feel, and that I'm not being unreasonable." He continued after a pause where he expected his father to reply. "I'm sorry I wasn't very social as a child, and I'm sorry I may be saying that I'm ungrateful for my friendships, but it's not a betrayal to want to meet new people who are better peers."

"Would you be this understanding if it were Gerrika or Chanin who wanted to take a break from you?"

"Maybe, maybe not. That's not the point. The point is that *I'm* the one with the new opportunity here. If the situation were reversed, it would be my problem and I would have to deal with it. Besides, they both took shines to new people too. And if we start to grow apart then it all works out, right? It's not like this is new. They have always been closer to each other than to me. Feeling like you're third-wheeling friends is not fun. Maybe this is the only way this can go from here. Either way, you won't have to be burdened by your unhappy son."

"I have not once implied that I have been burdened by your mood. Ever." The professor said, between his teeth.

"You didn't have to. I see how I've affected you. I see the way you look at me, both here and in class. I'm sorry that I haven't been the most grateful person in a while, probably forever, but you can't blame me for wanting other friends. Friends who challenge me intellectually like only you have before. I'm not saying Chanin and Gerrika aren't smart, but they don't think about things the way I do. I *need* this, dad, and I think I need Morell Edland."

Not knowing what else to say and wanting to spare his father from further conversation, Dreden turned his back, heading for the door.

"This sounds like an infatuation, Dreden." He jumped off his bed, rushing to his son before he could reach the door. "I need you at least consider that that's all it is. I don't want you to do anything you'll regret."

"There is nothing that I would regret more than staying here, poor and miserable, instead of going to really live my life. I'm sorry, but I think this is something I need to do. I promise I won't forget my other purpose while I'm there. I'm going to find out about those bastard soldiers."

His father didn't say anything. He felt a sting in his heart from including 'poor' before miserable. He never doubted that his father had done everything possible to give him a good life, and now that his father wasn't going to be a professor at Faeriebridge for much longer, it was only going to get worse for them.

"Please, son," His father sniffed. "this is too much."

"Faeriebridge let you go. You were already planning on moving away and teaching somewhere else, leaving me here to finish my classes without you," Dreden reminded him. "this isn't that much different. I'll be back, I promise, and I'm going to find those evil men."

He wanted to hug his father, but he felt that the moment for that was already passed. Dreden turned his back in the next second, not wanting to see his father's eyes get any more watery or let him see that he had been fighting tears for minutes.

And if he was being honest with himself, Dreden didn't know how much he wanted to get the murderous men anymore.

Chanin shook her head. "They didn't even believe me."

"Screw them." Gerrika spat. "You don't need that from them. I seriously don't understand the point sometimes in dealing with parents. They're always going to speak to you like a child."

"I assume that it went poorly with your father?" she asked.

"Is it that obvious?"

She smiled softly. "Your tone and that bag on your shoulder are pretty telling. Looks like your hand took a beating too."

"Yeah," he crossed his arms, hiding his bruised hand. A night breeze had returned. "I exploded a little bit. But if I'm going to explode at anyone, I'm glad it was at him."

The pair walked up the walkway, four street corners away from the university. Neither of them had anywhere to go anymore, so going about the town after the active late-night hours with no one to bother them was a better alternative to nothing.

"I might not be an expert on opening yourself up to others, pal," A group of other students, two humans and two avehos passed them on the sidewalk. She paused until they were out of earshot. "but alcohol is a funny thing. Sometimes it makes us say things that we've kept to ourselves for too long."

The aveho kept his eyes forward. She knew he was aware of what she was talking about. "I felt like an ass after saying that. Dreden was just trying to have a good time."

"He didn't take it hard. I'm positive he had no idea what you were talking about."

Gerrika cleared his throat. "That was intentional. Just saying 'I don't care what you say' doesn't specify anything. I should clear things up with him. It would make one less thing that's weighing on me. After the mess with my father, I don't need anything else like that bothering me."

"You know that Dreden is a good guy." Chanin added. "He doesn't mean to be arrogant and condescending, and he especially doesn't mean to hurt you. That's just who he is. He is very much the professor's son."

"Oh, but I *love* his father." Gerrika smiled. "He's like one of the coolest people I've ever met, and with his bushy brow and pointed nose he looks enough like an aveho already."

"You're terrible." she laughed.

"It's a complement! Certainly, I would never compare someone's looks to mine with hurtful intent."

There were never any crowds so late at night. There was nothing open except some taverns, but even those knew that most of their patrons, being students, were too busy to still be out. That made the sight of a lone traveler coming from around the block that much easier to spot.

Chanin and Gerrika prepared to motion to the side to allow the traveler to pass but paused as they recognized their friend's fallen red face.

"You don't look too well, bud." Gerrika told him.

Dreden took a deep breath, turning his head and exhaling away from them. "It's been a long day. I'm tired and I'd like to go anywhere but home."

"We were thinking of going to the same place." Chanin said. "Walks around the Town Square never did us harm."

"Mind if I join you? I sense that you two wouldn't be out here if things had gone ideally for you at your homes, and it looks like Gerrika's got his schoolbag packed."

Chanin and Gerrika told him about how their parents had reacted to their news. What Honja had said to Gerrika didn't surprise him at all. It was perfectly in line with what his father typically had to say about anything. It was Mister and Missus Adderfoth's reactions that got him more fumed up.

"I think I would have preferred them to think I'm crazy." she explained. "Even after I showed them the different currency, described the city to them in great detail, and offered to escort them personally to Heathback in an effort to prove myself, they doubled down on their convictions. They just think I'm lying, and thus the two of you are bad influences on me."

"What reason could they think you have for lying?" asked the aveho.

"Ditching class for one, and they seem to have it in their heads that it's my way of getting back at them for their pressuring me to be a perfect student and get out of Kroonsaed before everything fully goes to shit. Sometimes it even seems like they haven't decided if they care about me too much or not at all."

Dreden and Gerrika shared a look. She didn't have to say any more for them to know what she was talking about. Her parents had once been well-to-do merchants, like a last drip of a tea bag remnant of an older world.

"They can't help it," Chanin continued, after walking the next street in silence. "always thinking forward has been their way of life forever. I'm the first in the family who is actually going to graduate from a university. They don't think that my focus in history is very useful. For people who only care about improving upon their own past generations, it seems especially funny that their daughter's study of history would be their undoing."

Gerrika shoved his hands into his coat pockets. "That's rough, Chanin. I'm sorry."

"Me too." Dreden said. "It looks like I'm the odd man out here."

"Your father is too nice to have driven you out." Gerrika said. "What did you do?"

"I...ugghhh. Sorry, not now. I'm happy to lend an ear to you, but I don't want to get worked up again. I'll tell you though, I could really use a drink now."

Chanin patted him on the shoulder. "Same here."

"You know what was good?" Gerrika said, with new enthusiasm. "That Magill's stuff at Keethkay's."

"Right," Dreden smiled. "that stuff made me feel like my liver was getting a massage."

Half an hour later they were tired of circling the Town Square again. They walked past the corner for the school taverns and butcheries, heading out into the woods. None of them were saying anything, but Dreden knew the same thing was on everyone's mind. They never took the dark beaten path out of town unless they were going to their usual hangout spot.

But that was no longer any normal spot, and Dreden knew that unless they intended to get close to the Sea again, they wouldn't set foot a mile away from there.

"Are we seriously not going to talk about this?" Dreden asked.

"I was just following you guys." Chanin replied.

"I was following you, following him." Gerrika stopped his pace, causing the two humans to halt as well. "Look, I don't mean to hit it on the nose here, but I'm not going back home. After packing my things as dramatically as I did, it would be really awkward if I came back."

Dreden felt their eyes on him now. He turned away from them, kicking up dust with his boot. "I... told my father I was going back to the other world. I promised him I wouldn't stop trying to find the people who tried putting holes in us."

He explained to them what his father said about the soldiers striking again. The two of them cursed at the news, but he couldn't help but notice a flicker of relief in both their eyes, and Dreden sympathized. If that were true, then they were just random targets, and it might not have been all about them after all. The first thing Dreden felt upon hearing the news was liberation, and whether or not his friends would admit it, he knew that they did too.

"And you get to see more of your boyfriend too, if I'm not mistaken." Chanin smirked.

Gerrika scratched his head. "Am I missing something here?"

Chanin's face fell after realizing what she said. "Shit, Dreden, I'm sorry-"

"No, don't worry!" Dreden shook his head. "It's fine. He's my friend too. Gerrika, I ended up telling Chanin last night at Keethkay's that I'm crooked. I'm a homosexual."

"Should I be disappointed?" the aveho asked.

"No, why would you be?"

Gerrika nudged his side. "Because we've known each other for years and you've never asked me out. Love has been here for you this whole time!"

"Sorry to disappoint you, friend," Dreden ruffled the top of his friend's head. "but I think I prefer men with fewer feathers."

"Please, don't spare my feelings. It's my feet isn't it? They're too big."

A rushing sound of the Sunitian Sea reminded them of how far they had come. Afterwards not even a chirping cricket or a hooting owl dared disturb anything else that the Sea had to say.

The trio returned their eyes to each other one more time. Dreden didn't need words to know what they were thinking. They were terrified, but they, like him, had already made up their minds.

"I just want you two to know," Gerrika said, his arms shaking from the roar. "that I would go to the end of the earth for both of you. I would take arrows for both of you."

Chanin wrapped her arm around him, kissing the side of his beak. "We'll be fine, G. We'll be with each other the whole time."

Putting his hand on the aveho's back, Dreden nodded, giving a smile to help calm him down.

As they approached the entrance to the caverns, the air around them once again became thin. They knew how the process worked, and it made them less terrified of what was happening. Dreden, more than anything, was glad that it looked like the Sea was going to give them another visit to Brunswald.

A sinking part of him, looking at his friends start to take what was coming, told him that every choice they made since meeting the murderous soldiers had set things in motion that could never be undone. And Dreden couldn't bring himself to promise anything to either of them.

CHAPTER 16

The Prime Minister told everyone not to disturb him because he was taking a meeting. That wasn't quite true, but that didn't stop his associates and his secretary from slipping things under his door.

War was the last thing he wanted on his mind, and ever since the disaster in Andayt, it was all the buzz. Skaltbard and Andayt had been intermittently at war for hundreds of years, and now that an incident causing thousands of deaths had occurred in their capital city, their people wanted justice. But what were they going to do? Declare war on their earth for the earthquake?

It would come back to Skaltbard somehow. It always did.

Charles Dowlepot allowed his assistant Jess inside so she could refill his pot of tea.

"Thank you."

"Of course, sir," she nodded.

He smiled, waiting for her to leave before continuing his reading. The books from the National Library that Loid had given him weren't a help yet. He didn't know the best place to start, so he began with the most recently published book. *The Sunitian Sea and International Business* had been in print for just over a year. Besides being painfully boring, it didn't have anything useful for his personal research.

He shoved it aside and picked up the oldest one. It was the eight-year-old *The History of the Sunitian Sea*. Surely if the author had dedicated an entire book to the Sea's history, there would be something telling in there. Something that could tell him about what was happening and why the strangers had come.

It was a large volume, so his face fell when he saw the title of the first chapter: Mick Jowns. It was going to be a tedious exercise, but if he didn't already know that, he wouldn't have checked out all the books from the library. His mind flashed back to the point in his conversation with Loid where Mick Jowns was mentioned. Surely no coincidence.

"Maybe it means something." Charles laughed to himself. "Okay, Mister Jowns, help me figure this out."

He started from the top, which was a short biography of the man:

Mick Jowns (pictured below) was a promising philosopher and natural philosopher (scientist) starting in his first year of university at the Hinbarg School of Natural Philosophy. While still a student, he shocked the world with what would go on to be his greatest discovery: The Theory of Evolution by Natural Selection. While the university clergymen urged the admissions board to expel him for his radical ideas, his theory quickly gained ground in universities across Skaltbard. While many of his peers in the natural philosophy department refuted his findings, his discoveries and writings done during his entire semester in the wilderness are permanently etched into both human history and what is now mankind's understanding of his place in the world.

That was all stuff the Prime Minister already knew. Everybody knew about it. The introduction continued to discuss how Jowns's ideas forever changed philosophy, quickly moving away from theological-centric camps in favor of humanism and what would later be called Practical Jownsism, which described a way of looking at other life forms from the lens of the only species that could understand the theory.

Charles looked down to the bottom of the page. Photography hadn't yet existed a hundred years ago during Jowns's time, but the little portrait was impressive. Mick Jowns couldn't have been more than twenty-years-old. He was seated, arms over his lap in a seamless black suit and a red cravat. His teeth looked nonexistent. A lack in visible gaps in between them gave the appearance of just one large tooth in his mouth. His eyes were wide open, as if all the knowledge and wisdom contained in his young mind needed more room.

This is the boy who became the first Prime Minister of Skaltbard, Charles thought. *He led the movement of humanism that ended the divine right of kings. This boy grew up to nearly single-handedly do it. He also rid the world of what was written about the Sunitian Sea a hundred years ago when the Sea first manifested.*

It was written that his purge of scientific literature was because he wanted to rid the libraries and other houses for higher learning of lies perpetrated by the crown for thousands of years, but as someone with power, Charles knew sometimes even the worst things could seemingly be justified.

"Why did you do it, Jowns?" The Prime Minister asked the small painting on the page. "What were you trying to hide? What did you succeed in hiding?"

A knock on the door took his attention away from the page. He cursed to himself. Nobody ever listened.

"Not now! Come back another time!"

"Charles? Charles, it's me!"

"Loid? One second!"

The Prime Minister shut the book and opened the door. The librarian's hair was a mess. Where he wasn't balding, loose strands of hair hovered like spider webs. He held his hand against the doorway of Charles's office, out of breath.

"What's the matter, Loid?" he asked.

His friend let himself catch a few more breaths. "It's horrible, Charles. The library...the library has been ransacked!"

"What do you mean?"

"I mean what it sounds! It's like a goddamn hurricane went through the place! Books are everywhere!"

"Was anything taken?" Charles asked. He ushered the librarian into his office, offering him a seat opposite himself at the desk.

"It's going to be weeks before we can be sure." Loid said, taking his seat. "Nothing is where it should be anymore. It's as if someone just wanted to wreck the place inch by inch."

Charles closed his fists on his mahogany desk. "That's terrible, Loid. I'm sorry. I assume you've contacted the police?"

He nodded. "They looked the place over and under. They're not sure how much they'll be able to do. They've been scouting for potential witnesses, but it doesn't look good. They're saying it was probably the work of dozens of people. No one person could do that much damage in such a small time frame."

The Prime Minister knew that the National Library's hours were the same every day. They were open until 2 in the morning and reopened four hours later, with the exception of a two-hour break in the evening from 4 to 6.

"It is simply not humanly possible for one person to do that much damage in less than two hours." Loid shook his head furiously. "No no no. It had to be a gang, and they were looking for something."

"I take it you have no idea what that could be?"

"No idea, but based on the fact that *every* section of the library is a mess, I'm going to go ahead and say that they didn't find it. Good luck to them, I say! The National Library has the largest collection of books in the hemisphere. If we don't have it, then I don't think anyone does. The worst part is that we're going to have to close the library until this is all fixed."

"I'm so sorry, Loid." Charles said, patting his friend on the arm. "If there is anything I can do, don't hesitate to ask me."

The librarian inhaled, showing his teeth nervously. "That actually brings me to why I'm here. This may be a little awkward, but I'm going to need back the books you checked out this morning."

Charles had to laugh, but stopped when Loid's expression didn't change. "Why would you need them back?"

"Strictly inventory purposes, I assure you." Loid said. "We've known each other since we were kids, and you're the Prime Minister, so I always forgo the usual paperwork when you check out books, but I could still get in trouble for doing it for you. The owners of the library are going to have a close eye on all of us until it's all sorted out."

"I see. Don't worry. I understand. Remind me, who owns the National Library?"

"It's been owned by the Edland family for many decades."

"*Not* the government?"

"No. The library was failing many years ago, and the Edlands saved it. It now belongs to them more than it belongs to the state."

"Ohhhhh." Charles covered his face with his palms, laughing as he wiped them down his chin. "I just can't be free of that family, can I? Very well, friend, take the books. I only got through one of them today. Just keep them on hold for me until this is all fixed. Sound fine?"

The librarian stood up, shaking Charles's hand. "Thank you so much for understanding. You're really doing me a big favor here. Want to go out for a pint?"

"Sorry. Not tonight. Venka and I are going to Palasol's for dinner. Speaking of which, I should probably freshen up right now."

He helped Loid with the books before wishing him a good evening. After the librarian was out of his office, Charles sat back down at his desk. It didn't make sense to him, and he didn't know why he felt the need to do it, but after his friend knocked on his door, he had torn out the first few pages of the *History*.

It probably wouldn't be long before Loid noticed the pages were missing, but Charles wasn't done reading. He couldn't say for sure why, but he knew there was something to find there.

Cipre couldn't remember the last time a book had done it to her, but she found herself unable to put it down.

Just as she expected, it was unlike anything else she ever read. Minkompa's prose was better than many of the top award-winning writers, and he had a seamless way of getting into the characters' heads. He chose their words the way a bee might choose a flower. It seemed so natural, something so forward that Cipre's subconscious might have nodded, saying 'of course'.

"Consider me sold, my friend," she said to herself, alone, sitting on her couch.

She didn't want to get ahead of herself, but if she played her cards right, *this* could be the book that Mirthinout pushed to be the big hit of the year. Sure, Morell Edland was a good writer, but as the main editor of the novel, she never felt that it represented the core values of her publisher. That, or worse, it didn't represent *her* values. There were things about *A Mad Past* that were undoubtedly excellent, and even intelligently funny, but she couldn't kick the feeling that it wasn't what the literary world currently needed. It probably didn't need another book by some rich boy.

Maybe it needed a book by a lonely dragon.

"What are you reading there?"

She instinctively shut the book. Matry stood looking at her through the kitchen doorway.

"You scared me." She laughed, hand over her chest.

"I've always been praised for my abilities as a guest. I'm light as a moth and I've never snored."

After coming back from her second visit to Minkompa, she found her friend sitting at her porch with a couple small luggage bags at his legs. Apparently, his flat was undergoing safety inspections after the quake, and everyone in the building was going to be evicted for a couple days. He had nowhere else to go without his daily travel becoming a major liability, so she offered him her home for the next couple days.

He walked into the living room with a glass of cider in hand. "Must be a good book to grab your attention like that."

"It is. You have no idea."

"Who's it by?"

"You wouldn't believe me if I told you."

Matry took a seat in a chair opposite her. "*Really*?" He sipped his cider, shaking his head in amusement. "How many guesses do I get?"

"You don't get any." She smiled, tucking the book at her lap and covering it with her arms. "You don't get any because it is impossible for you to guess correctly."

"It's not you, is it?"

"I wish it were me." she beamed. "I'll be honest with you; I haven't been feeling really confident at Mirthinout lately. It's the stories we've been getting the last couple years. They've been good, but it's been too long since we've had a groundbreaking piece of fiction. Everyone is all hyped up about what I'm working on, but frankly, I don't see it as everyone else does."

"You don't think Morell Edland's book is groundbreaking?" he asked.

"There is some potentially great stuff in there, but none of its ideas strike me as 'ahead of their time'."

"That's a bit surprising." He put his glass on the table after a couple more sips. "Morell Edland is a fearless radical. I wouldn't expect any less from a young man like him. I would kill to be the one to edit *A Mad Past*."

"Go ahead," Cipre extended her arms outward, as if readying to embrace an elephant. "do it. I'm right here. Put a stake in my heart!"

Matry bent over, laughing, before finishing with a clap. "Don't tempt me, woman."

"You'd never have it in you." Cipre said, smirking. "Anyway, I'm not getting the fulfillment that I used to from the job, and I think this book would make an excellent addition to our lineup for the year. I think we should do what we would have done for Edland with this book."

"That one you got there?" He pointed to the thick volume that was still tucked at her lap. "And does this book have a name?"

It had taken her a while to notice its title. The leather covering was old, or at least it was poorly kept, but there was stenciled into the cover a title that had taken minutes of dusting and cleaning on Cipre's part to uncover.

"It's called *The Century*." she said.

"How ominous." replied her friend. "Look, I've known you for a long time, Cipre, and you've always had a great instinct for these things. If you want to storm into Radoff Dell's office and tell him about your fancy new author and show him the book, I'm all for it. Screw Morell Edland!"

She put the dragon's book down on the table in front of her. "I feel really good about this. I'm going to finish it tonight and send it over to Dell's place tomorrow."

"That's the spirit! Put that book down. You've been cooped up in here all day. Let's go out for a pint or something."

It sounded good to her. She knew that she was just going to be thinking about *The Century* the entire time, but getting out would do good to clear her head.

She had no idea what her boss was going to think about Minkompa's book, but Cipre had a feeling stronger than any she ever had before that she was doing something good. Whether Minkompa wanted it or not, his words could shift a civilization.

CHAPTER 17

They completely bypassed the crowds this time around.

Based on their two trips so far, it seemed like there was always a crowd huddled around the rocky port where the Sea came in. People murmured again, this time not so loudly, even though the crowd was much larger, drawn to the fact that something unnatural had occurred earlier in the day. As Dreden's senses returned, he felt their presence spark another light quake, but it wasn't enough to knock any of the viewers down.

The three didn't say anything. They just gave a quick wave to the crowd while they rounded the corner where the barrier was lowest. A few people from the crowd started to follow them down the street, but when Dreden, Chanin, and Gerrika paid them no mind, they paused, stuck like flies in amber.

"Seems like we're becoming regulars." Chanin noted.

"I'm not sure how that makes me feel." Dreden turned around. No one was watching them, but the people they passed on the street were noticing Gerrika again.

The aveho kept his eyes forward, avoiding all eye contact. "I hope it happens sooner than not. I'd rather people not still look at me like I'm some extraterrestrial forever."

"Some people might kill for that kind of attention." Dreden replied with a small smile.

"Right, but in those cases the attention is probably deserved. It's not my fault I'm the only aveho here."

It sounded like Gerrika had more to say, but accidentally meeting the eyes of a passing group on the other side of the street quieted him. They paused, smiling and pointing at him, but only Dreden and Chanin saw them do that.

"I wouldn't take it too hard." Dreden said. "I'm sure that back in our world there are many places where humans don't know what avehos are, and even the other way around."

"There are many corners of the world that probably haven't been explored yet." Chanin added. "Don't dwell on it. Don't show them what an aveho is. Show them who *you* are. You'll feel all the better for it."

"You're right. I know you are."

They rounded the street corner, passing along one where dozens of artists were showing their art on the walkways and bands were playing music. They provided enough of a distraction for people to not notice either of them or Gerrika for a few minutes.

Chanin took his talon hand in hers as they walked. Dreden wanted to say something or to give him a pat on the back, but he couldn't find it in him to commit. He sympathized with Gerrika's problems and wanted to help him out, but he didn't know if he could help someone when he had so many of his own problems to sort out, and therefore any attempt at consoling him would make Dreden turn the whole situation into something that was only about himself.

Thankfully they remembered how to make the journey back to Keethkay's. It had been a simple ride in the police carriage when they had been detained, and the city seemed very walkable, so even if they couldn't find it, someone would have known where to go.

The tavern wasn't as busy as it had been the day before. It was still the late afternoon. Dreden guessed it wasn't after five o'clock. The crowd, in what Dreden would assume was their middle-to-upper class rags and hats, sat at the bar talking about the ailments of the city and the world in excited tones, as if they were fans of some serialized story, trying to figure out what the writer was going to do next, and the alcohol the bartender served them was like some great piece of storytelling that had come before, helping them in their predictions.

And at the far end of the room, alone at a corner table for four people, was the man who had made such an impression on him.

"I guess I won't have to look for him later." Dreden shoved his hands in his pockets.

"He really *is* here all the time, isn't he?" Chanin said.

Several moments passed where Dreden just moved his waist and legs around nervously, while Gerrika and Chanin just stared at him.

"Do you intend on standing here with us all day?" Chanin asked.

"Of course not, I'm just really nervous-"

Gerrika grabbed him by the back and shoved him into Morell's side of the room. He yipped accidentally, and it was loud enough to catch the writer's attention.

Morell Edland turned his head up, and his eyes jumped as a smile spread from ear to ear. "Dreden Sharpstand! Didn't know you would be back so soon."

"Yeah, I was pretty surprised myself." He wiped his face, trying to fight the building redness. "Morell, you remember Chanin and Gerrika?"

"Yes, how could I forget?" He shook Dreden's hand, moving along and doing the same with the other human and the aveho. "May I be so bold in asking what brought you back so soon?"

"Maybe another time." Dreden said. "It's a little rough."

"You know what, fellas? I've been sitting on my ass here alone all afternoon trying to write something halfway decent. I think the three of you are just what I need. Come on, let's get out of here. Let's get some dinner. Sound good?"

"Perfect." Dreden turned to his two friends. "That works with you both, right?"

Chanin stepped back. "No, actually Gerrika and I are busy. We have plans for tonight."

"I could eat." Gerrika said, oblivious.

"No, you can't."

"Oh!" The aveho took a step back with her. "I just remembered that we *do* have plans. Maybe another time, Morell."

"Wait...wait...wait," Dreden turned around to them, speaking in a hushed tone. "Please, you can't leave me like this."

"Don't worry so much." Gerrika smiled.

"No, I'm *begging* you, I'm not read-"

Chanin took him by the hand. "You'll be fine." She raised her hand, waving goodbye as she ushered Gerrika out of Keethkay's. "Have a good dinner, you guys, and night, if we don't catch up later!"

"Pleasure as always." Morell returned the wave. "It wasn't just me, right? That was a little weird?"

"They're a little weird." Dreden replied, wiping his brow. "Would you still want to go get food even though it's just the two of us?"

"No, absolutely. Hey, wait a second!"

Dreden and Morell rushed outside to catch Chanin and Gerrika as they were continuing down the street.

"You two, no point in carrying that large bag around all night." Morell reached into his breast pocket, presenting Gerrika with a key. "Here, stay in the lodging upstairs again. Don't worry, the landlord owes me a favor or two. Based on how big that bag is, it seems like you don't intend to make this just an overnight trip."

Gerrika took the key, thanking him. "It's a long story. This means a lot to me. You're too kind."

"You can pay me back by telling me that story one of these days." Morell gave him a friendly point as he and Dreden continued down the road. "If you need anything, don't be shy!"

Dreden could feel the weight of his two friends' gaze on him and Morell as they rounded the corner. Morell adjusted his notebook bag over his shoulder as they passed a street full of mulled wine and cider vendors.

"Where are we going?" Dreden asked.

"One of the best restaurants in town. Palasol's. Anyone who's even visiting Brunswald for half a day needs to try their goose. It's truly the envy of the Northern Hemisphere."

"Great!" Dreden rolled down his sleeves, feeling extra cold from his nervousness. "I think I'll have to have you order for me. I don't know anything about being in those kinds of restaurants."

"Then I guess I'll just have to teach you, won't I?"

It was like something out of a fairy tale. Dreden never imagined there was such a thing as the kind of luxury that Palasol's aimed to provide, through sounds, scents, and company.

The clicking and clattering of dishes and silverware was enough for Dreden to self-consciously lower his hand to his empty pockets. He found himself happy that he was apparently with one of the wealthiest young men in the country.

"Seems like the kind of place one would need a reservation for." Dreden mused.

"Certainly, unless you know the owner."

"Will any of your friends be joining us here?"

Morell shook his head. "No, but I plan on meeting some of them later tonight at a tavern. You're welcome to join, of course."

"Keethkay's?" Dreden asked.

"I've been there all day." he said. "No, you'll like the new place."

They waited by the entrance for a couple more minutes before the server showed them to a table for two that just opened. Dreden thought he must have looked like a toddler, shooting his glazed eyes around from the windows to the little shiny plating along the corners of the menus. The little folded napkins resting on the corner of the table did nothing to ease his excitement.

Dreden's eyes lapped the menu. "Tell me what to get, my friend."

"First thing, *everything* here is excellent. I told you about the goose. It's my personal favorite, but the duck and the pheasant are no less impressive."

"I've got enough on my mind right now, Morell, I don't think I need to stress about what to eat at the best place in town, especially since I'm underdressed compared to you." Dreden smiled, putting his menu down. "Just get me whatever you get."

Morell made a clicking sound, shooting him some teeth. "Don't worry about that. You look fine. Besides, if you're here long enough we'll get you some nice clothes."

"I've always wanted to wear a white shirt like yours. Back home, white is hard to wash, so it can only be worn once, so no point in investing in it."

A server came to their table a minute later to take their order. Morell ordered the two of them a glass of twenty-five-year-old Archman's Red Wine, and for food, Morell ordered them the goose with bread rolls and a side of assorted salads.

After the wine came, their conversation got much livelier, and the more sips of wine Dreden took, the easier it was to forget that the two of them weren't alone in the restaurant. Their conversation fires were watered out when Morell looked over Dreden's shoulder and his expression fell. He couldn't tell if it was from a good or unpleasant surprise, but the next thing he knew, Morell was removing the napkin from his lap and was on his feet.

A middle-aged couple was enthusiastically greeted by the staff. They took the man and woman's coats and hats, giving them a last cheery hello as the two of them followed a server's lead to a table on the far end of the restaurant.

The man didn't look very old, and neither did his wife. They were dressed just the same as everyone else around, with the man in a sharp tan suit and a clean-cut head of hair with the woman, who Dreden assumed was his wife, wearing a shiny blue dress. She was the one who recognized Morell, so she tugged at the man's arm, and a new life came into his tired eyes.

"Mister Edland," the man said, shaking his hand. "I heard you like to come to Palasol's but have never actually seen you here."

"Only every other Thursday, Mister Dowlepot," Morell laughed. "Ah, Venka, lovely as always." He leaned in and embraced her, kissing her cheek. "I would assume you're too good for a place like this, sir, after your surge in popularity."

Charles Dowlepot shook his head, smiling. "Never. I think most of the bakeries on Main Street would back me up here. I don't know if you realize it, young man, but lately I am not able to escape your parents."

"I'm sorry about that." Morell replied. "I've said it before, but I'll say it again: I am not my parents. I do love them as a good son should, but I have always been open about how different we are, especially our politics."

"I didn't intend it in a harsh way, but it has made my job interesting for sure." Dowlepot's eyes met Dreden's. "How rude of us. Morell, please introduce us to your friend."

"Funny thing, actually." Morell said. "I'm sure you're familiar with the three visitors who came in from the Sea. This is one of them. Dreden Sharpstand, meet Prime Minister Charles Dowlepot."

Upon hearing those words again, all of Dreden's excitement drained from him.

"Is that right?" Charles asked, cheery. "I hope your visit has been excellent so far, Mister Sharpstand."

The Prime Minister extended a hand to him. He didn't take it. He couldn't. For all he knew this was the man who had sent men to try to kill his father and his friends.

"I'm going to need to speak with you." Dreden told him, eyes locked on Dowlepot's like a hungry hawk's.

Dowlepot cleared his throat, passing it off as a laugh when his hand wasn't shaken. "What about?"

He told him. Several times through his story Morell tried to interrupt him, telling him that it wasn't appropriate to be bringing it up at dinner, but Dreden was persistent. Dowlepot didn't make any move to silence him, instead taking it in like any other bit of feedback he got on a daily basis.

"Believe it or not, young man," said the Prime Minister softly, after he had finished. "I have unanswered questions on my end as well. Not as personal as yours, but I am doing my own investigation. In the meantime, all I can promise is that I knew nothing of any world beyond ours and I *certainly* did not send any men there to assassinate anyone. I'm afraid my word is all I can give you right now."

Dreden didn't know what to think. The person talking to him didn't appear to be the kind who would have random people killed, and he did believe him when he said that he wasn't aware of Kroonsaed's existence. Taking Dowlepot's word was all he could do at the moment, and he didn't want to cause any further unpleasantness for his wife or for Morell.

"Thank you. I'm sorry, but you can see why I would need to speak to you."

"Perfectly understandable." The Prime Minister offered his hand again, and this time Dreden shook it. "Let me know where you'll be staying. If I figure something out, you and your friends will be the first to know about it."

With passing goodbyes, the Dowlepots found their server again and were shown to their seats. When Dreden sat back down, he could feel Morell's judgement.

"That wasn't appropriate of you." he said.

"Are you sure about that? Because what would you do if you were in my position?"

Morell went back to adjusting his napkin over his lap and took a sip of a new wine that was delivered during their dialogue.

"Look, Dreden, it doesn't make me look very good to bring you here and talk to the Prime Minister, the *Prime Minister*, like he was some kind of petty criminal."

"He's not *my* Prime Minister." Dreden replied. "He doesn't tell me what to do."

"Please see this from my point of view. I'm a regular here. These are my people. I could be the one who gets scolded for your behavior, or worse yet, my parents can hear about it."

Morell ended his sentence with a smile, causing Dreden to return the face. "Sorry, but I'm not going to forget about why I'm really here. I made a promise to my father."

"And we'll figure it out." Morell extended his arm across the table, briefly cupping Dreden's hand in his. "Now, if you can do me another favor, just forget about what's weighing on you and enjoy tonight. You made a good impression on my friends last night, and I think they'll be happy to see you again."

It was another twenty minutes before the food arrived, and whether it was because he was starving or that Morell was right about the goose, it was outstanding. Halfway through the meal and more than three quarters into a bottle of wine, he found himself not even wondering what his friends were doing.

CHAPTER 18

Gerrika wanted to drop his things off in the room first. He and Chanin didn't have any set plans for the evening, so they thought walking around the city would do themselves good, and maybe clear their heads a bit more. The rooms were generous sizes, especially compared to what they were used to. Though it wasn't much of a contest compared to the average size of a house in Kroonsaed.

"I was being serious though," he told Chanin. "I *could* eat."

"What do you feel like?"

The pair exited the flat and took to the streets. The sun was falling and the electric lamps lining the streets began to go to work.

"I don't know. I liked what we had for breakfast."

"I imagine places like that bakery aren't open for dinner." Chanin said. "I still have the money Chief Milbrey gave us. Surely it's enough for something around here."

They continued around for several streets aimlessly, looking through every window of an open store that served food. After a few looks and taking in the scents fuming from the stores' exhausts, they kept on going.

"I'm really not picky," Chanin said. "and I'm starting to starve. I say that we just roll the dice for the next place we see, even if all they serve are shark pies."

"I know that's not supposed to be serious, but we don't really know all the culture in this place, do we?"

A loud bang stopped them both in their tracks, and a slight burning smell assaulted their noses. It came from around the corner. Gerrika and Chanin looked at each other as if waiting to see what the other would do. Then they both started for the corner at the same time.

"Aww, shit!"

The source of the smoke and the curse was the first store on the left. The majority of its front façade was an open area, with a large door the size of a wall pulled up like a curtain along the ceiling. A man and woman were standing under a giant metal beast that was spewing smoke like a dragon's throat.

Chanin peeked her head into the room. "Are you guys okay?"

The pair looked at them, their faces covered in soot. When they saw Gerrika they smiled, and their teeth looked whiter than a night star with their dirty faces.

"Oh, hey!" the woman cheered. "You must be two of the visitors?"

"That's right. We are." She took a couple more steps into their room, with Gerrika sheepishly behind her. "I'm Chanin, and this is Gerrika. I'll tell you; we don't have anything like *that* where we come from."

"Is that right?" said the man, scrubbing his hand with a wet cloth. "I'm sure you figured out that we don't have anyone like *that* here."

He pointed to Gerrika. The aveho knew the man was joking and trying to smoothen their introduction, but when he looked at him without a hint of amusement on his avian face, he coughed, returning to Chanin.

"Like what you see?" he continued. "It's not easy work, but based on current international tensions it looks like it'll be necessary. I'm Allin. Allin Gumary. This is my wife Sidra."

"We're engineers." Sidra said.

"What is it you're doing here?" Chanin asked. "Looks and sounds really important."

Sidra took the wet cloth from her husband's hands, wiping her face with it. "I guess you can call it a 'motor-horse'. There's starting to be shortage of horses for public use due to the building war effort. We're trying to solve that problem in this little garage of ours. Everyone knows what kind energy powers boats and ships, and we're trying to create an internal system with this boy of ours to function like the real thing."

"What kind of energy would that be?" Chanin approached, in awe of the motor-horse.

"We're trying to make a steam engine compact enough to fit inside this thing," she continued. "and we're workshopping with a lot of different natural fuels to produce said steam."

Allin brushed sweat off his forehead. "The problem is getting the coal and the water hot enough, but not too hot for a machine of this size. It's extremely prone to over-heating, but if we can figure out a way to stabilize the temperature levels, then I think the two of us will have a real winner on our hands."

"Not to mention an early retirement." Sidra added.

Chanin couldn't take her eyes off the machine. It was shaped like a horse, with a long metal neck and a large weight where the snout would be for balance. From 'hoof' to head it stood a few inches over six feet tall and was as long as any horse she and Gerrika were used to seeing.

"Will it be possible to ride one?" she asked them. "Or will it strictly be for carriage-pulling?"

"It would be rough on the ass for sure." Allin laughed. "But possible? Yeah."

She circled the motor-horse, admiring its structure and looking at the bits of hardware in the machine's belly. The couple had turned the engine off, but it was still smoking noticeably out of the exhaust at its side. Neither of them had ever seen anything like it, and based on what the Gumarys were saying, no one in the city had yet to see anything like it.

When she finished, she turned back to Gerrika, her face lit as if starstruck. "This is the coolest thing I have ever seen."

"Me too." he replied. "Just imagine what people back home would think of something like this. Witchcraft for sure."

Chanin turned back to the engineers. "Would you...I suppose it would be too much of a bother if we watched you work for a little bit?"

"Not at all!" Sidra cheered. "It would be good to finally have an audience, or anyone to admire our genius to boost our egos."

"You're too kind." Chanin smiled.

"Wait, what about food?" Gerrika asked.

Allin put his hand on his wife's shoulder. "If you guys are hungry, we could always make you something. It's been a while since we've had visitors but I'm sure we haven't lost our ability to entertain."

She turned to the aveho, almost jumping with excitement. "Want to stick around? I think this'll be so much fun!"

"Nah," Gerrika swatted his hand, covering his beak shyly. "as cool as it is, I'd rather not spend my night with boring machines."

"No! No come on, G, it will be a lot of fun."

"You have fun here, Chanin. I'm confident that this city has something different for me tonight. Besides, brainy things have a habit of not getting done when I get involved."

She took his talon hands in hers. "I don't want you to be all alone. Are you sure you're going to be alright?"

The aveho nodded. "I promise. Don't worry. I can take care of myself." As she looked at him, Gerrika could tell she wasn't sure if she believed him or not. "I'm *fine*. I'll meet other interesting people. I'll tell you all about it tonight, or tomorrow morning at breakfast. It'll be good for me."

She wrapped her arms around him, locking him in an embrace that went a bit too long for Gerrika's comfort, involving her hand moving up and down his spine as if she were a mother consoling her child.

"Come back if you change your mind." she told him.

"I will." He gave her a last smile to remember as he turned around and headed out of the garage.

They finished their bottle of wine and even started on a second one. Neither Dreden nor Morell could find it in themselves to finish the second bottle. They weren't too drunk yet, but they wanted to save room for their next stop of the night.

In the end they ended up gifting the rest of the wine to a random couple at the table next to them. They thanked Morell profusely, and all Dreden could do was stand there and continue to pretend that he believed he belonged there.

The place Morell took him to was a bar called The Royal. It was apparently the oldest tavern in all Brunswald. The crowd was intimidating, but Dreden felt solace in walking in Morell's shadow. The inside was at least twice as large as Keethkay's, and more than four times as crowded. The pair had a hard time finding wiggle room, but Morell seemed to know where he was going. Part of Dreden's anxiety was quelled when Morell raised a hand in the air, shouting something that was silenced by the laughter and clinking of glasses on tables, but somehow one of his friends heard him, and they greeted each other with a hug.

"Get any work done on the next great novel?" A young, clean-shaven man asked him. He looked to be about Morell's age.

"Very little. The atmosphere at Keethkay's wasn't doing anything for me today."

"No rush, right?" Came a woman with glasses from the corner of the table, also his age. "Mirthinout is still shut down for business, isn't it?"

Morell found a spot at the corner of the adjacent table. Another party had already claimed it, but it was so crowded that no one would notice. "For the time being, but no doubt the editors are still at work, just not in their offices."

Based on how many people were listening to Morell, Dreden guessed that there were six people in his group. Two men and three women, besides himself. Dreden never found himself comfortable in a group of more than five people, so the situation did nothing for his comfort, even after all the wine.

"And you are?" One of the other women asked, forcing everyone's eyes onto Dreden.

"Right." Morell took him by the elbow, tucking him closer into the table. "None of you were at Keethkay's yesterday. I have the pleasure to introduce you all to a new friend of mine. One of those three visitors that everyone keeps talking about."

Dreden went around to the five friends, nodding and taking their names even though he knew there was no way he was going to remember them.

"You're Dreden, then?" asked the young man who had first greeted Morell.

"That is what they call me. Dreden Sharpstand."

"I'll bet it is." He winked.

Morell shrugged his shoulders, smiling with all teeth. "What does that mean, Davon? What does that even mean?"

"I think it's a sex thing." answered Marrie, the first woman.

"I can see that you're all intellectuals." Dreden smiled.

A wave of light laughter swept the table. Dreden felt relieved that Morell's friends seemed so easy to talk to, even if not all of them had his sense of humor.

For the first half hour of the night they mostly talked about friend-group stuff, leaving Dreden to sit most of that conversation out. With the buzz of the wine from earlier starting to fade, he wanted more to drink, lest he feel too sober to continue drinking.

He nudged Morell's side for his attention and asked him if they were going to order anything. He apologized for not getting the order done earlier, and he ordered two bottles of Magill's for the table which arrived five minutes later, and Dreden filled his glass before the other bottle had touched the table.

In two sips, Dreden instantly felt more talkative, ready to insert himself into any point in the conversation where he had something coherent to say.

"What do you do?" asked the third man. "I mean, where you come from."

"I'm a university student. Faeriebridge University. My father is a professor there."

"No wonder Morell took such a shine to you." Came another one of his woman friends. Dreden was pretty sure her name began with an 'L'. "I'm sure you two have a lot to talk about, despite coming from much different places. What kind of stuff do you study?"

"Literature mostly." Dreden took another sip of whiskey. "Also a bit of natural philosophy-"

"Science." Morell told his friends.

"And philosophy. You know, the 'why are we here?' kind of study."

"Oh!" Davon cheered, getting his nose out of his glass. "Well, I'd like to think we're *all* sort of philosophers here, though none of us may be as good as Morell. You read anything from here yet? Anything by Mick Jowns?"

Dreden turned to Morell. "Who's Mick Jowns?"

"A brilliant man." he replied. "You would love him. In Skaltbard he's essentially credited with shaping modern society." Morell paused, focusing on filling his glass. "If you have no plans tomorrow, I'll take you to my favorite bookstore in town and pick up some of his works. Even if you're here for just a few days you've *got* to read Jowns."

With another sip of Magill's down his throat, Dreden was unable to hold his normal smile, and any attempt to retain it would only create a crooked smirk that invited more honesty than it would probably produce.

"Sounds good to me." Dreden said. "You know, I've always said to myself that I'm way ahead of my time, and the idea of getting to discuss philosophy with you would be all the data I need to prove myself right and satisfy the ego of my twelve-year-old self."

Only Morell and Marrie heard what he said. As the booze went from the bottle to their bodies, so split the conversations. The more they all drank; Morell gradually became less interested in what his friends were saying and opted to stay in an intense side-conversation with Dreden. Philosophy was most of what they discussed, with Dreden surprised by their overlap of ideas and terminology.

Dreden had to confess to him that, while he was familiar with most schools of thought, he had never been able to commit to one and claim that that was what he believed. Morell told him, over the course of a glass, that he missed the times when he was just that way.

"But you're soooo smart." Dreden said, almost drooling. "Why would you trade it for the chronic indecisiveness that I have?"

"Because, my sweet Dreden," Morell smiled bitterly. "nothing crushes a person's spirits as to have such big ideas and live in a world of small minds. It's an impotent feeling, especially if you have parents with the kind of power that mine have." He coughed, his face showing red from drunkenness like the night before. "I don't say this to many people, and it's probably easier to say it to you because we don't know each other well yet, but I haven't been the happiest man."

Dreden's smirk appeared again. "Neither have I. What's your excuse?"

"Most people in the city know who I am, and they have this idea of me as this rebellious young man who's at odds with his family at every political point. It's not always true, of course, though my philosophy is much more egalitarian than what my parents are used to." He took a deep breath and another sip of whisky. "I want to be better than I am. I really do, but there are just things about who I am and how I was raised that make me fear I'll never be that person. It's what turns me to my writing. Storytelling always has been and always will be a beautiful thing. Part of me wants to create a story to inspire a social revolution, even though deep down I don't think I'm the person to do it. I'm too stuck in my parents' shadow."

"My father is a poor professor." Dreden swirled a finger in his empty glass, aimlessly. "I can't say that I have the same problems you do with your parents, but I've felt that I'm too much like my father. He's a great guy, but a very unhappy one, even before my mother took her own life."

Morell didn't have any response. He simply stared into Dreden's eyes as if they were black holes and his gaze was a hapless comet. Slowly he brought his head down until the side of his face was resting on Dreden's shoulder.

Before the intimate moment could make Dreden more nervous, an echo of surprised gasps rang through the bar, though they were largely contained by the doorway. Whatever was the cause of the gasps was something that most people were too busy or drunk to notice.

A familiar-looking avian appeared through the cracks in the crowd and found the two of them quickly enough.

"Gerrika!" Dreden cheered as he stood up, regaining his footing. "What are you doing here? Where's Chanin?"

"She found something interesting to do. May I?"

Morell kicked a stool out from under the table for him. "Please."

Gerrika took a seat. Some inebriated people turned their heads to him to see what everyone had been looking at, but didn't care enough to look for long.

"You guys are drunk, aren't you?"

"Yeeeeaaah just a little bit." Dreden said, falling back down on his seat.

"Nice," he said, as if his friend had just told him he wanted to take up croquet. "anyway, Chanin and I were wandering around the city and we found these two engineers. They were a very pleasant couple, working on something pretty cool that Chanin wanted to learn more about."

Dreden took an unused glass from the center of the table and started filling it for Gerrika. "Then what happened?"

"After exploring for a bit longer, I got bored and wanted to see what you guys were up to, hoping to join if it wasn't a bother."

"Not at all!" Morell said. "We're just sad you couldn't join us at Palasol's."

"That's actually how I found you." Gerrika picked up the glass Dreden prepared him, starting with small sips. "I went there and one of the servers told me you were heading here, and thankfully I found you easy enough in this crowd."

"Tell me more about yourself, Gerry." Morell said.

The aveho paused, briefly amused by his new nickname. "I go to the university with Dreden. That's actually how we met. We met in a history class we had to take as-"

"As wonderful as that is," Morell interrupted, suppressing a small boozy belch. "Dreden and I were actually in the middle of a really interesting conversation. Your species does philosophy, doesn't it?"

"Sure, we do, but that doesn't mean that *I* do."

"Come on! Get yourself involved here."

"No, this works out well." Dreden said, his eyes moving uneasily between Morell and Gerrika. "Gerry, you're in a philosophy class right now."

"Because it's a requirement." replied the aveho.

"And you just got your graded test back, right? And you didn't do well?"

Gerrika frowned, putting his glass of Magill's back on the table. "You know that's the truth. I told you that like two days ago, *privately*."

"No need to get testy, friend." Morell replied. "Tell me what kind of stuff you've been reading. Perhaps the two of us can help you out with it. What have you been reading outside of class?"

"Gerry isn't really one to do unrequired reading of his own accord." Dreden took another sip, hiding his smile behind the glass.

The aveho cocked his neck to the side hard enough to crack a walnut. "It's 'Gerrika', friend. That's not really true anymore, is it? I bought those plays from the vendor the other night that I've been breezing through."

Dreden tapped Morell on the shoulder. "Right. Those plays. Between you and me, Morell, the playwright that he's reading isn't exactly on track for any awards, certainly nothing literary."

Gerrika leaned back in his seat, staring at Morell and crossing one leg over the other. "This is what you guys do? Hmm? You just sit down with your rich little friends and your rich little booze and you people get to decide what's good art? How would you feel if someone discussed something you wrote the way that you bring other people down?"

Morell clicked his teeth. "I have a book contract with the top publisher in the entire country. If someone doesn't like it, then screw them. They never achieved what I did."

"Gerrika, we're not trying to bring anyone down here." Dreden said, with an increasing mumble. "You're my friend, and I think that it's part of my duty as a friend to try to get you to expand your worldview through this kind of culture."

"And you think Winds Wilk can't do that for me?" asked the aveho, sharply.

"Why would you ever want to read something that Wilk writes?" Morell laughed.

Dreden and Gerrika locked eyes, sharing confusion, briefly sobering the tension that had built between them.

"You know who Winds Wilk is?" asked Gerrika.

"I've been hoping to forget about him." Morell smirked, downing the rest of his whiskey.

"How is that possible?" Dreden asked. "I saw one of his plays in Kroonsaed, and that's where Gerrika bought the plays."

"Oh, I weep for all creation if there are any other worlds out there plagued with his nonsense." Morell snickered again, nudging Dreden to smirk with him, but he wouldn't. "Seriously, Gerry, forget about him. You don't want to read him. Last I heard, the state of his personal life wasn't any better than his plays."

Gerrika jumped to his feet, almost taking the whole table with him. "Fuck you, pretty boy. Just because you don't like what someone has to give to the world doesn't mean that you should root for his misfortunes."

"Whoa…whoa…whoa." Morell raised his hands, still laughing. "That's not what I said."

"Maybe not literally," Dreden replied. "but the tone of your voice suggested it."

"Was that so? Fine, I'm sorry."

No one said anything for a few seconds. Gerrika stood there, staring Morell down, occasionally shifting to Dreden, who was trying to telepathically calm him. A few people from neighboring groups had stopped to watch their fight.

Taking a deep breath, the aveho turned around, kicking the chair back into place.

"Gerrika, wait!" Dreden got up, this time almost stumbling. "Come on, now. Don't take anything that we said too seriously. We're just trying to *help* you that's all. Would you expect anything else from us?"

A new fire appeared in Gerrika's eyes. "The two of you deserve each other."

Then he left, with their portion of the bar paused in silent contemplation.

"Shit, I feel like I was an ass." Morell said, wiping his face.

"Ohhhh we both were." Dreden let out a breath, resting his head on his elbow. "This is unreal. The two of us have *never* fought like that."

"Come on," Morell said softly, wrapping an arm around Dreden. "don't dwell on it too much. New surroundings can be intimidating. I think your friend killed my mood for this place for the night. Want to get out of here?"

Dreden fought a blush. "Where would we go?"

"My place? We could talk more, sober up, and maybe you can start reading *A Mad Past*. It'll take your mind off things."

"That sounds like a good idea."

"Though it's pretty large. Odds are you'll only get to a small piece of it tonight and have to leave a lot for tomorrow morning."

"Tomorrow morning?" he asked.

"You're a smart man, Dreden." Morell leveled his eyes. "Did you not realize that I put *you* in my lodging above Keethkay's for a reason?"

Dreden turned away, unable to hide his fluster. "What's that like here? In Brunswald? In the country?"

"Being crooked?" Morell exhaled. "It's certainly rough for some. Especially in places where the bishops still have a lot of power, but here in the city?" He shook his head. "Not a very big deal, especially when you have a lot of money. At that point, homosexuality is almost just a fashion choice. So...do you want to go?"

"Please," Dreden adjusted his collar, wiping the sweat from his neck, surprised by how well he was holding himself. "and let's get some more booze."

CHAPTER 19

Gerrika's feet hurt from walking around the city all night, but he was in no mood to have anyone staring at him and try to talk to him. Despite his tiredness, he went out of his way to find unpopulated alleyways to travel through to get back to his lodging.

He was ashamed to admit it, especially after the encounter with Dreden and Morell he just had at The Royal, but he really wanted to drink, and he still had money that Chief Milbrey had given him.

Entering Keethkay's was a bigger spectacle in his mind than it actually was. Opening the door with a quick tug, from both exhaustion and frustration, didn't earn him any attention. The night was aging. The crowd had already peaked, leaving the aveho with less privacy than he wanted.

He recognized the bartender, Stavans, from the night before, and the man had no problem recognizing Gerrika.

"Good to see you again," the bartender said, washing a glass in the sink.

"Hey." The aveho took a seat at the bar. He was the only one there. "I'm still unfamiliar with the currency here, but how much rum can this get me?" He plopped a single bill on the bar counter. It had the number 20 on it.

Stavans picked up the bill, smiling to himself before looking back at Gerrika. "Are you serious?"

"I am."

"You want to use *all* of this on rum?"

"That's the idea."

Stavans took the bill, sliding it into the cash box and bending down to the bottom shelf below the bar. When he came back up he had bottles of Deed's Dark Rum in both hands.

"Oh, I didn't realize it was that-"

The bartender bent down a second time, shuffling some bottles around before coming back up and placing two more bottles of rum on the counter. The aveho was left sitting dumbfounded at the four large bottles of liquor that no creature on earth could finish in a night.

"Go knock yourself out." Stavans smiled at him, returning to his cleaning of the glasses and silverware. After wiping one clean, he handed it to Gerrika.

The aveho grunted, slowly opening one of the four bottles in front of him and pouring himself a glass. It was quieter than it had been when the three of them joined Morell and his friends in the party room. Of course, there were fewer people in the bar now, and there was no music being played from anywhere. According to the front sign, Keethkay's was supposed to be open for another four hours, but the place was probably going to be full empty by then.

"To life, my friend," Gerrika raised his glass to Stavans. "to life and terrible art."

Stavans gave him a sympathetic smile and picked out an empty glass from his clean ones. He filled it up with water from the tap and clinked it against Gerrika's. "I usually toast to endless human stupidity."

"It's not just your species that's stupid." He turned the glass around in his talon fingers, watching the swirling liquid. "Believe me, there's not one of you that has anything on how I've been the last day."

Someone tapped Gerrika on the shoulder. He hadn't even had a sip yet and he was ready to tell whoever wanted to ask him something or take his picture to shove it, but turning around, he recognized the man.

"Excuse me," the old gentleman said. "I don't suppose you remember me, do you?"

The aveho blinked. "You're the piano player from yesterday, right?" The man smiled, nodding. "How have you been, sir? You play again tonight?"

"I did. It went very well. How about you?"

Gerrika turned away, taking his first sip of rum. "I think I've made a real fool of myself for the last twenty-four hours."

"I'm awfully sorry to hear that." The man took a seat at the barstool next to him.

"Please, help yourself." He gestured to his four bottles. "No way I'm finishing this."

"I suppose a little more won't hurt my playing." He poured himself the equivalent of two shots and downed one of them in the next breath. "If it makes you feel any better, none of us yesterday thought you were a fool."

"You mean when I sang?"

"It was wonderful." The man finished the rest of his drink, pausing as he simply stared at the aveho for a moment.

"Thank you." Gerrika forced a laugh from the awkward pause. "Is that all you came to say to me?"

"No. Sorry, I was hoping to ask for a favor." The man leaned in closer to his ear. "I'm on break now, but I'm supposed to be entertaining an event with various politicians from around the country. I'm afraid they just won't leave."

"You want me to chase them out or something?"

"Nothing like that! What I mean is...I've run out of material for the night. Is there any chance you would like to help me entertain again?"

The aveho put his drink down, interested. "You want me to sing again?"

"You would obviously be paid for your time." The musician put his palms together as if he were in prayer. "I think having them see and hear something as amazing as you would make them leave the city in high spirits. If we work quickly, I think I can make a tune for other songs you know. What do you say?"

Gerrika looked over at the entrance to the room. Not much could be seen from the outside, but it looked just like it had yesterday, only the people in there were noticeably older. There was no music, the only sound being the constant laughing and conversing between the people who had probably not met each other until tonight. If that were true, then Gerrika would not be such an outsider. He thought that, maybe, he could be just like any one of them.

"Sounds like a good time." He smiled, shaking the man's hand. "I've nothing better to do."

"This is extremely good." Dreden said, as his legs dangled in the air, nose-deep in the book. "I mean, the prose itself is better than pretty much anything you'll find them teaching at Faeriebridge."

"Maybe you should take my copy back for distribution." Morell was sitting up against the back of the bed.

Turning to the next page, Dreden brought his arm to the floor where his empty glass and a bottle of gin sat. He poured himself another couple ounces, taking a light sip from it as he continued onto the next page.

"Oh, and there's a map on the front and everything."

"My editor, Cipre Lane, thought that including maps of Lady Hanning's travels would be a good visual tool." Morell replied. "I thought it was a good idea too, and she has her job for a reason. I love how it turned out."

Dreden squinted. Even though the two of them had sobered up in the hours since leaving The Royal, and after they had their romantic activities, they were still drinking, and it wasn't doing well for his concentration while he was trying to read.

"We're both still drunk and tired," Morell laughed. "I won't take it as an insult if you want to stop reading."

"I know, but I still wanted to try. I'm a fast reader."

Saving his spot with a bookmark, Dreden returned his concentration to the map on the first page. Whether it was the illustrations and the wonderfully rendered seas and mountain ranges that made up the Northern Continents, or just the fact that he wanted to learn as much about the new world as possible, he was captivated.

"This is what your world looks like?"

"A large part of it, anyway." he replied. "Ignore the Deadlands. They're essentially unpopulated and no part of the story takes place there. I'm not sure why the artist included it."

"They look absolutely beautiful." Dreden turned his head back to Morell, showing him his drunken smirk again. "I already feel like I've been everywhere Lady Hanning has."

Morell returned his look, and the two of them stopped as they stared at each other again. Dreden couldn't hold off his smile for long and chuckled to himself as he turned away.

"How do you feel?" Morell asked.

Dreden knew he was talking about more than just the book and the booze. "I feel outstanding. I feel better right now than I've felt since before I was a teenager."

Morell nodded into his glass. "I appreciate the compliment, but you do yourself no favors by talking about yourself like that. You're not a teenager anymore. You're a man, and if I have to make you really love yourself properly, then I'm going to do it."

Dreden didn't know what to say. Even if he did, he wouldn't have said it. He didn't want to say anything to ruin the words that Morell had said to him, so he looked back at him over his shoulder, smiling and shrugging.

A tumbling noise came from the outside hallway. At first Dreden thought someone was trying to break into their room, but the rustling was coming from the neighboring door. He heard a voice curse from outside as the culprit struggled to get their key through the lock. After a loud kick against the door and the sound of the doorknob turning, Dreden looked back to Morell with his jaw open.

"Umm, is that who I think it is?" Morell asked.

Dreden bit his lip. "You didn't give that room to anyone else?"

He shook his head. When the crashing from the outside hallway subsided, Dreden knew he couldn't just lie down on the bed not knowing how his friend was doing. He threw himself off the corner of the bed and started for the door.

"At least put on a shirt, you animal."

"Right," Dreden's face flushed with his smile, as he tossed his shirt back on.

He stepped out into the hallway. The neighboring door was wide open. Now that he was right outside of it, Dreden could hear stumbling coming from the inside.

Putting his head through the door, he could see Gerrika bent over in the corner, digging something out of his bag. He ended up bending over too far and he hit his head against the wall. Dreden winced, and he must have made a sound because his friend turned around, covering the black feathers on top of his head with his hand in pain but smiling all the way.

"Who put that wall there, am I right?" He threw his head back, laughing.

Dreden took his good spirit as an invitation inside. "How are you feeling?"

"How am I feeling? How *am* I *feeling*?" He raised his arms up and spun around. "I am fantastic!"

As he spun around, loose clumps of bills fell to the floor. From Dreden's experience learning how much bills were worth in Brunswald, it wasn't cheap change that was spilling off Gerrika's clothes.

"But you're fine, right? *We're* fine, I mean?"

"We're wonderful, pal. We're all wonderful!" The aveho took off his buttoned coat and dropped it to the floor, just noticing all the money that had fallen off him. "Damn, I'm going to be finding money on me for daaaaays. You know when you go to the beach and you can't stop finding sand on you? That's me now, but with money. Dreden, I think it's safe to say that breakfast-" He pointed to himself, shaking his head like an excited dog. "is on me!"

"Where did all of this come from?" Dreden asked. He didn't want to seem too passive, especially with how much he was currently worried about his friend.

"You know who's generous? Drunk lawmakers! They just wouldn't stop tipping me! To be fair, I had my fair share of drinking too." Gerrika turned around, almost tripping on his coat. Dreden moved to help him, causing the aveho to laugh more. "I was at Keethkay's. The piano player from last night wanted me to sing for the crowd again, so I did, and they *loved* me! I even sang that song again, Sky Man, the one you and Chanin said was a downer."

Dreden helped Gerrika onto the bed, so they were both sitting on it. "I suppose we said that. Bud, I'm sorry if that bothered you."

"It didn't. No, I agree. It's depressing, especially when you know what the song is really about." Gerrika took a deep breath. Through it, Dreden felt something start to swell up in his friend. His drunkenness was a sign, but he wanted to believe his friend was happier than he had always seemed. "There's an aveho legend about how we lost our wings. Being a Sky Man was the most impressive thing you could become. Sure, everyone had wings, but many avehos were too scared to fly, and even more couldn't fly for very long, stamina, you know. The story goes that a young aveho has a Sky Man for a father, and he admires him so much that he wants to become a Sky Man when he grows up. But his mother...well..." He sniffed, exhaling. "She tells him to pretend that his father is already dead. He belonged to the sky now, not to them. She tells him to pretend that his father is just a memory, and that every time he visits it's just a pleasant memory, but not to forget that his father is already dead. Then one day, they hear that his father really did die."

"Gerrika, you can stop if you want-"

"No, I'm not going to." He wiped the corner of his eye, sniffing again. "Even though his father died, flying too close to the sun and having his wings burned away, the son doesn't lose his desire. When he grows up, he becomes a Sky Man too, and eventually suffers the same fate as his father. Anyway, according to the story, every one of us became a Sky Man, and we just learned to survive the fall. It was like a mass, prideful self-destruction. Oh! How fun it would have been to have wings, wouldn't it, Dreden?"

"Amen, Gerrika." He smiled, rubbing his friend's back. "I've always thought that if I could be any animal, I would be something that flies, and for that reason. It might be a sad story, but that's all it is."

The aveho wiped both his eyes again, turning to Dreden, putting a hand on his shoulder. "Let's stay here forever."

"Gerrika…"

"I'm *never* leaving." he said, sounding the most sober now. "Can you blame me? There's nothing for me back home. Back in Kroonsaed, I'm not interesting. There's nothing special about me. I'm not a scholar, I'm not an athlete and I don't have any special talents, but here? Here I have the voice of a fucking angel. And I'm the only aveho here, so no one can take it away from me."

"I'm so sorry that Morell and I were such asses to you earlier."

Gerrika sat up, taking another deep breath, forcing a frown away. "Yeah, you both were. It's okay. We've known each other for years and have never had a personal argument. It was bound to happen one day."

"Maybe it's this place." Dreden looked around at the room. "Brunswald is getting to our heads."

"Or maybe we're all just bastards to begin with and this place is just bringing it out in us." Gerrika shook his head, keeping his crooked beak smile. "Look, I know that I'm still drunk, but I have to tell you something."

"I need to tell you something too." The human cleared his throat. "There's a lot I've been keeping to myself for a long time, and-"

Gerrika shoved his shoulder. "Not now. I don't want this to turn into another thing, especially with what I'm going to tell you. Dreden…I was wrong. You don't deserve Morell. You deserve better than him. I don't trust him."

"I know he didn't make a good example of himself earlier," Dreden said. "but trust me, I got to know him well tonight. He's not just some stuck-up rich boy. He's really sensitive, and if you could have heard the way he talked about things-"

"I know. I know." The aveho raised a hand. "I believe he's gotten to you, but I still don't trust him. Call it a hunch or intuition or whatever, but I wouldn't get too attached."

"Okay." Dreden took his friend's wrist in his hand. "Just promise me you won't say anything to him or be rude. He is the one supplying you with this room, you know?"

Gerrika snorted. "You see the money on the floor? Soon I'll buy myself my own building. Also, I've decided that I'm going to find Winds Wilk."

"You are?"

"I don't think it's a coincidence that this world also has a playwright by that name. He came from our world, Dreden, and now he's here. I need to know how he did it. How he managed to survive here as an artist this long. Better yet, it can probably help us solve the mystery of our worlds too."

Gerrika threw himself on his back, grabbing at the bedsheets with both hands, trying to get comfortable.

"Ohhhh I'm so tired."

"Please get some sleep." Dreden stood up and helped him with the sheets, since he was incapable of tucking himself in.

There was an empty trash bin on the other side of the room. Dreden picked it up and brought it to the foot of Gerrika's bed in case he needed to throw up any time during the night. When he said goodnight, his friend didn't say anything, possibly already knocked out from everything.

As he left the room and went back to his bed with Morell, he wiped a tear from his eye.

Second Interlude
Marseali's Café. 1000 miles away from Brunswald
Giobana, Borgetta

Cally was the one to pick up their order tonight. They alternated who paid every week, which wasn't a problem since they pretty much ordered the same thing every time they came to Marseali's Café.

"Okay," Cally said, carefully balancing the tray on her hands as she stood over the table. "I've got the house ale for Jobe, the glass of wine for Rina, and a regular cup of coffee for Biham."

"Thank you," Biham took the coffee in his hands. It came with a tiny spoon which he used to mix the sugar.

Jobe and Rina took their drinks with smiles. They also said 'thank you' to Cally but their words were swallowed by the crowd. It was unusual for the café to be packed that much on a Sunday night, but summer was approaching. A lot of the crowd might have been university students staying out late to forget about their upcoming exams or to reward themselves for taking them, regardless of the outcome.

It would make the four friends feel a bit out of place, since they were all in their late twenties.

Jobe took a sip of his ale and licked the foam off his lips. "I say, it's getting harder and harder to keep up appearances around here."

"You old man." Biham snickered. "What? Do you think that going out for a drink once a week is beginning to harm your liver?"

"Nothing like that! I'm just saying that more and more every week, it seems like this place is becoming a young man's world." He paused, noticing that Cally and Rina were staring at him. "A young *person's* world, I mean."

The pleasant sound of small wooden boats sailing along the canals by the café was why the four friends always tried to get seats on the outside, or when they couldn't, like tonight, they tried to stay within ear's reach. It was calming, and the soft swishing from the rhythm of paddle on water did something that a drink couldn't. It was order. Constant. You could depend on it.

"You might still be good-looking, Jobe," Rina put her glass down, turning it in her fingers like a toy. "but you're not going to be that way forever. I'd be wary of how much longer it'll be attractive for you to complain about the modern youth."

He gave her a closed-lip laugh, leaning back in his seat. "Maybe, but that doesn't make me wrong, does it?"

"Many a person throughout history has looked stupid even while telling the truth." Biham said.

"It's not-" He raised a finger to his lips, thinking. "It's not a matter of being right or wrong. It's just a matter of perspective. It's how I *feel*. You can try to invalidate it, but even if you've convinced me I'm a fool, I might still feel the same. That's just how people work."

"I hear you saying a lot of nothing right now." Rina laughed. "And you've just started your beer."

"Come on, let's leave the poor fella alone." Biham told her. "Look, we come here every week and talk about what's new with our lives and we can't help but complain, especially since it seems like the world is going downhill more and more every day, but I think we should actually use some brain power today."

Rina stirred in her seat; brow raised. "Big words, Biham. What do you suggest?"

"Let's pretend we're all philosophers for the night. Sound good?"

Everyone seemed amused by the idea, even Cally, who had grown silent since bringing them their drinks. She smushed her lips together like an excited child and shrugged.

"I guess we're all on board." Biham took another sip of his coffee before proceeding. "If it helps, we'll make this all about current events. In international news, it seems that the Prime Minister of Skaltbard has had an interesting week."

"Are you referring to the growing potentiality of war, or are you talking about the three aliens that landed in the capital?" Rina asked.

"Both. I mean, something isn't sitting right with me. It sounds way too convenient for me. I think the whole thing was staged."

"They didn't *land*, Rina." Jobe cut in. "I heard they appeared out of the Sunitian Sea. As in, one second no one was there, and then *they* were."

"Horseshit, I say." Biham sat up. "They say there were witnesses, but everyone who knows anything about detective work knows how unreliable witness testimonies are. Besides, they all could have been bought."

Rina asked: "To what end? What would that achieve?"

"It would turn everyone's attention to Brunswald, as well as the whole of Skaltbard. It's got the kind of sensationalist feel to it that would make everyone forget about international tensions."

"See, we all hear you," Jobe nudged Rina with his elbow. "but we know what you're truly saying. The fact that you're religious makes you unable to even entertain the idea of intelligent life elsewhere."

"That's a bit of an ad hominem, don't you think?"

"It's true." Jobe and Rina smiled to each other, then turned to the still-silent Cally, who mimicked their grins.

"That doesn't even work out." Biham said, now with more of a flame of debate spirit in his eyes. "Your point is invalid since the apparent aliens are human."

Rina shook her head. "Only two of them are. The other is some weird bird thing. How did they stage that, Biham? Jobe and I saw the bird's picture in the paper."

"You say that as if you don't know that Brunswald is famous for its theater." Biham raised his hands up, as if to accentuate his point. "*Faked.*"

They could feel patrons from bordering tables start to turn their heads around and listen to their conversation. Some of the parties had grown silent. Others, from what they could hear, had adopted their topic of conversation and were already as lively as theirs was.

It seemed Rina had forgotten about her wine, and her glass was left alone in the corner of the table. "There's no shame in admitting it, Biham. If this were true, it would shatter your entire worldview." She turned to Jobe, who hadn't forgotten his ale. "I say we both go to Brunswald and get a picture with the bird."

"No way. I don't like birds."

"He's called an aveho." Cally said.

The three of them looked at her, momentarily stumped, before Biham continued.

"That's a fail." Biham threw back his head and let out a single laugh. "To address your latest point: would it shatter my worldview? Maybe. Maybe not. I don't think that the point of life is to constantly be in pursuit of knowledge that you can't even use for the greater good simply for the sake of knowledge. Okay, let's say bird-people exist, now what does that do for us?"

"Ooooh, now we've transitioned to the meaning of life." Rina said. "Who wants to go next? Who wants to give their tidbit on the meaning of life?"

Rina turned to Cally, who simply stared at her, inviting the next question.

"Cally," she said. "you managed to pull that 'aveho' word somewhere out of your ass. If you feel smart tonight, answer the question. What is the point of life?"

"I think the point of life is to suffer." she said, not skipping a beat.

Her response almost made Biham choke on his coffee. Jobe and Rina turned their attention to him, not hiding their amusement.

"That seems strange coming from you," Jobe told her. "considering that you, more than anyone I know, are in constant pursuit of pleasure. Normally by now you're looking over our heads trying to spot your next carnal conquest. What's wrong tonight?"

"Nothing's wrong." She extended her bottom lip and shook her head. "It's really a simple question. It's not hard to figure out. When you get down to it, none of us *need* to be conscious, do we? Sentience is a burden. I guess we can never know for sure, but it's easy to say that there are countless organisms in our universe that thrive without any shred of self-awareness, and they live, breed, and die like we all do. Which begs the question, what's the *use* of being aware?"

"It's so we can know right from wrong." Biham said. "That way, we can make moral choices."

Cally turned her head from him, cringing. "That doesn't make any sense either. If no organism is aware, then that doesn't necessitate the need for moral judgement. If we are all shitty to each other, then no one can blame us because we don't know any better, and in a world where no one is aware, none of us feel pleasure and pain or have an immortal soul if you believe in such a thing, then there's no point. Morality is useless.

"Therefore, my young friends," she tapped her glass to get their attention, as if she didn't already have it. "the point of life is either self-destruction or suicide, which are not two sides of the same coin but are the same side. Self-destruction, I would say, is the middle of the coin and suicide is the edge. There is a species of rodent that only lives to mate and die. Upon reaching sexual maturity, it quite literally fucks itself to death. Now, a rodent absolutely has exponential more awareness than something like an amoeba, but it's still doomed for self-destruction. It's natural for the old to wither and die, and it's still self-destruction whether one is *aware* they are doing it or not. That's the beauty of it. It's beautiful natural selection.

"Then I must ask you," Cally took a toothpick out of her pocket and placed it between her teeth. "if unaware microorganisms complete their purpose and die just like you humans and every other aware creature, why do we need consciousness? What evolutionary gain could it bring? All of us could look exactly how we do, come to this café and act like we're friends, without sentience. We could all be automatons, and no outside observer would be able to tell the difference. Why are you alive? Why am *I* alive?"

Rina turned from her, looking at Biham and Jobe with a forced grin. "This is weird right? It's not just me? Cally, you're never like this. What's wrong?"

"You know," Cally slipped the toothpick out of her mouth, pointing it at Rina. "you all keep calling me 'Cally'. Why?"

"Because that's your name." Biham spat.

"No. No it's not. I don't have a name, and if the three of you had been paying attention, you would have realized that I'm not Cally. It can be surprising; the things we don't notice about the people we love. Cally has green eyes." She rolled up her eyelids as far as they would go, causing the three friends to retreat in their seats. "I have blue eyes. And when I signed for the bill before getting you your drinks I signed with my left hand. Cally is righthanded."

"Let's just assume we're playing along with this." Jobe said, almost knocking his drink down with his unsteady hands. "If you're not our friend as you claim to be, then how did you know what our usual orders were?"

"And how do you know us?" Rina asked. "It can't be a coincidence that you look exactly like her."

The one they called 'Cally' crossed her arms over her chest, as it rose and fell from contained laughter. "I am...I am everything that *isn't*. I am everything that could have been. I am every life, organism and chance that *could* have happened but didn't, as became the course of the universe. I knew your orders because I knew everything that has never happened, and I *am* everything that never happened. If I am everything you all have never done, then I know exactly what you have done. You all...all of you at this table and everything that has existed, I know all about, because I know everything that I am."

"You're speaking like a lunatic, Cally," Jobe put his hand out to hers, but she wouldn't take his hand. "we know you've been under a lot of stress lately."

"I. Am. Not. Cally."

The air around the one they called Cally seemed to grow fuzzy, and there was a swishing, rubbing sound that filled their ears as if they were full of water.

Then Biham realized that the noise from the boats in the canal had ceased.

The body movements of the one they called Cally became like something moving through a room where the lights kept flickering. In one moment she was smiling, and then a tear had formed in the corner of her eye, and then her skin flashed black as if she spent days in an oven.

"Sorry about that." she told them. "It happens sometimes when I get a bit worked up. As I was saying, because I am everything that never existed, I can take infinite forms. I can't literally become someone that exists. No no no. There needs to be deviations, as I have said."

"Where's Cally?" Jobe asked, now fighting a tremble.

"If what you say is true," Rina could feel every eye in the café on them now. "that's how you knew what the bird was called?"

"Cally is...elsewhere. As far as the aveho, not quite. Dreden Sharpstand, Chanin Adderfoth, and Gerrika. I have a special interest in the three of them. The wonderful Kroonsaed Three! I think there is something that they can help me with."

"What could those strangers have that you could want?" Biham asked.

"I've already told you," the one they called Cally scolded. "maybe you haven't been paying very well attention. Beyond them, I do have another purpose, though I'm afraid everyone here won't like the sound of it. I have been busy the last few days, toiling, laboring, suffering. Why am I alive? Earthquakes aren't alive as far as I know, and neither are hurricanes and wildfires. Why am I *alive*?"

Her increasing despair caused Biham to rise out of his seat and start to make a run for the door. Before he could even turn around, he found himself being forced back down onto his chair as if some invisible man were throwing him back down.

He screamed, looking back at the one they thought was Cally, who was sitting still.

"I didn't excuse you." she said, between her teeth. "It's so easy for you humans to just run from problems. It's so easy for you to avoid unpleasantness and anything you don't like. You have the agency to make yourself what you please, but you can never imagine my life. Can you even imagine what it's like to have been born out of the most outstanding evil ever committed by mankind? No? Looking at your clueless faces I can see that you have no idea what I'm talking about. But I never forget. The omnipotent never forget."

"Who do you think you are?" Biham forced a laugh, sweat building on his forehead. "God?"

"I wouldn't say that." She twirled the toothpick around in her fingers. "No, God is the creator. God makes things. That's not what I do. I do the opposite. I guess you can call me…the *Un*maker." She got up out of her seat, now everyone who worked at the café was frozen watching her. "I'm bored of you all, and I'm afraid I have a job to do, but I will give you something I didn't give the Bellsignor or any of the other thousands that I killed in Andayt yesterday and Brunswald before. I'm going to give you a chance to beat me."

The Unmaker let loose the toothpick from her hand. It landed perfectly on its tip on the other side of the table.

"I will not kill everyone within a block radius on one condition. I want you to snap the toothpick in half."

Biham, Jobe, and Rina didn't move, unable to decide if her words were more terrifying than the fact that she had just broken physics.

"Come on!" She said, dragging her voice into a beg. "Please, just one of you try, give me something to smile about later."

The standing toothpick was closest to Biham. Slowly, wary not to prick himself on the tip or fall victim to whatever other games the Unmaker might be playing, he picked it up. There was no puncture mark on the tablecloth below it.

Putting two fingers on both sides, he put his thumb in the center of the toothpick and pressed down.

And pressed down again. Harder and harder a third and fourth time.

It wouldn't bend.

"What the...?" Biham wiped his brow. "This isn't possible."

"I *am* what is possible, friend." The Unmaker smirked. "I am magic and science together. It's truly a dear shame that you couldn't break the toothpick, a lot like how it was a shame the cooks in the kitchen accidentally put gunpowder in their cookies instead of sugar. A rookie mistake. To me they taste exactly the same, and I smell them going into the oven right now."

"That's ridiculous." Rina said. "That's something that's way too stupid to happen. Even if it did, no way it would take out the street."

"It's happening because I made it. I unmade it. Right here and now, the universe plays by my rules. My will be done."

The inferno that followed was like a carnival game to the Unmaker, and anything that wasn't incinerated became vaporized by the Unmaker's gaze.

With a smile, the being that had been the dogman in Andayt shifted into a new form, taking a dive into the silent canal.

CHAPTER 20

It is important for every person not delusion themselves with beliefs that have hardly improved since the beginning of human civilization. There is no one in the sky that hears our prayers or who gets to tell us what is right and what is wrong. It is important to remember that we are all just animals.

Charles Dowlepot put the book down. Jowns was making for some interesting reading, but it was early in the morning and he had been ignoring his coffee. The pages he tore from the library book didn't do anything but provide him with some breadcrumbs of quotations from the first Prime Minister. The Library was still closed for the investigation, so he had to resort to actually paying for books from the nearby store.

He hadn't expected to run into Morell Edland and his visiting friend *again*.

It didn't help that they were all there for the same author. Blane's Books didn't have a full shelf of Mick Jowns's work, so they had the awkward task of figuring out who would get which books. The Prime Minister felt that he got most of the goods, but as someone who had neglected Skaltbard's favorite scholar all his life, he couldn't be sure.

In his hands he held Jowns's *On the Creation of the New State*. It wasn't his most famous work, since his most widely read were science books, but in it he aimed to express his ideas for the perfect human society. Charles may have had about a one-hundred-year lead from Jowns's day, but the man's influence in the country was magnificent.

Sipping his cooled coffee, he continued through the text: *From a young age, I always felt out of place. It was as if there were a big stain on a nice rug and I was the only one that could see it. The stain here, of course, being the days of the monarchy. I couldn't think of those lesser animals in the castle without grimacing. They did nothing to deserve their place, and they had the pride, the audacity to try to tell us how to live. And why? Because that's how it's always been? I shake my head as I write this. Even if my Theory of Evolution hadn't come about or had a sliver of truth in it, I still would have amassed an army and taken them all out. Divine right of kings? There is nothing divine in being a protector or a ruler, especially when it is unearned. As in nature, the affairs of history should be awarded by the survival of the fittest.*

Charles leaned back in his seat, taking it in. Those didn't seem to be the words of someone who would appreciate the more egalitarian spirit that Skaltbard had adopted since the end of the monarchy. He had to read the last paragraph over again to make sure he understood correctly, but the words were unchanged.

He went on: *Then, my reader, I wish to pose a question that may challenge your comfort. What use is there to believe in a deity that won't challenge your extinction in the face of a superior creature? You say you were made in God's image, but you are unwilling to accept the idea of a god in constant evolution as we are? What a strange wonder it is to be a human. In the world we've created, there is no creature that is free of our judgement. We have the might to wipe out what we deem undesirable, a feat that God is either incapable of doing or unwilling to entertain of their own accord. Therefore, reader, the question of the existence of a supreme deity is immaterial if there is no use for them. A better, and the real question, is not if God exists, it is whether God exists…yet.*

"Wow," Charles took another drink of his coffee. "I can see how this isn't one of his most read books."

Despite his fascination for what he had read, there was a lot that was unsavory about it, and certainly some passages could create almost a religious fanaticism of Jowns's philosophy.

Though I suppose it would be strange, Charles thought, *if the brilliant mind behind the Theory of Evolution didn't build his entire worldview around the idea. If it wasn't him, then someone else would have done just the same.*

A knock on his door stopped his thought, and suddenly he felt he had to shake his head like dice in a hand to regain himself.

"Yes, please come in."

The pair that entered his office made him sit up. It had only been a few days since he'd seen them, but Charles felt he hadn't had a chance to escape them since.

"Keeting…Janely!" he rose from his desk and shook both of their hands.

"A pleasure as always, Mister Prime Minister." Janely Edland smiled.

Charles felt that she must make a fortune every time she showed her teeth, considering how forced it always looked.

"Likewise, sir," Keeting Edland tipped his black bowler hat, keeping it on his head.

"What brings the two of you here this early? There wasn't another earthquake was there?"

Charles tried for a laugh, but it didn't pass with either of them.

"Thankfully not yet." Keeting put his hands in his pockets, walking away from the door as it was shut behind them. "We just felt we owed you a personal visit."

"As a thank you for that excellent speech you gave after the earthquake." Janely cut in. "And we felt that we owed you an update on our service to the city."

The Prime Minister had a few extra chairs in the corner of his office. He set them up around the coffee table in the middle of the room, as well as one for himself. His wife Venka had put on a pot of tea for herself earlier, so he offered them a cup of tea, but they both declined.

"It's been better than we could have anticipated." Janely said. "It would be cruel to refer to the quake as a blessing, but it seems like this might have been just what the city needed right now. The majority of people who lost their jobs and homes will be making more money now than they ever did before the disaster."

"That's an awfully bold claim," Charles replied. "It's only been a couple days. I would think that that's not even enough time for the proper paperwork to be filled out for this kind of mass event."

"Bureaucracy be damned, sir." Keeting said, adjusting his glasses. "These people need our help. We have the means to give it to them which means that we have the moral obligation to. We've given them shelter and food. Obviously, we can't expect the ones needing work to start right away. They just went through a tragedy, and some of them lost friends and family."

Janely put her hands together, pointing them at Charles. "They're going to need counselling. For some people it may take a while, but we at the Edland Estate have created a step-by-step process that we intend to follow down to the dot. We've already put all the funding aside, so we know money will not be an issue."

The Prime Minister downed the rest of his cold coffee, holding it in his mouth a couple seconds before swallowing. He needed the extra time to consider what the Edlands had told him.

"Thank you for this." Charles let out a breath. "As usual, I would rather you schedule a meeting with me beforehand, but the fact that it's good news does make me feel better."

"As we said," Janely said. "the full story should be in the paper tomorrow morning, but we did strongly feel that we owed you a personal visit."

Keeting smiled, for the first time that morning. "As we like to say in the family: 'We do whatever we can'."

"I suppose then that I'm almost an Edland myself." Charles laughed, this time earning smiles from the two of them.

The Edlands got up from their seats as the Prime Minister started ushering them to the door. They discussed the idea of another meeting in a week or two, but Keeting became distracted by the book that sat on Charles's desk.

"That's some good reading you've got there."

Charles turned to his desk, picking the book up in his hands and showing it to them. "I just bought it this morning. I take it you've read Jowns before?"

"Many times. We both have." Keeting took it from Charles, reading the title. "*On the Creation of the New State*. Yes, I've read this one. Not since my university days, but I've read it."

"It's very fascinating." Keeting turned it around, reading the back cover before returning it to the Prime Minister. "Made me realize how little I've actually read of him. Strange right? The Prime Minister of Skaltbard being unfamiliar with Jowns? By the way, your son seems to be doing well."

"You've seen him lately?" asked Janely.

"I've actually seen him twice in the last twenty-four hours." Charles said. "First I caught him at dinner and then I found him at Blane's Books this morning. Though he wasn't alone either time. I don't mean to be a gossipy goose, but it seems like he's getting close with one of the visitors."

"The visitors?" Keeting turned to his wife. Their eyes lit up. "The ones that came from the Sea?"

"That's right. Dreden. Dreden Sharpstand was his name."

"Is that right?" Janely cocked her brow.

Charles put his fingers up. "Just thought I'd let you know. How's his book doing?"

Janely turned her head to her husband's ear. She whispered something, but the Prime Minister couldn't make out what it was.

"I'm afraid we must be going, sir." Keeting said. "A pleasure, as usual. You can probably expect us next week."

Charles was too surprised at the turn of events to follow them to the door. He stood still as a stone by the corner of his desk, rubbing his jaw with his palm, just trying to figure out what had happened.

A minute later another knock came from the other side of the door. This one was much more urgent than the Edlands' knock.

"What?" he asked with a bigger bite than he intended.

It was his balding, mousy-looking aide, Skitt. He hadn't seen him since before his speech following the earthquake in central Brunswald. He was looking as timid and non-confrontational as ever.

"Skitt?" asked Charles.

"Sir, I don't mean to be rude," his aide wiped his eyes, finally making eye contact. "but what is it that you've been so desperately looking for this morning?"

"Looking for? What are you talking about?"

"With all due respect, Charles, it looks like a tornado went through this place."

From two rooms away he heard his wife scream, and a glass broke against the floor.

He shoved his aide aside, rushing into the living room.

Nothing was where it had been. His bookshelves were a complete mess, with most of them on the floor and more than a dozen feet away from the shelf. The furniture was all overturned with chairs on their sides and couch cushions flipped over as if someone were desperate to find spare change.

Charles darted to his wife, who was dressed in nothing but a bath towel.

"Are you alright?" he asked.

Venka nodded, already taking deep breaths. "I'm sorry. I didn't mean to scare you. Who did this?"

"I don't know. You didn't hear anything while you were bathing?"

"Nothing. I couldn't have been in there for more than fifteen minutes."

The kitchen drawers and cabinets hadn't fared any better. In the center of the room, where the couch had normally stood, were broken pieces of wood all around the areas where the flooring had been chipped. Someone had tried to get under the floor.

Someone was looking for something.

"*Shit*," the Prime Minister swung an angry fist through the air. "It was the Edlands. They intentionally were keeping me in my office, distracting me from this!"

"The Edlands were here?" Skitt scratched his head. "You sound a bit paranoid, sir."

"I'm not. This is just like what happened in the library yesterday. This can't be a coincidence. Dammit, I need to tell Loid about this."

"I'm afraid all of that will have to wait." Skitt grabbed him by the arm, and Charles had to fight every ounce of his will not to slug the man in the face.

"And why is that, Skitt?"

His aide tugged at the cuff of his shirt, and all the Prime Minister could do was follow. "There has been another disaster. I'm afraid another country is screaming for blood."

"Please tell me it isn't Gontland or Borgetta."

"Borgetta, sir. There's been an emergency meeting scheduled, and if you don't show up, then world war is all but certain."

A telegram from Radoff Dell came for her in the morning. Cipre was happy. She worked through Minkompa's book quickly enough to deliver it to her boss's home before the end of the night. With Mirthinout's building still under inspection, he invited all employees to his home if they had anything important to share.

And she felt she did.

He told her that he would try getting to it as soon as he could.

Which apparently was last night, since he wanted her to meet with him at her soonest convenience.

Dell's home was a thirty-minute carriage ride from hers. She had never been before. It was a cozy-looking two-story home located on the edge of one of Brunswald's wealthier districts. Cipre couldn't see why anyone would want to go out of their way to find a home in his parts, since besides more living space, the homes were still the same distance apart. One wouldn't be any safer from an earthquake or a fire with the way they were organized.

The front door opened as she was paying the driver. Radoff Dell stood holding the door for her as she approached.

"Pleasure to see you, Cipre." he said. "I hope you've had a good morning."

"I had a later start than I hoped for," She shook his hand, shrugging. "but I'm here, and I must say I'm excited for the possibilities before us right now."

"Good. I'm glad to hear it."

He showed her around his home, at least what could be seen from standing at the front door, then took her into the living room. His wife and kids were out for the morning, so it was the perfect chance for them to discuss business uninterrupted.

After receiving the telegram in the morning, Cipre hadn't made time for breakfast, so Dell brought over some coffee and a few little pastries for her to have. She thought about declining, but they smelled better than anything she could find on her street corner, so that thought went out the window.

"So, you've gone out and discovered a new client for yourself?" he asked.

Cipre put her little plate of pastries on the coffee table and sat down on his couch. Radoff took a seat on a lone chair adjacent to her.

"I have, and…it's kind of an incredible story."

"Is it? You'll have to tell me it. I hope I don't keep you in suspense too long." He laughed, narrowing his brow as he always did. "Kidding. I read the book."

Cipre took a sip of her coffee and wiped her palms on her legs. "Great! So did I, obviously. What did you think?"

"Before I get into that answer, Cipre, I know I've asked you this already, I must ask again: is there another reason why you're not so certain about Edland's *A Mad Past*?"

"I wouldn't say so. I've been open about what I think of his work and even meeting him a couple times didn't help my enthusiasm. Radoff, I want to take on something radical. I want to work on a story I think will make a visible difference in society."

Her boss inhaled, turning his head. "That's a pretty lofty goal, Miss Lane, especially when it involves saying no to Morell Edland."

"I wouldn't think of it as saying no." she replied. "I'm not saying we shouldn't publish his book. I'm just saying that I think we should put all our focus behind something that can really make a difference. I think this book; *The Century*, is that kind of book."

"I see what you mean, but you might be selling Edland a bit short in your assessment. He may not be the most radical person around but he's subversive, and I'd say his book is as well."

"That might be, but I do stand by this book."

"Ah yes, I think we should get to the book now." Radoff picked the hefty volume off the table, trying to wipe some of the ancient dust off, but to no avail.

"Cipre, you've been one of the best editors Mirthinout has had in a long time, so it is a completely new feeling to be at a loss with you."

She felt the blood start to drain from her head, and she swallowed. "What do you mean?"

"The book. It's...it's..." he swirled his hands around each other, trying to think. "...uninteresting."

"You think it's boring?"

"Some of the time. When it isn't, it's pedestrian, which isn't a lot better. I mean," He leafed through the pages, giving each a quick look before closing it and returning to Cipre. "the prose is the best thing it has going for it. I'd go as far as to say it's haunting at times, but the story...I'm sorry, Cipre, I just don't think it's there."

"Are you biased against these kinds of stories?" Cipre asked, still feeling flushed. "Fantasy stories about old worlds and magic?"

"I can't for sure say that I'm not. We don't get many of them at Mirthinout, as you know. Look, I think we have a winner with *A Mad Past*. It's perfect. It's historical fiction with critiques from modern sensibilities and values. The way Edland balances both of them is better than any other attempt at it I've seen. I think we should choose the better story and the more useful genre. Maybe one day we'll get to historical fantasy."

Cipre blinked, remembering her food and taking a bite of a pastry. "The story has magic and kings and knights and all that stuff, but I wouldn't call it 'historical' fantasy. I would just call it fantasy."

"Except that these characters that...what did you say the author's name was?"

"Minkompa...Minkompa...Bookman."

"Minkompa Bookman?" Radoff smiled. "Exotic. As I was saying, many of the people in this book, as far as I can remember some history, actually existed."

"What do you mean? You mean *most* of them?"

He nodded. "King Madan was the last king of Skaltbard, and all his knights mentioned by name I believe were all real, as well as all the aristocrats and noblemen. There were, however, a whole lot of other characters that were definitely made up. History was my focus back in university, if you can believe it. That being so, I would have liked to have been given descriptions of what the characters looked like, but all the ones that were made up weren't even given any defining features. They could have looked like ten-foot-tall ape-men for all I know, and there's a lot else that isn't shown or explored. I have no idea what the book is trying to say, if it even has something to say. It sometimes reads as if this were the most boring university textbook ever.

"All this is to say," Radoff continued. "that I'm just not seeing whatever you're seeing."

Cipre crossed her arms over her legs. "I really think you need to consider this more."

"Look, as I have said, I strongly value your judgement, Cipre, and showing me something I happened to not like isn't going to change anything, but before you try to sell me on this book more, I want you to be sure that it's the book you're really trying to sell me. Make sure you're not trying to sell me the author."

CHAPTER 21

Dreden and Morell met Chanin at Spetter's Bakery a few blocks away from Blane's Books, which was only a fifteen-minute walk to the site of the broken middle of the city. Morell asked him if he wanted to see where the disaster had hit the hardest, but Dreden said he didn't want to. He was too hungry to go on a longer walk.

They met briefly while they had returned to their lodging after visiting the bookstore. Chanin heard they were awake and the two of them invited her to breakfast. Dreden thought about checking if Gerrika had woken up but Chanin said she hadn't yet heard him get out of bed, and that he was probably still asleep.

"Or he could have gone out by himself this morning." Chanin wondered, when they had returned to the subject at breakfast.

"Probably not." Dreden drank his coffee, as he held one of his new books on his lap. "Considering his state last night, I doubt he would have been in a condition to want to wake up early."

"What happened?"

Morell moved to tell her about it, but after Dreden turned to him he stopped.

"He…" Dreden said slowly. "had quite a night at Keethkay's apparently."

"Good for him!" she cheered. "I was worried after he left me last night. Sure, he always puts on a brave face, but I could tell that he was on edge."

"He has been since we left home. Enough about him, tell us more about the scientists you hung out with yesterday."

There was no indoor seating in Spetter's. The only room indoors was a line for customers to stand in while waiting to order their food, but the outside was aplenty. The three of them shared a long table with two umbrellas to protect them from the growing late-morning sun.

Dreden hadn't brought any other clothes with him after leaving Kroonsaed, so Morell loaned him some of his. Whether Morell or Chanin noticed it or not, Dreden's demeanor was already different, as if being in the new clothes was like a drug to his brain. He didn't ask her about last night. He *told* her to tell him about it.

"It was a lot of fun." Chanin smiled, putting her elbows on the table. "They are two of the coolest people I've ever met. I can only pray that I have that kind of relationship with my husband one day."

"Who did you say they were?" Morell asked.

"The Gumarys. Allin and Sidra Gumary."

"Don't believe I've ever met them."

Dreden turned to him, wiping breadcrumbs from his lips. "Really? I cannot believe that there are people you've never met."

"Believe me, there are many people I haven't met, some because I've gone out of my way not to." He turned his eyes to the book Dreden had under the table. "You come out of your reading daze just to make fun of me?"

"And what would your father say if he knew you were reading while people were trying to talk to you?" Chanin teased.

"I honestly think he's done that hundreds of times in his life." Dreden put the book on the table, his finger saving his page. "Can you blame me though? I've never read philosophy that was such a page-turner."

Chanin leaned in, reading the book's title. "*The Human Animal; the Relationship Between Natural Selection and Contemporary Ethics*. Sounds a bit dense. You think this Mick Jowns guy is worth reading?" she asked Morell.

"He makes for more important reading than almost anyone else you'll find here." Morell told her. "Like I was telling Dreden last night, he is responsible for the abolition of the monarchy and the birth of modern society."

"This is some serious stuff, Chanin." Dreden resumed his reading on the table. "The stuff scientists back home know about biology seems incomplete when you see what Jowns says about evolution. However, despite how much I am enjoying him, he also seems… problematic."

"You're not alone there." Morell said. "Most of what he wrote was brilliant, but he was also just a man, a man who was born more than a hundred years ago.

No one, no matter how bright, can really escape the fact of where they were born and raised. We can't judge someone who lived that long ago by modern values."

"Yes and no." Chanin raised her eyes, looking more interested in their conversation. "History is my focus back home. It sounds a bit foolish to me to expect my professors not to take sides when discussing the past. I would argue that the study of history is also a study of morality."

Morell nodded to himself, pleased with her contribution. "Judging a civilization and judging an individual are two different things."

"True, but we often talk about an individual rising above their society: a diamond in the rough kind of thing. I can't think of an example in history when a society overcame an individual, at least in the same kind of way."

"According to Jowns, it's happened here." Dreden said. "That individual is God."

"Impressive," Morell clapped. "I don't hate religion. I don't think anyone really does, but with the rise of the Theory of Evolution as well as Jowns's prolific writing, the people of Skaltbard really started outgrowing religion."

Morell went on to give them a bit of a recent history lesson. After the fall of the monarchy, the main body keeping religious leaders in power, the authority of the church had become nonexistent. Despite the rise in belief in scientific facts over religious faith, there were enough people who remained loyal to the governing of the church that Jowns gave back a portion of their power.

It wasn't what they remembered, but religious leaders didn't have any other choice. At times, their vote was the deciding vote on a new law, but beyond that, some scholars referred to the power the church had left as a 'consolation prize' from the fall of the monarchy.

"None of us are religious." Dreden said after he finished. "Kroonsaed has historically been a secular city-state. It's a much different business when you have two species, humans and avehos, under the same laws. They had their religions and we had ours, but it's not really a pressing issue anymore."

"I'd like to visit this Kroonsaed of yours one day." Morell sipped his tea. "I'll bet I could learn a lot, as you've learned here. But that's not just it. You should take these books back with you, Dreden. Shouldn't be selfish and keep Jowns to yourself. He's definitely one of the smartest men to read no matter where you are."

"How often are the smartest men the most moral men?" Chanin asked.

Morell smiled, pointing a finger at her. "I like you." He dug into his breast pocket and looked at his watch. "As pleasant as this has been, I'm afraid I must be going."

"Where are you off to?" Dreden asked, almost standing up.

"A business meeting. My parents want to step their feet into the photography industry, and when they want to start something new, I'm usually the one they get to handle the pleasantries and introductions."

"Can I expect you back before lunch?"

"Probably not. These things usually…" Then Morell smirked with the corner of his mouth. "Second thought, come with me."

Dreden was already on his feet, shoving his chair back under the table. "You sure about that?"

"It'll be fun! These things can get dreadful when it all falls on my shoulders. Besides, hearing that I brought you with me might get under my parents' skin, so it's a win-win."

Turning to Chanin, Dreden said his goodbye, promising that they would meet up later in the day for drinks or for dinner. As he sidled up to him, Morell took him by the arm and kissed him on the lips. There were a lot of people around, and Dreden couldn't help but turn red.

Looking back at Chanin, he saw her almost knock over her silverware in surprise before tightening her lips and giving him a nod of approval.

When Dreden and Morell were out of earshot someone pulled out Dreden's seat and sat down, groaning as they did.

"Have you been here the entire time?" Chanin asked, taken aback from her friend's sudden manifestation.

Gerrika propped his feet up on the chair in front of him. "Yes. It's been an interesting morning for me."

"How did you know we were here?"

"I was on my way back from the Clothing District when I saw the three of you. I hadn't eaten yet, so I thought I'd grab some breakfast here at Spetter's."

The aveho, except for his typical boots, was donning a whole new wardrobe. The brightness from the sunlight being reflected off his new vest made Chanin want to cover her eyes.

"You could have joined us." She told him, amused. "Why didn't you?"

The aveho tucked his arms at his sides, taking in a breath. "Because…"

"What happened between you and Dreden?"

"What makes you think something did?" he asked defensively.

Chanin took a sip of coffee, making sure that he could see her smile behind the cup. "You guys can't get anything by me. I know when things are up."

"Since you guessed, it wasn't really him. I mean it was, but it was mostly Morell. After I left you, I met them at a place called The Royal and they were both very drunk."

A server approached him from behind. She was probably in her late teens and had curlier hair than anyone in Kroonsaed. "Excuse me, would you like to order something?"

"Oh?" Gerrika smiled. "I've just been sipping water waiting for Morell to leave, I guess I should. Umm I'll have one of those little ham pie things you have in the display case, and…do you have anything with alcohol at this time?"

"We're known for our Gin Sunrises." she told him. "It's gin with a combination of three fruit-"

"Sounds delicious, I'll have one."

The server took the empty cups and plates from the table as she turned away.

"I take it you don't like Morell?"

"I don't have a good feeling about him. I actually told Dreden that last night before I passed out on my bed. Don't worry, I apologized to him and he apologized to me." Gerrika cleared his throat, adjusting the collar of his new shirt and fixing his vest. "Now, to get the elephant in the room out of the way, what do you think of my new clothes?"

Chanin looked his new clothing up and down, starting out level but unable to keep a straight face for more than a few seconds. The sharp, piercing blue of the vest made almost a painful contrast between the colors of his feathers. The yellow of his talon hands and the blue around his collar seemed as dull as a butter knife.

"You look like an upper-class peacock."

The server returned with the aveho's drink and his ham pie, which Gerrika thought looked significantly less flaky than the one that was in the display case. He thanked her and slipped her a tip of a ten dollar note, which she took after staring at it for a few seconds and left with a pleased smile on her face.

"You mock," Gerrika cocked his head. "but I wouldn't expect the likes of you to know the first thing about fashion."

"For as long as I've known you, you've basically worn the same outfit every day."

"Just checking your memory, girl." he joked. "Fine, you got me, but I don't think this shade of blue even exists anywhere back home."

Chanin met his eyes. "There's no reason for me to be concerned here?"

Gerrika let himself breathe a moment and took a gulp of his Gin Sunrise. "I've been a bit troubled lately." Chanin leaned forward, hands together on the table and giving him her full attention. "It's hard…like…can I ask you, what's usually your first thought when you wake up?"

"Usually? Usually it has to do with everything I have to do that day, but even before that…" She blinked. "I remember that I'm a woman."

"And you can't be blamed for that." said the aveho. "What I mean is…seeing Brunswald has changed my reality. I'm not a fool, Chanin. I know that things back home aren't perfect. Aveho and human relations are better than they've ever been, and even though most people in my life have been humans, I've never seen myself as anything other than just one of the guys, but the last couple nights," He took another sip of his cocktail. "being an aveho was the first thing to come to mind when I woke up. It made me uncomfortable. I'm a freak here, Chanin. I feel like, if I'm not constantly interesting, the people here are going to throw me away, and I'm not sure if I could handle that. I said it when I was drunk last night, and I will say it again: I don't want to go home."

Chanin didn't say anything. Gerrika didn't think that she knew what to say. She leaned over and took his hand in hers. He curled his fingers around hers, keeping his eyes away and watching random people along the street pass by. He took his first bite of the pie, ripping off the front with his beak as if decapitating it.

"Don't keep this kind of stuff to yourself for too long." She said, when the moment was over. "Dreden does it all the time and you know how messed up he is."

Gerrika let himself laugh. "Compelling point there. Anyway, not unrelated to what I was saying, I got mail this morning."

"You've already got mail?"

"Yup! It was from one of the people I met last night at Keethkay's. As luck would have it, he is the owner of the Lesting Theater in the best part of town."

"What's the Lesting Theater?" Chanin asked.

"Fuck if I know! But apparently, if I'm interested, I have been scheduled for multiple nights there. Though, if I'm going to keep singing, I think I should write some songs of my own."

Chanin rose out her seat, locking him in a hug. "That's unbelievable! Damn, Gerrika, just promise you'll remember us when you become such a big deal."

"I'll never forget you, Jeffrey."

She playfully slapped him across the face, as he tried brushing her off, moving his chair over and almost accidentally taking the whole tablecloth with him. The noise earned sharp looks from the patrons nearby, and they went from annoyed to surprised when they saw who was sitting at the table.

After finishing his food and drink, Gerrika and Chanin went for a stroll down the street. The aveho's bright blue clothes shined like a dying comet in the city sun.

CHAPTER 22

All three of them would have been lying if they said that their first full twenty-four-hour day in Brunswald wasn't the most fun they had in a long time. But they wouldn't have said that to each other, as they all got together, for the first time of the day, a couple hours before midnight.

"It's weird how warm it gets here, even at night." Chanin told them as they walked. "It's kind of nice."

They didn't want to meet at a restaurant or a bar or any other place where they could get interrupted or become victims of more photo-shoots. While they were at lunch, Morell told Dreden about a park a couple miles down the road from their lodging. He said it was his favorite place to take a walk and get his inspiration. Dreden figured that since it was so late at night there wouldn't be much foot traffic.

There were still many parts of the city he hadn't seen, but there didn't seem to be much crime in the area, and the park looked like it was no exception.

"That's one thing I already miss about Kroonsaed." Gerrika said. "I like the cool summer nights. My room was always the coldest in the house."

Dreden and Chanin shared a look behind his back.

As they strolled down the stone path through the park, watching the ground and kicking their feet at small pebbles, most of their conversation was silence. They all knew what each other was thinking, and to each of them, putting into words what was on their mind could possibly do more harm than good.

After circling the park several times, they came upon a vacant bench big enough for the three of them. They took a seat on it to give their legs a rest.

"Get any work done on the lyrics you're going to write?" Dreden asked Gerrika.

"Very little." he shrugged. "It's not as easy as it seems. You always hear songs that have such *plain*-sounding lyrics, but being the writer of those lyrics suddenly gives you a different perspective."

"Then don't make them plain." Chanin said. "What do you want to write about?"

Dreden hunched himself over in his seat, thinking. "They say the best writers of anything write about what they know, or better, write about what they love. You need to ask yourself what you love."

"I love ham."

"I think you might hit a dead-end sooner than you want there." Dreden laughed.

"You probably don't even need perfect words." Chanin added. "Considering how much they love your voice, the words themselves take a back seat."

The aveho nodded. "Fair, but I'd feel more comfortable with myself if I could come up with good stuff. The songs I know from back home are good, but I need more stuff, especially since singing that Sky Man song is bumming me out."

"You don't have to sing it." Dreden said.

"It's their favorite." Gerrika sighed. "It's my greatest hit. I tried getting by without singing it last night, but they knew. Somehow they already knew about it and they started asking for it."

"You could look at it as the price for being talented." Chanin smiled.

Gerrika gave a half-laugh, shrugging it off as his eyes visibly cleared with a new thought. "Earlier today after we hung out, Chanin, I found a couple people who I met through Errick Lesting. The one that owns the theater I was invited to. He knows where Winds Wilk lives. I think I'm going to be paying him a visit sometime this week."

"Found him already?" Dreden asked. He had to bend over to see the aveho, since Chanin was sitting in between them. "I hope you get what you're looking for from him. Despite what someone like Morell thinks of him, success is success, isn't it?"

"Sometimes success can be the worst thing to happen to people." Chanin crossed her arms over her stomach. "A lot of people aren't cut out for it. People can kill themselves over desires their whole lives and then not know what to do when they've been fulfilled. Worse yet, sometimes it's everyone else that takes the hit. There are tons of sore-winners in history."

"You're a ball of good cheer tonight." Dreden nudged her.

"I feel the opposite. I don't know, guys, I feel a lot less stressed than I used to. I should be worried about missing my classes and my future and all that, but all I feel right now is calm. Probably has to do with being around machines all night yesterday with the engineers."

Dreden adjusted himself. The wooden bench was doing nothing for his back. "Let us in on it once you've figured it out. I'm going to be needing it for my writing I've started."

"So now everyone is a writer but me?" Chanin shook her head in jest. "Makes sense that Morell's creativity would rub off on you. I always found it weird you never did much writing of your own, Dreden."

He told them about what he had started, about how he wasn't sure if it was going to be philosophy or fiction or some mixture of both. All he knew when he started was that he had something inside him pounding like a beating heart and he had to get it out. Putting some thoughts into words was calming, which was additionally soothing considering how much better Dreden had been feeling in the last couple days.

When their conversation had died down, the trio sat on the bench in silence for minutes, just watching the sporadic passing of late-night walkers or small crowds of what looked like university students finding areas to settle and eventually migrate somewhere else. The sound of a light breeze through the bushes and trees earned the attention of all their ears, as if even the clockwork natural events of the world of Brunswald had secrets that were begging to be heard.

With the three of them needing to get some sleep, they said their goodnights and hugged it out, pleased that their first day in the new city had gone so well.

It would be days before three of them got back together again-

-because the days that followed felt to them like their last year at Faeriebridge University had come and gone, and what was only natural would follow. Dreden, awake late at night grasping at the corners of his bedsheets for comfort, once dreaded what would happen to him once he and his friends graduated. Kroonsaed hadn't experienced any form of economic boost since before he was born, and if what was happening to his father was any hint as to what would happen to him, he would find himself always nostalgic for his university days.

That thought terrified him. It terrified him because now near the end of his third year at the university, he had spent all of them being unhappy. He tried shrugging it off when asked about it, or when having a conversation with a friend or someone he didn't know well, as if it were a cold or a rash. When that happened, he thought it meant that he had to go stretches faking smiles and enjoying the company of Chanin and Gerrika, because no one would want to have his company if they felt he was dragging them down with his emotional ills.

Bigger than that, Dreden worried that it wasn't just that he was in a constant state of depression. Perhaps that's just who he was, like his love of reading or the color of his hair. Perhaps he was incapable of being anything else.

But Brunswald was an *out*. It was an alternative that none of them could have seen coming. It was a chance to escape what Dreden had long felt had already been decided for him. Maybe he didn't have to be poor there, maybe he didn't need to be miserable there...

Maybe he would no longer be burdening his friends there...

He didn't know the answer to that, and the opposite might have been true. Besides the fact that they all were staying in the same building, they stopped seeing each other for a few days. It was just what happened when you left school, Dreden thought. You start to lose touch with the people you knew there. It wasn't intentional and there wasn't any malice, it just happened on its own. New environments called for adaptations. They called for evolution.

His time with Morell made him forget about those things, or at least not care about them for a few days. A part of him that had long been unfulfilled in his relationship with Chanin and Gerrika had been calmed in just a few days. When he was with Morell, he no longer feared being unhappy forever or feeling like he wasn't spending time with *his* people, as he had told his father before he left Kroonsaed.

Gerrika and Chanin noticed the change in his behavior, but didn't say anything. The two of them had their own things as well, which helped them. The aveho, despite the worries he had about being famous, was adored every time he opened his beak. Sitting at the piano in Keethkay's, he tried to recall what he had learned while taking piano at Faeriebridge. Music was a requirement for graduation, and he felt he had to keep improving himself. As he had told Chanin, he had to stay new.

Chanin, despite her lifelong devotion to history, was growing so quickly in her knowledge of mechanics that the Gumarys almost had to calm her down. They loved her company and, as the days went by, her surprising contributions to their work. To their surprise, she would often start something brilliant by saying "Back home we have this thing…" which would end up being a great idea. It was certainly humbling for them to learn from someone who had seemingly come from a much less-advanced society.

All the while, as the Kroonsaed Three were, in their own ways, having the times of their lives, the Prime Minister of Skaltbard was living in hell. After his home had been ransacked, he was dragged into emergency meeting after meeting where he had to forget all his other troubles about the Edlands and the three visitors and focus on stopping the three most powerful countries in the world from going to war.

Everyone wanted blood, and as Charles Dowlepot learned, everyone, including him, wanted a scapegoat, since they couldn't figure out what had really happened. Reminding them that Brunswald had suffered a disaster as well did nothing for their empathy or other consideration. The representatives from Andayt and Borgetta were clear: someone was going to have to pay.

Three days after the ransacking of his home, now that all the meetings for the next few days were over and dealt with, Charles finally had the time to confront the people who had been inconveniencing him for much too long now.

I believe, to a large extent, that the goal of philosophy is not to create something timeless or perfect enough to last forever, but almost the contrary. I think, for the preservation of our species, philosophy is something that we should one day outgrow. The goal is to perfect philosophy, as I have strived to do with both my writing and scientific pursuits. If it is perfected, it can possibly one day be instilled in all homo sapiens like the common manners we learn as small children or even something as inevitable as opposable thumbs.

It is my hope that I am one day forgotten, with my life's purpose fulfilled. It could run contradictory to progress. I wish to become almost a force of nature, like the wind or thunder, nameless, powerful, but gone once the storm is over.

That was the last passage from *On the Creation of the New State* that Charles had read, still on his mind as he left his home and caught a carriage to go confront the Edlands.

"Excuse me, sir, you can't go in there." A guard told him, putting a hand on his shoulder.

"Horseshit! I'm the goddamn Prime Minister, and if I want to get in, I'm going to get in!"

The other guard at the front gate gave him a shove. "It doesn't matter who you are. The Edlands are very clear about who comes in and who doesn't."

"I'm here by myself." Charles felt his heart rate rise. "I didn't get anyone else involved as a courtesy to my *friends* here. I could get the police involved, but I've opted not to."

"Let him in. It's okay."

Standing at the front door, a few dozen feet away from the gate, was Janely Edland. She was completely dwarfed by the size of the building above her. The Edlands' home was a thin fifteen-story building that overlooked every other structure that was in view of the Brunswald Pier. It was a few miles outside the main metropolis, but from the roof of the home, you could probably see everything from the middle of the city to almost even Borgetta across the sea.

The guards let him through. He brushed the collar of his suit, where the guard had touched him, and shook hands with Janely as she showed him into the building.

"I assume you're here because of what our guards did?" she asked.

"Your guards made the mess in my home?"

"It couldn't have been us, Charles, we were speaking with you at the time."

He grunted in irritation. "I know that. It doesn't really matter *who* did it. I want to know *why*."

"We knew this day would come, eventually. Fear not, we've prepared for this."

They passed by the staircase. The Prime Minister moved to go up, but Janely grabbed him away.

"Where are you taking me?"

"The top."

She pressed the button for the elevator. They waited in silence for a few seconds for the mechanism to find its way back to the ground. With a click, the doors opened.

It seemed like an hour to Charles before the elevator had finally climbed all fifteen floors of the Edland Estate. He was on edge the whole time, with Janely Edland's typical cold demeanor amplified by the seriousness of whatever it was she intended to show him. He didn't know if he should have been more scared of what he was about to be told or of a surprise knife to the gut.

The door opened, revealing to him that the top floor of the home was just one big room. With the elevator doors retracted, he could see everything in the room.

Everything and everyone.

In total there were about sixteen people in the room, all seated around a center table. The first one he recognized was Janely's husband, but there was no one in the room that he hadn't met before.

Loid the librarian was seated in the corner, along with a couple other heads of the National Library. Even Skitt, his aide, was in the crowd.

"Consider me impressed." Charles said. "Looks like everyone was in-the-know about whatever the fuck is going on except me. Anyone want to tell me why?"

Keeting Edland got out of his seat, taking a stand next to his wife. Everyone's eyes were on the Prime Minister. It made him want to curse more. He wasn't used to feeling like he wasn't the one with the power.

"It's a long story, Charles," he told him. "but if you're willing to listen calmly, then we'll tell you the whole thing."

"The whole thing?" The Prime Minister raised his arms in confusion. "And what, pray tell, is the whole thing? What does it deal with?"

"Deals with you more than anyone else, sir." Skitt said. "It's our understanding that you've already been trying to figure it all out for yourself."

Charles nodded, knowing. "This has to do with the three visitors, doesn't it?"

"Them and the disasters that have plagued the advanced world this week." Janely said.

"Here, Andayt and Borgetta?"

Everyone in the room nodded.

"You should really take a seat, Charles." Loid said. "Like we said, it's a long story, and you're going to have a lot of questions, but there is no question that won't have an answer."

He knew that trying to get into a verbal battle with everyone in the room wasn't going to do him any good. More than anything, Charles wanted answers. They were the whole reason he came.

"Fine." He breathed, finding a seat on the couch in front of everyone. "Lay it on me."

Telling the Prime Minister the whole story took almost an hour. It wouldn't have taken so long if he didn't ask a question every other minute, but everyone was patient with him.

When it was over, a disturbed Charles Dowlepot put his clammy palms on his face, trying to wipe away the disbelief.

"I can't believe this." he said, sounding as if he were fighting tears. "I can't believe this. I can't. I can't. Loid, for fuck's sake we've known each other since we were children. How long have you known about all this?"

"I learned when we were university students, Charles," he said, eyes straight with no hint of sympathy. "even back then I knew what I was going to be in my life. We librarians are sort of the keepers of history, if you think about it."

"And the ransacking of the library? That was all fake? It was all you?"

Loid looked over to the other librarians in the room, and then they nodded:

"You understand that now, Charles." Loid said. "You now know what we're looking for, and why it's so important."

"I understand alright. I understand that you're all basically mass murderers. You're criminals, and you only serve yourselves!"

"You know that's not true." Janely spat. "We don't serve ourselves. We serve the Prime Minister. We serve *him*."

She gestured to the portrait in the middle of the room. Charles recognized the portrait as the exact same one that was photographed in the book on the Sunitian Sea he had been reading. It was Mick Jowns as a young man. His perfect smile and his bright blue eyes almost coming to life underneath the paint.

"It's him," Charles stared at the portrait as if it were a ghost. "everything happening is because of him. The boy, Dreden Sharpstand, thought I was responsible for attacks in his home." He shook his head, smiling. "It wasn't me. Of course, it wasn't me. It was Mick Jowns. What's next, are you going to tell me he's still alive?"

"He is still among us, in a matter of speaking." Keeting said.

"There's something you haven't told me. Why was I never told? Why do the librarians and my aides know this and not me?"

"It's not what Jowns wanted." Skitt told him. "He wanted the burden of knowledge for the Prime Minister position to end with him. He thought that the fewer the people in power there were who knew the big secret, the less of a chance it would be discovered and fought."

"Though that hasn't stopped every Prime Minister from finding out one way or another," Keeting continued. "but once they've known, they all made the right choice."

"What happens to me if I don't make the right choice?" he laughed. "Are you going to kill me?"

"I'm sure there's no chance it'll come to that." Janely smiled, turning around to her husband.

At his wife's glance, Keeting went over to the bookshelf in the corner of the room. He bent over and dug down into the bottom level before extracting four books, which at the next look, Charles realized weren't books, but spiral-bound notebooks.

"What are those?"

"They're Jowns's Final Testaments." Keeting said. "Here is all the information you'll need about Jowns, including his own writing and reflections as well as accounts by people who knew him regarding his state of mind during the most pivotal moments of his life." Keeting slapped them down on the table. "We want you to read these before making a decision about what you'll do next."

The Prime Minster paused, staring at the notebooks as if something were about to spring out of them. "What do you expect me to do with the visitors, hmm? What do you want to be done to the aveho?" he asked, having just learned the last word from the story he was told.

"The *invaders* and the bird will be dealt with soon enough." Janely said. "In fact, we believe we could use them. Once we find what we're looking for, we actually believe that we're going to need them."

With all eyes now on him, Charles sheepishly stood out of his seat and picked up the notebook that was on top of the pile.

He took it in his hands. The penmanship on the cover wasn't perfect, and it looked like it took Jowns a few tries to carve into it, but the title read:

WHAT I DID TO THE OLD WORLD OF
MAGIC AND SORCERY AND WHY

CHAPTER 23

"I didn't ask you to do that." the dragon said. "I didn't ask or want you to do that."

Cipre raised herself slightly in her seat. "I think you meant to, Minkompa. Look, I've been in the publishing business for many years now, and I think that this book has the potential to make a lot of difference in people's lives."

She had told him about the meeting she had with her boss, about how she read through the whole thing in a day and had to get Dell's opinion on it. When she told him what Dell had to say about the book, Minkompa didn't have any reaction. Cipre felt that everything she was saying was probably like trying to explain calculus to a frog, but she was determined to get through to him.

She was determined for his book, *The Century*.

"And how long ago did you say you met with him about the book?" Minkompa asked.

"That was three days ago."

"And you think there's a chance he's changed his mind already?"

She shook her hand. "You're missing the point. It's not about trying to change his mind; it's about trying to show him how wrong he is about how the public will receive the book."

The dragon looked away, facing the many rows of books that lined the walls. Cipre followed his gaze before his eyes returned to her.

"Can I ask you something?" he asked.

"Yes," she said. "but I also have questions for you after."

"Fair." She saw his back rise and fall in a large breath. "Be honest, Cipre, why do you like the book so much? Are you sure you're not seeing things that are in it that aren't really there simply because of what I am?"

She wasn't expecting him to ask that. It was a good question, but it was a question she knew the answer to. "I can't possibly read it while not having you in mind, just like I can't help but look at a work differently after I've met the author. I've always thought this was good practice. I'm not a critic, Minkompa, I'm an editor. I think understanding the author that I'm serving makes my job many times easier." She gave him a smile, and he returned the gesture by turning his head lightly, giving her open eyes, which she figured was sort of like his smile. "And it actually ties in perfectly to what I want to ask you to do."

"What would that be?"

"I want you to come to Mirthinout with me."

Minkompa laid down his neck, looking like he was fighting the urge to cover his whole face with his paws. "We've been over this. I know my place. I'm not going anywhere. That book is only between you and I."

"It doesn't need to be." Cipre got up, then plopped herself down next to his massive arm. "Last time I was here, you told me that you don't feel like you have a moral obligation to help anyone. If I may, as a friend, I will try to convince you otherwise."

She told him about Morell Edland's book, about her life so far as an editor as well as how being a witness to the destruction in the middle of Brunswald changed her. Prior to the event, she was having doubts about the value of her work with Morell's book, and she told him that she didn't think their meeting was a coincidence, and neither was the fact that she genuinely had a love of the book he wrote.

When the dragon asked what it was about the book she liked so much, she told him that she thought Radoff Dell's problems with it were its strengths.

"You show a mode of history where, while you took many liberties with real events, showed things in a spectacularly *real* way." she told him. "The story itself seems as unbiased as it could be, but your prose tells something extremely personal and heartfelt. In this day, I think there is something especially valuable in that."

She was going to add 'and the fact that you're a dragon will make everyone want to read your book', but she thought that much was obvious to him.

The dragon was silent for half a minute before giving in. "I'll consider it."

His tail, which at its base was thicker than a group of tree trunks, curled around his side until it smacked Cipre on the side of the arm. It was clear that it was intentional, and she countered by elbowing him in the side.

"Hey!" he whined.

"You started it!" she laughed. "Considering your size, I'm surprised you felt that."

"You were going to ask me something, Cipre?"

"Oh yes. I was." Sensing the nature of what she was going to ask, Minkompa rose up on all-fours and adjusted himself so he was facing her again, giving her his full stare. "I know this probably makes you uncomfortable, but have you felt like you weren't alone here again? There was another disaster in Borgetta, and it can't be a coincidence."

"I have," The dragon looked like he was fighting a shudder. "but I can handle myself. I've lived long enough to know how to get over little frights."

"How did you know about Charles Dowlepot? Can you really hear so much while being under here?" She felt that he didn't want to be pressed with a ton of questions, but they were burning her since she had last seen him.

"It wasn't from any of my books, if that's what you mean. My tunnels go pretty much everywhere under the country. I was actually able to listen to his speech after the quake in person. You see, I *so* want to be caught up with current events, but it's just so difficult, you know?"

"Do you know about the three that came out of the Sunitian Sea? Do you know about the humans and the bird-person?"

That one stumped him. She could see it in the deep whiteness of his eyes. Something was cracking in the back of his mind that made it seem like the dragon would forget to breathe.

"People came...*out* of the Sea?"

She nodded, keeping her eyes locked on his face. He didn't let her keep it for more than a few seconds. The dragon started to shake his neck again and his paws shot to his snout in stress.

"None of that makes sense. No no no, that's not right. That's not supposed to happen."

"It surprised everyone in the city too." She adjusted her tone, hoping it would calm him down a little. "It seems like it's a good thing. The imaginations of everyone in the city are boundless now because of the strangeness of the incident. Granted, it seems like some people are trying to push their luck by jumping the fence and getting close to the Sea, but nothing else has happened." she laughed.

Her voice didn't do anything. Minkompa sat up on his haunches, covering his eyes with his claws and bending over, locking himself in a circular embrace like a small insect.

"I'm sorry, Cipre, I think you should go." He told her, his voice under his paws. "I have a lot to think about and I'm very stressed out. I hope you'll come back soon."

She didn't want to fight him. Trying to get him to come out of his ball would probably do more harm than good, especially since she didn't know what it was about her question that caused him that much distress.

Wanting to leave with a final consolation, she approached him and gave his massive snout a couple rubs. His eyes were closed shut, but his body felt like it loosened up at her touch.

It might not have been much, but it gave her enough of a positive feeling to let her be able to approach the situation with a more hopeful attitude.

Gerrika and Chanin weren't in their rooms. Dreden figured that they were probably out doing their own things, but he couldn't be sure. It had been days since the three of them last hung out.

He had seen both of them in passing and had gotten a drink with them individually, but nothing more than that. In the moments he had with them, they seemed like they were doing fine.

For the first night since arriving in Brunswald, Dreden didn't know what to do. During the day he had taken a carriage ride with Morell to see the coast and the beaches, which were brighter and better looking than any Kroonsaed had to offer. Morell told him that he would likely be busy at night, but that he would still probably be able to meet him at his friend Davon's flat in the evening.

Now, tired of reading the Jowns books he got from the bookstore, he was on his way to Davon's place. He had only been there once a couple days earlier when Morell wanted to pick up a few documents, but he remembered how to get there. His place was only a couple blocks away from The Royal.

"Hello, Marrie," Dreden greeted.

Morell's friend Marrie was standing outside in the hallway smoking a cigarette. When she saw Dreden approach, her eyes lit up and she almost accidentally crushed the cigarette in her hand.

"Dreden! Hey!" she said, tapping the ashes in the tray she held. "What are you doing here?"

"Finished all my books." He smiled with half his mouth. "Tried to get a little writing done too, but nothing was coming to me. After that, I thought I'd hang out with you guys while I wait to see Morell."

"Oh, that's sweet. Yeah, I could go for a beer. Want to head downstairs?"

"I think I've been drinking a little too much the last few days, to be honest. Would you mind if I just waited inside for him? Is Davon here?"

Dreden motioned for the door to the flat, but Marrie stepped in front of him, clamping her hand on the arch of the doorway.

"No, I think he went downstairs. He might be at The Royal right now."

He looked at her hard, though making sure not to change his tone or seem hostile. "What was that for?"

"What was what for?"

"It's not like I was going to go in or-"

A laugh came from inside the flat. Recognizing it as Morell's, Dreden turned back to Marrie, who was putting out her cigarette, her face turning red.

"He's here?" he asked, stepped towards the door. "Why didn't you tell me that?"

Dreden opened the door and only got one foot in the flat before he spun his head around back to the hallway, taking rushed steps down the hallway.

"I see, then," he crossed his arms. Suddenly the hallway felt a lot smaller, as if it were all that was between him and the rest of the universe, and Marrie was there, who wouldn't meet his eyes. "I see that's why you were standing there."

"Dreden!"

He turned around. The door was now all the way open. Morell stood there, shirtless, buttoning his pants back up before following Dreden down the hallway.

"Dreden, don't leave yet."

"Why shouldn't I, Morell? It looks like I wasn't wanted here anyway."

"Come on. Don't be like that."

"Don't be like what? Hmm? Don't have a normal reaction to being betrayed?" He looked away from him for a moment. Marrie was gone, probably into the now more vacant flat. "How long have you and Davon been together?"

"Much longer than the two of us have, if that's what's bothering you."

"And you never thought about bringing that up?" Dreden asked. "We've basically been together nonstop for the last four days and you *never* thought to bring that up?"

"I'm sorry, but I didn't think that you would understand." Morell adjusted his pants again. They were all that he was wearing. "You're not from around here, and you came from a totally different culture. I was going to tell you." He put his hand out, putting his fingers on Dreden's shoulder.

Dreden swatted his hand away. "I'm not where I come from. I'm not who my parents are. I'm *myself*, Morell. I would have thought that you would have realized that from the days we've spent together. Paint it however you want, *hon*, but this is a betrayal."

"We never made that kind of agreement." Morell said. His face lit up as he was unable to hide his teeth. "Never. I've never kept myself to one person and, I'm sorry if this bothers you, I'm not starting with you."

"I hear you, alright, but why do I feel as if this all could have gone a bit easier if you had been honest with me? If I didn't have to catch you in the act to know that you'll sleep with anyone!"

"Marrie was supposed to hold the door in case you showed up." He sighed, shaking his head.

"Yes, let's all blame this on her!"

"Do you feel entitled, Dreden?" Morell raised his voice. Dreden could hear the neighbors shuffling around from the sudden change in volume. "Do you feel entitled to me? To my lifestyle? Do you think that just because you're a smart boy you deserve to be happier than others?"

"How does that have anything to do with it?"

"I know you. I should, right? We've spent almost this whole week together. You have an arrogance to you. Whether or not it's justified isn't important. What is important is its effect on everyone around you."

"It's all about me then?" Dreden said, fighting the urge to punch Morell's bare chest. "It's all my fault. I have one thing off-putting about me and suddenly I deserve this?"

"*Listen* to me." Morell hissed. "You're beginning to bore me, Dreden. No one owes you anything. You haven't been wronged, at least not in the way that you seem to believe that you have. Just because you're a smart boy from a poor family doesn't mean you're entitled to be with someone like me. You're flawed, Dreden, and I like you anyway."

Dreden wasn't sure what he was doing with his face, but he couldn't look at Morell anymore. He turned around, facing the stairway he had come from, wondering what would happen if he just darted out as fast as he could. Would Morell run after him? Or would he go back into the room with Davon?

"I'm sorry if you're hurt. I truly am, but we've been spending too much time together. I really don't think it's good for you. You have two other friends from home to spend time with. Relax, get some sleep, sober up."

"I'm not drunk." Dreden spat. "I haven't had a drink since lunch."

Morell raised a hand to calm him, as if Dreden were an enraged bull. "Relax, get some sleep, and we'll talk tomorrow. You're not stupid, Dreden. By this time tomorrow, you'll have realized how unnecessary your outburst was. I think this is a really good moment for you."

Either he was out of things to say or he was out of courage to say what he was really feeling. Regardless, Dreden didn't want to spend another second in that hallway. He turned away, looking over his shoulder at Morell one last time before trotting down the stairs and back to his lodging, feeling farther away from home than he had ever felt before.

Getting back to Morell's flat, he had no idea what to do. It was probably too late for him to go out. Not that he wanted to. Dreden did his best not to make a sound in between coming up the stairs and opening the door, in case Chanin and Gerrika were home.

He sat alone in a chair at the corner of the room, with no light except the light from the moon and from a tiny lamp. Dreden grunted to himself as he brushed his hair through his fingers. He was feeling a lot at once, but nothing he was feeling had a chance of calming him down.

What have I done to deserve to be lied to? he thought, tightening his teeth in his mouth. *I've never lied to him about anything. This is the man I left home to be with? As if there's no one as smart as him back home. As if I have a chance with anyone at Faeriebridge. No, I've never been good at meeting people like that. I've never been good at letting people get to know me.*

Maybe that's what's happened to Morell. He's gotten to know me too well and now that's the end of it. Maybe I should have put on a show for him and hide who I really am.

Maybe Gerrika and Chanin are going to leave me too.

That did it for him. He couldn't sit down anymore. Dreden threw himself to his feet, looking for the nearest thing to throw against the wall.

A Mad Past was on the table next to him. He motioned for it, but then stopped himself. If he damaged Morell's book, he knew that he would regret it, no matter how hurt he was by him.

He paused for a moment, but the rage was all still there. One of the books by Mick Jowns Morell bought for him was on his bed. That book belonged to him, and it was a gift from Morell. Yes, it would do nicely.

Winding up in a quick motion, as if he were going to chuck it over a cornfield, he launched it against the wall. The book opened up in the air, making a swishing, flapping sound before colliding against the wall. It wasn't a big book, so it didn't make a ton of noise, but the amount of energy it took for Dreden to throw it that hard helped calm him down. Suddenly he needed to breathe.

In the impact, the last page of the book had come loose. It dangled out of the corner of the book like a little creature trying to crawl out of a cage.

Dreden cursed to himself. He always liked keeping his books in perfect condition, but he knew he should have thought about that before throwing it.

Picking up the book, he opened the back flap to adjust the loose page back where it belonged.

His mouth dropped open upon seeing the page.

He had read four books by Mick Jowns, but on none of them did he bother looking at the portrait of the author at the back of the book. The portrait showed Jowns as a young man. It wasn't a clear picture. It looked like the publisher of the book had taken a photograph of a painting, so it was black and white and a bit fuzzy, but he didn't need a perfect look at the man to know that he had seen Mick Jowns before. He had seen the man in Kroonsaed.

"Oh, fuck…"

He was immobilized by the photo but had to pull himself away. Dreden put the book back down on his bed and rushed over to the far table where Morell's novel sat.

Opening the front cover, Dreden looked at the map of the character's travels.

A map of Skaltbard and the surrounding nations.

This time his head was clear. He wasn't swimming in drunkenness or under Morell Edland's spell for the night. He was sober and angry.

He saw on the map what he should have seen those nights ago.

This can't be a coincidence, he thought, his mind rushing left to right. *All the pieces are on my table now. I just need to see how they fit.*

Closing the book, Dreden sprinted out the door and banged on Chanin and Gerrika's doors hard enough to wake a passed-out drunk. When neither of them answered, he ran down the stairs and out the door, ready to spend all night looking for his friends if he had to.

CHAPTER 24

Gerrika was nervous. A lot of it was carried over from his performance at the Lesting Theater, which to everyone there, was an outstanding success.

He didn't know if any of the songs he had written were any good, but the crowd loved them all the same. He didn't even sing Sky Man, but everyone was pleased.

Now came the true source of his anxiety. As he stood in the hallway outside the flat of the only writer he had ever enjoyed, the aveho couldn't keep his fingers still. Looking at his watch, Gerrika saw that he was still early, but he knocked on the door anyway. It was late at night, and he didn't want to keep Winds Wilk up more than he had to.

The door opened, and he caught his first look at the playwright.

"Mister Wilk?"

Winds Wilk stopped the door against his shoulder. He was a lot younger than Gerrika had anticipated. He couldn't have been more than a couple years over thirty.

A pair of sunken eyes blinked at the aveho. They looked like they were the oldest part of him.

"As I live and breathe," Winds gave him an uneven smile, eyeing him up and down. "an aveho at my door."

"I know it's obvious," Gerrika said. "but I'm the one that sent you the letter. You told me to come at this time." He extended his hand. "I'm Gerrika."

The playwright looked at his hand, then back up to him, leaving him hanging for an uncomfortable time before he finally took it. "Come in. No use wasting more time."

Gerrika followed him inside, turning his head and looking at all the decorations and ornaments around the flat, but most of it wasn't so pretty. It looked like his home might have once been nice and clean a long time ago. There was a feeling of culture and company a lot like the feelings he got from his own lodging above Keethkay's, but like a sweet pie that had long been eaten, it was only the saliva-inducing scent that remained.

Winds himself dressed halfway between tailor and tramp. It was as if he wanted to put *some* effort into his appearance simply for his own sake, but not having a desire to let anyone see him.

"You know I'm an aveho." Gerrika said, as Winds showed him to his couch. "Is what I asked true? You're not from here, are you?"

"No. No I'm not." Winds threw himself onto his chair by the window. The flat was eight floors above the street, so it offered Gerrika a nice view of the city. "Uggggghh, did I really ask you to come here this late?"

Gerrika dug into his jacket pocket, opening up the letter Winds had sent him. "You did, see? We agreed on the time because I just came from a show at the Lesting Theater. It was the only time I could see you."

"Right. Right right." Winds grimaced, tapping the side of his head with two fingers as if trying to knock out something loose. "I guess you're a big celebrity now, aren't you, songbird? You gather a flock every time you open your beak?"

"Something like that." Gerrika replied, softly. "Umm, look, I don't want to take up too much of your time, but I love your writing."

"Is that right?"

The aveho nodded. "And that's saying a lot. I've never been a literary person. I've never read much. Your plays are the only things I've ever found myself enjoying."

The playwright was back up on his feet, as if struck by something. "Can I get you something to drink, kid?"

Gerrika blinked, watching Winds almost trip over his own foot as he approached a table embedded against the wall. It looked like he had half a bar, and his stumble made him realize that Winds was certainly not sober.

"Sure. I'll take anything. Whatever's easiest."

"I'll get you a gin and tonic."

Winds poured gin into the glass for Gerrika before topping himself off.

"Here you go. Here's your *g and t*. I'm all out of tonic so you'll just have to take the g."

Gerrika took the glass with a smile and a nod. He looked into the liquid and saw his reflection before taking a sip.

"Tell me," the playwright plopped himself back down on his chair, half an ounce of booze spilling onto himself as he did. "what do you like about my plays?"

He took another sip, trying to do it quietly. "I think you're very funny. It's probably subjective, but I think the ones I've read are clever."

"Thank you. I devoted a lot of my young life to making people laugh."

"Funny thing, though." The aveho leaned over in his seat, trying to keep Winds's attention, as the playwright's eyes seemed to look everywhere but him. "I didn't know who you were until about a week ago. My friends and I saw a performance of Pigamist at the theater by campus."

"You go to Faeriebridge?"

"Yes...well...not anymore. I don't intend on finishing my studies there."

Winds swirled his neck around so he could take a gulp of gin. "I didn't finish there either. I was too distracted. I wrote when I should have been studying. I'm from Kroonsaed too, if you haven't figured that out already."

"No, I got that," he tried a smile. "and that brings me to why I'm here, Mister Wilk. See, I've gained a lot of fame around here for my voice, but I don't want to be a singer. I want to be a writer like you."

Winds gave a loud choking sound as he threw his head forward, spitting out some of his drink. Gerrika didn't realize until he saw the up and down of Winds's spine that he was laughing.

"*You* want to be like *me*?"

Gerrika tightened his grip on his drink with both hands. "I do. I don't think there's anything wrong with that. There are all kinds of writers like you that don't get the attention they deserve because they aren't 'literary', and I want to help those writers by becoming one. I think you deserve to be taken seriously."

Winds put down his half-finished glass of gin, staring at the aveho's face for the longest time so far. "Can I give you a piece of advice?"

"Yes, please."

"Go home, kid. Go home while you can. You should be thankful you're not repulsive to the people here."

"I don't see how that's supposed to help me." Gerrika narrowed his eyes.

"I've never been good, kid. Never. Ask anyone in Kroonsaed who knew me. I was a big dreamer as a student, like you are. I had ideas and the ego to believe that I had something great to share with the world." The playwright picked up his gin again, downing the rest of it as if it were water from an oasis. "As it turns out, I'm not very bright. I truly thought I had written something groundbreaking when I wrote my first play, and you know what my friends and family told me after they read it? Hmm? Huh? They said it was funny. It was a funny little thing."

"They *are* funny little things."

Winds's fist pounded against the arm of the chair. Gerrika flinched. "I didn't want them to just be 'funny little things'. I wanted to be subversive. I wanted to be brilliant for fuck's sake! You know what I did? To save the image of myself in their eyes, I pretended to shrug it off. I told them I loved what they had to say about my work and if they wanted to look for something brilliant or subversive in it to go ahead, but it wasn't my intention. I kept hoping someone would one day see how great my work was. Because what was the alternative? The alternative was accepting the fact that I'm a fucking moron, a moron that only does little things. Every time after that when I wanted to be bright and brave, they said they liked my other stuff better. I'm a moron, songbird."

"That's not what you are, Winds! You're not a moron, and you're certainly not one to me."

"Now I feel so much better." Winds smiled, fire lighting his eyes like a midnight sky. "A random aveho thinks I'm not a moron. Kid, I hated what they thought about me in Kroonsaed. When I came here, it was by some freak incident with the Sea, just like you, I'm sure. I never wanted to go back, and because I look like everyone else here, I was able to fit in, which you can't do. I've been here almost ten years. You know what I've learned? No matter what world you're on or wherever in the universe you are, people are people, and they break your fucking heart."

Gerrika shuffled his feet together, unable to come up with anything comforting. "I'm sorry, Winds."

"No, I'm sorry." He shook his head. "I'm sorry I invited you here. I'm sorry that I'm not someone that can help you or even give you anything encouraging. I think you should go, kid. I'm in no mood for company anymore."

The aveho got back on his legs, leaving his unfinished glass of gin on the center table. "I hope you feel better tomorrow."

He didn't watch for the playwright's reaction. Gerrika tried leaving the flat without seeming in a hurry to get out. He didn't want Winds to think he had something against him, regardless of how badly their meeting went.

Before he closed the door behind him, he heard a glass shatter against a wall.

Charles had been postponing the reading all day. Even with what he now knew from the Edlands and the others, he knew there was even more that he would learn from reading Jowns's Final Testaments.

He left the Edland Estate feeling like he was being followed, but that was just his paranoia. They didn't need anyone following him. With everything they had, he figured they could probably deal with him at any time they wanted.

Now, sitting alone in his office, four books put together by Jowns were spread out across his desk. He couldn't decide which one to start with. They were surely all equally disturbing in their content, and there was no way to tell which one would ease him into the truth before it got to the more awful stuff.

It has to be done, the Prime Minister said to himself, trembling before the books. *I know too much already. There is no going back from this, especially if I want to keep myself safe.*

A knock on the door almost made him yip. His wife Venka peeked her head inside.

"What are you doing alone in the dark?" she asked.

He didn't know how to respond, and before he could have a chance to make any sound with his mouth, Venka saw the books in front of him.

She nodded to herself, knowingly. "You found out, didn't you?"

He threw his arms in the air in surrender. "I give up. I seriously give up. Am I the last one around here to know the truth about Jowns?" Lowering his voice, he looked to her again. "How long have you known?"

"The Edlands told me the day you were appointed to Prime Minister."

"Ever consider going into theater?" he sneered. "You've had me fooled, and your little performance when you discovered our home in shambles was award-worthy."

"You have a lot to think about, Charles," she said. "and you have a lot of reading to do. I'll leave you to it. Don't worry, I won't wait up for you. Take all the time you need. If it's any help, I would start with that one there."

She pointed to the one that had been on the top of the pile when he received the notebooks at the Edland house. The one that had a cover reading: *WHAT I DID TO THE OLD WORLD OF MAGIC AND SORCERY AND WHY.*

After she closed the door, he picked it up, examining it as if it had some kind of demonic power inside that would be let loose if not handled properly.

Charles Dowlepot knew his life would never be the same once he read.

He threw his eyes right into the words.

If you are reading this, Jowns's notebook began, *then I am still successful in my mission to end the old ways. I don't know who you are, but I expect that the account I'm about to give you will come as a great shock. You will undoubtedly have many questions as to not only why I did what I did, but HOW. Bear with me, reader, you will have all your answers soon enough.*

Before you even think about judging me, I must remind you that the world in which I grew up looked nothing like yours. Where you now have apothecaries and drugs and have all forms of science taught in schools, I had magic and wizardry. Yes, you read that correctly. Magic was everywhere in my young life. Magic is what cured our illnesses, magic is what we used in battles, MAGIC is what we turned to when we needed help.

And I despised it for that reason.

One did not need to be smart to be a good wizard, or to be able to do magic at all. One also didn't need to be physically strong.

Do you already see the problem here?

How is humanity supposed to advance when their most powerful resource can be used by anyone? The animals don't use magic. A slow rabbit isn't able to get the best of a speedy wolf by casting a spell. Why should humanity work any differently? That's why science earned my permanent devotion. The early scientists were mocked for being "impractical" and "useless". In a world of magic, who needed it? But they were all too stupid to see that we'd all grown so fat off our reliance on magic that we hadn't had real progress in a long time. Magic allowed genetically superior men to be held down by their inferiors. It had to be done away with forever, in order for the supreme civilization to realize itself.

But before I set myself out for the great task of freeing mankind from the shackles of magic, I dealt with a set of chains that had LONG been holding humanity back since even before there had been an organized study of magic thousands and thousands of years ago. I set myself out against the feathered undesirables.

The elimination of creatures called avehos.

EPILOGUE

He saw Chanin catch him in the corner of her eye, but when there was no one else that looked like him anywhere in the city, that's all it took for someone to notice him.

"Gerrika?" She stopped, standing over him. "What are you doing out here all by yourself?"

The aveho was sitting down in the corner of an alleyway tucked between a bookstore and a residential building, with drooped eyes showing that neither his new clothes nor the empty bottle of beer in his hand could keep him company.

"Passing the time," he told her with a chortle. "didn't know what to do after my show and I don't feel like going back to the flat, so this looked like a nice little place."

"You could at least be standing. It's probably filthy back here. Don't want your clothes getting ruined."

She took him by the hands, helping him back up to his feet. He dusted himself off on the back and tossed his empty bottle in the dumpster against the wall.

"Ugh…thanks. I answered your question, now tell me what *you* are doing here."

Now that Gerrika was up, he and Chanin started down the street. It was now after midnight, so there was a lot less foot traffic. "I'm coming back from the library."

"I thought I heard the National Library was closed."

"I went to a university one. The University of Brunswald Library. I was doing some studying."

"Chanin, the point of being away from Faeriebridge is to *not* think of school." She brushed dirt off the back of his arms. "We can't all be talented artists, G."

"Talented?" The aveho shook his head. "Hardly. I just do something that every aveho can do, but hey, I shouldn't complain. I should be thankful I'm not repulsive."

"Now why would you say that?"

"Forget it. It's just something someone said to me."

"They don't sound like someone you should give a rat's ass about."

A few people passed them on the sidewalk sporadically, followed by a group of three people who were clearly drunk. Gerrika and Chanin let them pass, while the aveho shied away hoping none of them would take notice of him.

"Maybe, but it's easier said than done." He saw Chanin yawn, which caused him to do the same. "I'm so damn tired. I want to sleep for twelve hours. Do you have plans for tomorrow? Maybe we can eat at Spetter's again."

"That's actually what I was going to talk to you about," She stopped her walk, pausing in front of her friend. "I've been thinking a lot about us being here. I know how you feel about being here, Gerrika, but my story is a little different."

"What do you mean? You seem like you've been finding yourself alright here."

Chanin poked the ground with her boot. "I've had a lot of fun in Brunswald, but I need to think more seriously about my future. The three of us do."

"I don't think I have a lot to worry about. Do you have any idea how much money I made just tonight?"

"That's not the point. It can't go on forever, bud." Gerrika sharp gaze was making it hard for her to keep her eye-contact. "I'm going home. I think I need to."

"*You* need to go home? *You?*" Gerrika slapped his talons against his legs, throwing his head up, his black head-feathers seemingly flapping in amusement. "I didn't realize that your time shadowing engineers has been so stressful."

"Calm down, Gerrika. It wouldn't be for good. I need to see my parents again. I need to go to class again before I've made up my mind."

"You don't know half of the pressure I've been under the last few days." he said. "No matter how anxious you feel, I soooo guarantee that I've had it worse, and now you're saying you can't take it? You're leaving us?"

She shoved him on the shoulders. "That's because you've been putting an absurd amount of pressure on yourself!" Chanin looked away, covering her mouth with her palm. "We're still just university kids. For damn's sake, last week we were at the campus bar not knowing what the hell to do, but we didn't care, did we? At least I didn't. You, me, Dreden, we all have things that make us unhappy, but at least we enjoyed ourselves with each other, just being students and having the worries that students have, and now it's like the two of you are trying to grow up overnight and it doesn't work that way! The two of you are setting yourselves up for misery and I don't want to go down that road."

Part of him knew that Chanin was right. It was the part of him that had been in constant anxiety over the last few days. Everything she told him was something that he thought to himself earlier, but had shoved away in favor of a more pleasant idea of reality. But he still wanted to fight her, as if it were her that had really been the one to upset him.

The sound of running feet stopped the aveho as his beak was open to speak. He and Chanin turned to see an out-of-breath Dreden come to a grinding halt upon seeing them.

"Dreden?" Chanin asked. "What's the matter?"

Dreden was bent over, breathing as if he had just outrun a tiger. "I...finally found you guys. I have something to show you."

He dug into his pocket, taking out a small book page that was wrapped in a larger one that had a map on it.

"What are those?" Gerrika asked.

"This is big, guys." He let out another breath, wiping his mouth. "I might have figured out why we're here. Look at this." Dreden showed them the page he had torn out of his book. "Does this man look familiar?"

Even with the lighted electrical lamps lining the walkways, Chanin had to take the page in her hand to get a good look at it. Her face changed color at the recognition. Gerrika noticed and plucked it out of her hand so he could see it.

"Where did you find this?" Chanin asked.

"In the back of one of the Jowns books Morell got me. The man you're looking at is Mick Jowns himself."

"He shot at us!" Gerrika beamed.

"I know how this is going to sound." Dreden said. "It might all be crazy, but there are too many things here that just *can't* be coincidental. Think about it: we get transported to some alternate world where humans exist, and they speak the same language we do?" He shook his head. "Guys, this isn't a different world. This *is* our world."

Gerrika didn't look convinced. "How could that be? Not only am I the only aveho here, but no one has ever even heard of my species."

"That I don't have an answer to, but I can show you this." He unrumpled the larger page he had taken from his pocket and handed it to them. "Morell showed me this map of the travels of his protagonist a few nights ago, but I was drunk and didn't see it then." Pointing to the edge of the map, there was a large mass of land far outside the main focus, many many miles across the sea from Skaltbard. "See that? See the coast along that continent?"

They did. Chanin rubbed the corner of the page as if trying to see if it would reveal buried treasure, but she didn't need any further confirmation to know what was read all over her and Gerrika's faces.

"That's where we live. It's the Saedian Coast." She passed the page to Gerrika, who was still eating it up. Chanin blinked twice in confusion. "No, this can't be right. We don't come from a place that hasn't sailed across the world before. A place as advanced as Skaltbard? We should have made contact a long time ago, and we should have known about all these other countries too."

"Which brings me to my biggest leap." He put a hand on each of their shoulders, huddling them close. "The Sunitian Sea didn't take us to another world, I think it jumped us through time."

Neither of his friends looked like they had any idea how to respond. Chanin tried anyway. "What do you mean? You think we came from the past?"

"I don't know what to think anymore. All I know is that the philosopher I've been reading for days was the lead man who almost killed us back at Heathback that night and that we need to start taking this mystery seriously."

"If it's true that we're from the past, then there is something we could try."

Chanin broke herself off from the group for a moment. There was a lone woman on the other side of the street. She called to her, getting her attention and beckoning her to join them.

"What's this about?" the woman asked, as her face lightened up at seeing the aveho. "You're the visitors, aren't you? You're the songbird!"

"Yes and yes he is." Chanin answered quickly. "What year is it?"

"1110."

The three friends shared looks of defeat.

"That doesn't help us that much." Gerrika said. "That's the same year as it is for us."

"Hold on a second," Dreden said to her. "why is it 1110? Where does that number come from?"

"It goes back to the birth of the country." she told them. "The first year marked the start of the end of the old kingdoms. This is so wild! What does 1110 signify for you?"

"The unification." Gerrika answered. "The first time that humans and avehos began living under the same civilization."

She had a few more questions, but they didn't have time for her, so they dismissed her as kindly as they could.

They didn't feel they had gotten anywhere. The fact that it was the same year in Brunswald and Kroonsaed didn't bode well for Dreden's theory.

"Or maybe...maybe it makes no difference." Dreden brushed his forehead with the back of his hand. "Wait! Think about it, guys, if Kroonsaed has never made contact with Skaltbard, how is it possible that we have the same year? Sure, the reasons for the years are different, but this is an astronomical coincidence."

"What about Kroonsaed now?" Chanin asked. "Did Morell say anything about the place we think is our home?"

"He called it the 'Deadlands', saying they weren't populated. Shit, bring that woman back."

Chanin rushed down the street to catch up to her. It took half a minute for her to come back, looking more than pleased to be of more assistance.

"What else can I do for you?"

"You know the Deadlands, right?" She nodded to him. "Tell us about them."

"There's not much to tell. Explorers have gone back and forth to study them, but there's nothing there. Not even many animals. It's apparently a truly bizarre place. It's called the Deadlands for a reason."

They thanked her again, leaving the three with even more questions than they had before.

"What if it's not our home?" Gerrika asked. "The whole premise could be wrong here."

"My time-jump idea could explain it." Dreden said. "Something terrible could have happened to our home. It might sound insane, but what if the reason we were sent here was to find out what happened so we could stop it from happening in our time?"

Chanin turned from them, pacing back and forth along the walkway. "The time-jump idea could explain the language. Perhaps in the future we come into contact with Skaltbard and we end up sharing a language. The year is still what's getting me. If we really did travel through time, it's anyone's guess exactly how far in time we traveled."

"My head is starting to hurt." The aveho whined.

"Except there's still Jowns!" Dreden remembered. "We saw him in the flesh at Heathback before he and his two men disappeared into the Sea."

"And he's been dead for many decades, meaning…." Chanin looked up, doing the math in her head. "It might have been around a hundred years since he was alive and looked the way we saw him."

"I don't know about you two," Dreden said, huddling up with his friends again. "but this now has my full attention, and I only wish I could have been spending my time better here."

ABOUT THE AUTHOR

Currently living in Glendale CA, Brendan Walsh is a graduate student at Cal State Northridge. When he is not writing, he is either watching movies, reading comics, drinking coffee or thinking about what to write next. He is also a Dodger fan, philosopher, and a recreational madman.

NOTE FROM THE AUTHOR

Word-of-mouth is crucial for any author to succeed. If you enjoyed *The Century's Scribe*, please leave a review online—anywhere you are able. Even if it's just a sentence or two. It would make all the difference and would be very much appreciated.

Thanks!
Brendan

Thank you so much for reading one of our
Paranormal Fantasy novels.
If you enjoyed the experience, please check out our recommended
title for your next great read!

Dark Touch by Elle Lewis

Summon Fantasy Top 10 Fantasy Reads 2019